SERIAL KILLER WANTED

Also available by Nika Grace (Writing as Michelle Hazen)

Novels

Breathe the Sky

Unbreak Me

The Sex, Love, and Rock and Roll Series

Fill Me

A Cruel Kind of Beautiful

Playing the Pauses

Tie Me Down

Insatiable

Christmas With the Band

The Friends Make the Best Lovers Series

So You Think You're a Match?

Nonfiction

Kiss & Tell: How to Write Unforgettable Sex Scenes

SERIAL KILLER WANTED

A NOVEL

NIKA GRACE

CROOKED LANE

NEW YORK

Published in the United States by Crooked Lane Books, an imprint of The Quick Brown Fox & Company LLC.

Crooked Lane Books and its logo are trademarks of The Quick Brown Fox & Company LLC.

Library of Congress Catalog-in-Publication data available upon request.

ISBN (hardcover): 979-8-89242-759-3
ISBN (paperback): 979-8-89242-760-9
ISBN (ebook): 979-8-89242-761-6

Cover design by Meghan Deist

Printed in the United States.

www.crookedlanebooks.com

Crooked Lane Books
34 West 27th St., 10th Floor
New York, NY 10001

First Edition: October 2026

The authorized representative in the EU for product safety and compliance is eucomply OÜPärnu mnt 139b-14, 11317 Tallinn, Estonia, hello@eucompliancepartner.com, +33757690241

10 9 8 7 6 5 4 3 2 1

CONTENT WARNING

If you'd like to avoid spoilers, you can skip this page. However, if you have sensitivity to any elements, you may want to be aware that this book contains murder and physical fighting. It involves discussions of suicidal ideation, loss of family member, death of a young person, and suspected child abuse. There is NO on-the-page sexual assault or child abuse depicted.

If you or anyone you know is struggling with suicidal thoughts and feelings, please call or text 988. You don't have to decide anything today. Just know there's someone safe you can talk to about it.

Dedicated to my goddaughter, Savahna, who gave me the line that inspired this book. Never be afraid to speak up, because you never know how far your words might travel.

I SAW MY FIRST dead body in Walmart.

My mom sent me from two aisles over to grab one of those round disc things you stick inside the toilet. When I saw the man, he was reaching up to the shelf above the bathroom stuff, and then he fell.

It was so distinct, the moment between when he was and when he wasn't. How much of him was already gone before he hit the floor.

That's how I always remembered it, like his body was a sock puppet and the hand inside just disappeared.

Before that, I was scared of lots of things: the dog-monster under my bed, the squishy black stuff in the very end of a banana, the way my mother's face pinched down when she opened the bills every month.

But after that, I was only afraid of one thing: What was the hand inside of me?

Serial Killer Wanted

Willing victim for experienced murderer.
No rape, no torture, no amateurs.

You need to kill and I need to die.

Let's talk.

CHAPTER

1

Dani

I'M NOT THE kind of girl who believes in fate. I believe in death and taxes, and that the math will always come out in favor of the person with the most expensive calculator. Fate is a fairy tale for the kind of people who actually get happy endings, who can afford sedans with heated steering wheels, and donate a dollar only after they've dropped six times that on a coffee.

It wasn't until I became a murderer that I felt the first itch of destiny. Before death started to follow me like I owed it something. Or maybe it owed something to me.

That's why I'm not as surprised as I should be when a CheepsList ad for a serial killer pops up on my phone. I wouldn't be sitting in my car outside a funeral home right now if I weren't already suspicious about fate. As signs go, this is the equivalent of running into your drug dealer outside your twelve-step meeting. But part of me still isn't sure.

Not about what I've done. That's simple enough. I still remember the first time, analyzing the blood spatter with eyes made critical by a thousand CSI shows and true-crime podcasts. Trying to decide how to adjust my story to convince the police.

I know what I can do, and that's no longer interesting. It's the *why* that digs at me.

Because that's the thing, isn't it? Either all this shit means something, or it doesn't. In my case, I'm not sure which is harder to live with.

This funeral home is my attempt to find out if there's something else I should be doing with my very particular set of skills. There's no other reason I would apply for an internship when I already have the kind of job that pays like you always need another one. I'm not naive enough to work for free, showing up bright-eyed and bushy-tailed to make some asshole's coffee in the hope that it'll teach me something about my future. I might just be desperate enough, though, because a career as a mortician would be an easy answer to the equation of Me + Death = ?

I don't like this new development, though. I eye the mortuary sign, then cast a restless glance at my phone. There's no way that classified ad is a coincidence, not now, not today. It's a tap on my shoulder from something I'm trying to ignore. I'm three months clean since my last kill. At least, the one I was hoping could be my last.

I flick out of CheepsList and into social media, but all the posts are about the latest news—rich, corrupt men making policies that are about to make the rest of us even poorer. I stab off my phone screen and yank open my car door handle even though it's still too early for my appointment.

The heat of midday closes in around me as I cross the street toward the funeral home, sweat already prickling under my nicest top. Should have worn heels for an interview, maybe, but I'm not shelling out twenty bucks at Target for a job that doesn't even pay.

I stalk into a quiet room of pastel carpet and stop at the claw-footed foyer table with its meek rack of brochures. Boxes of tissue are tucked knowingly into all the corners. In the room beyond, racks of coffins gleam.

It is a building made for weeping.

Slick-soled shoes whisper over carpet, and a middle-aged man appears. He's shaped by a cheap suit and a face that reminds me of lumpy banana pudding. The kind that's been left out for long enough to grow a skin across the top.

"Hello, and welcome . . . to Williams Funeral Home." The owner's voice hitches almost imperceptibly when he sees me.

Almost.

"I've always wondered about that. The difference between a funeral home and a mortuary." It's an honest question, but after his hesitation, my voice comes out sharp. I'm not helping my case, as my mother would say. Though I don't even know yet if I care to be making a case. Besides, he won't throw me out. Not now. He'd be too ashamed of what that meant about him. I just give him a tight-lipped smile and cross my arms so he knows we don't have to shake hands. I wonder if people ever refuse to shake *his* hand because they know he's been touching dead bodies all day.

"That's an astute question, missy. You must be our potential intern?"

I nod, staring him down like a dare to ask why I'm interning at twenty-six.

"Well, a funeral home is a full-service establishment, offering an array of supportive services, including grief counseling and multimedia funeral presentations. A mortuary focuses a bit more on the mechanics of body preparation and the paperwork of appropriate remains disposal."

Hmm. A mortuary might have been a better option. I doubt I have an untapped talent for grief counseling or multimedia anything.

But I follow him anyway, listen anyway. Ask to see the embalming facilities anyway. He takes me downstairs. Instead of smelling like dusty pews and Kleenex, down here the air is colored by disinfectant, chemicals, and the faintest tinge of rot that even the droning ventilation system can't entirely sanitize. I wait, knowing most people would be disgusted. Instead, I feel that same, familiar nothing. There has to be a reason for that gap in me. For why I can do what I do.

I let my fingers trail over the metal of the wheeled tables. The hoses and boxes of gloves. A scalpel and a few other tools are laid out and I touch them too.

It's rude. But I heard a musician once say that the way to choose a guitar was to see what feels right in your hands. Funny how it all comes back to that. How nothing will ever feel to me like it does to them.

"Can you . . . Um, please don't touch the scalpels. They're sharp and you're not trained."

I turn and he busies himself with straightening things.

"So when can I start?" I ask blandly, because I hate it when people won't look straight at me.

"I . . . the nature of the work may not be what you thought," he says. "I'm not sure you can handle what we need."

Oh, can't I?

I pick up the scalpel.

The look in his eye changes. I can't tell if that's what I wanted or not, but either way, he's looking at me now. I twirl the scalpel, and the metal is hard and cold as it spins across my knuckles. There's more than one way to test my purpose here, and the floor has a drain. The walls hold no cameras. When I made the appointment, I didn't give him a name.

"Miss, I—"

I take a step forward.

He took something from me with that look, and with one step, I take it back. One tiny knife is all I need to remind him how very alone we are in this basement. Me, the dead, and him.

He's a tall, white, middle-aged man. Even growing up with a banana pudding face, I have to wonder if this is the first time he's ever felt the cold trickle down his neck that whispers *you're prey.*

The man starts to edge away, but I'm between him and the only exit. He throws a startled look toward the cell phone resting on the table, but we both know it's too far away. To get to help, or to get away, he'll have to come through me.

The power in the quiet of this moment fills me back up as I stroll across the room. I like the way he can't quite lift his shaking hands as I set the tip of the scalpel beneath the knot of his tie. It reminds both of us that I'm more than a nobody with a crap job.

I wait, letting his shock trickle into shame as I give him a long moment to realize he could have tried to fight, and he didn't. He owns this building, this suit, all this money. But I own him.

The threads of his tie start to part under the sharp edge of the scalpel and I strengthen the pressure, deepening the cut. His back has come up against a cinder-block wall now and there's nowhere for him to go that's not closer to my blade.

He makes a sound, a heaving yelp of a sob whose movement only slices his tie faster. The blade glances off a button beneath and we both smell ammonia as the fabric of his pants darkens. What's left of his tie dangles in two ragged tails, like ruined legs.

I could walk away right now. I've made my point, probably.

But it pisses me off that when people look at me the first thing they see is weakness. They're almost always bigger than me. They *could* beat me, hold me down, sure. But I can erase them like they've never been.

So I do. I slip his own scalpel into his neck, finding the carotid with a quick flick of my wrist.

His heart is already pumping so hard the first blood comes out as a spurt, and it splatters my face. I should wipe it clean, but I like the way it feels hot on my skin when I meet his eyes one last time and arch an eyebrow.

Checkmate.

I won this round, but he's too busy clutching his neck to properly concede the point. Too bad.

I turn my back on the spluttering sounds he's making and pluck his phone off the desk just in case he makes it that far before he bleeds out. Wipe down every instrument on the tray that I touched. He doesn't try to stop me when I leave the basement, following twists and turns of corridors I shouldn't know already. But then, perhaps it's an innate talent of criminals, always knowing the way out.

I pluck tissues from one of the ever-present boxes and wipe the phone, which I leave innocently on his upstairs desk. Clean my face next, and the outside handle of the funeral home, third. Without a name in his appointment book or a single fingerprint left behind, this case will grow cold and die.

The bloodied scalpel, I keep. A small theft to remind me that he was wrong about what strength and weakness looked like. This bridge is burning behind me, but Williams Funeral Home doesn't feel like the sign I was looking for anyway. Not the way the CheepsList ad did.

I step out of the scanty pocket of shade by the front door and cross the street in the scorching Arizona sun. It's barely tepid compared to what it will feel like to work the fryer all evening at my shitty job. I close my eyes and inhale, ignoring the sweat that gathers under the band of my bra, because with it comes the warmth of the sun, absorbing into my black hair. Caressing my skin like a gentle touch I probably wouldn't accept even if I still had a girlfriend to offer it.

What feels right in your hands?

The question mocks me all the way back to my car, across the street I'll never drive on the way to the funeral home career that I apparently won't be having.

My real question is, *Why me?*

What does it mean that killing is so easy for me? It's a clue, it must be, but the larger mystery remains.

I pick up my phone, letting it glow in the palm of my hand once more. The CheepsList ad is like an answer.

So I create a new email address, and I answer back.

Because even if I'm still searching for the why, with a new body growing cold behind me, there's no arguing the what.

I *am* a serial killer.

CHAPTER 2

To: CheepsListAd8543493053@CheepsList server.com
From: FacelessMan00@gmail.com
Date: May 1, 1:20 PM
Subject: Help Wanted

What kind of person posts a CheepsList ad for a serial killer?

To: FacelessMan00@gmail.com
From: MVictimVolunteer@gmail.com
Date: May 1, 1:31 PM
Re: Help Wanted

The desperate kind.
Can you help me? Have you done this before?

To: MVictimVolunteer@gmail.com
From: FacelessMan00@gmail.com
Date: May 1, 2:04 PM
Re: Help Wanted

Dear Volunteer,

Talking to strangers on the internet about murders you've committed sounds like a great way to go to prison. And posting a help wanted ad for a murderer seems like it'll probably end with you skinned for a lampshade, so good luck with that.

Why would I put my ass on the line to help someone I give absolutely no fucks about?

Cheers,

Not Your Serial Killer

To: FacelessMan00@gmail.com
From: MVictimVolunteer@gmail.com
Date: May 1, 2:38 PM
Re: Help Wanted

Dear Faceless,

I figured somebody like you needs people to kill. Why not me? You'll be a hell of a lot more likely to get caught messing around with unwilling victims than you would taking me as a freebie.

But if that's not enough, just tell me what you want in return. Money, a kidney, a blowjob, whatever. Believe me, I'm so beyond caring.

Sincerely,

Volunteer

To: MVictimVolunteer@gmail.com
From: FacelessMan00@gmail.com
Date: May 1, 3:30 PM
Re: Help Wanted

Dear Volunteer,

I'll take two fresh kidneys and a million dollars. Cashier's check only, please, and you can mail it to Crazytown, USA.

Which is where you're clearly already living, if you think the kind of guys who'd trade you a blowjob for a bullet will take you anywhere you care to be.

I don't *have* to kill, for the record. I just can.

I don't know if you recognized my screen name—in *Game of Thrones*, the Faceless Men carry out the will of the Nameless God and bring death to those who need it. The Faceless Men have their code about who lives and who dies. Except in this case, I decide, not some invisible god who can be given convenient speech bubbles by whoever is in power. It also means if the wrong choice gets made, the error hangs on me, not God.

If you want my help, I want your story. I don't personally give a shit what you've done. But your blood will be on my hand, and I have to live with myself after this. You don't. If I'm going to keep doing this, I should probably do it for the right reasons.

Cheers,

Faceless

CHAPTER

3
Jeika

CHEEPSLIST IS BASICALLY my fairy godmother.

When my baby brother peed on the couch, Mom was between paychecks, but after one day of sitting on the floor, we headed to the little bird icon of the online classified ads. Four hours of scrolling pictures, a minimal amount of cash, and an annoying drive out to Scottsdale later, we had non-peed-on fake leather with reclining seats and cupholders. Legit cupholders. In the couch.

A couple of years later, when my little brother, Ray-Ray, forgot he had a social studies project until the night before? CheepsList, boom. One slightly used diorama of the Oregon Trail. Granted, his project was supposed to be on the Civil War, but this at least eked him out a C.

And when I realized the dorms are only for people, um, still *enrolled* in college and I needed a new place to live that wasn't my car? One ad for a room for rent later and I had a roof over my head without waiting for a credit check.

Lesson learned. CheepsList solves problems.

So when I needed to die, and I realized I wasn't up to the task, to the online classifieds I went.

Writing the ad was the hard part. I wasn't sure how to attract the exact kind of criminal I needed, so I kept it simple. After all, they can't be any worse at killing me than I am.

The day before yesterday, I tried to hang myself in the woods.

I thought gravity would leave no room for mistakes. After all, gravity doesn't get nervous or flinchy. It doesn't have feet that can slam, unasked for, on the brake pedal. Gravity has no fingers that shake and sweat so you can't even grip a knife. Doesn't have a mouth that goes gummy and dry so the pills stick to your tongue and bleed bitterness down your throat until you choke and spit them into the sink like the mangled, half-melted carcasses of your best intentions.

But even gravity can fail you when you can't tie a thirteen-loop noose properly.

There's a quiet whimper from the next room, but I steel myself. Not my problem.

Still, my stomach flips and growls, and I reach for the box of Teddy Grahams beside the bed. I'm always hungry, like the empty feeling that haunts me is begging for some kind of nourishment I can't give it. Bonus: the snacks quiet the churn. Double bonus: munching on something sweet distracts me and makes me feel almost okay. Not so much when my throat is this sore, but usually. I've been reading the last email from Faceless Man over and over, trying to decide how to answer their ultimatum, and it's got my stomach even more churned than usual. One thing's for sure: I can't tell them what I've done. There'd be nothing stopping them from taking it to the police.

But what else but the truth would convince them how badly I need their help?

Another small, sad sound comes through my bedroom door, and it scrapes at the underside of my heart. I jump up, cursing myself the whole time. My roommate's due back from class any minute. If she never has to walk her own dog, how is she ever going to remember to do it once I'm gone?

I open the door, feeling horrible for making Cooper wait. He perks up when he sees me but doesn't jump on me. He's all playful energy with Kia, his real owner, but with me he's more careful, soft. Like he's afraid to startle me.

"Sorry, boy." I run my hand over his silky head and he leans against my leg, instantly content. "Wanna get your leash?"

Now he *explodes*, nails scrabbling for purchase against the floor as he races back toward the door to get what I've asked. Kia adopted him as a rescue, and he's some mix of golden retriever that produced a sweet, happy fuzzmuppet the color of hot chocolate with a dollop of cream, like my mother used to make us at Christmas. I don't think he ever got enough to eat before he ended up at the pound, so he only ever grew a little past puppy size.

Makes him cute as anything, but I always pour extra in his bowl when I'm the one to feed him, which is . . . probably too often.

I take him outside and apologize with a longer walk than usual, but when we get back, Kia still isn't home. Again.

I don't begrudge my roommate her busy whirl of friends and classes and frat parties, I really don't. In a parallel universe, I'd probably be doing the same. It's just, I don't think she realizes how much pain Cooper's in trying to hold his bladder for all the hours she's gone. He's all bounding joy and enthusiasm when she gets home, and she doesn't hear the tiny whimpers that sometimes escape him in all those empty hours before she returns.

That's why I started driving over on my breaks from work to let him out and taking him to the dog park to run. Especially after I saw how rarely Kia bothered with anything longer than a five-minute visit to the sad little strip of grass by the road.

When we get back into the cool of the air conditioning, he tries to follow me into my room, but I crowd him out with my knees, a pang twisting in my chest. "Sorry, boy," I murmur. I don't want him to get attached, because I can't stand the idea of him whimpering at my door and me not being able to answer, once this is all over.

I try to ignore the tiny, disappointed sound he makes as he flops to the floor in the hallway, tags jingling. To distract myself, I pull my phone out of my pocket, going back to the email that's been tormenting me all day.

I have to live with myself after this. You don't. If I'm going to keep doing this, I should probably do it for the right reasons.

How the hell am I supposed to know what qualifies as the "right" reasons to murder someone you found on CheepsList?

The pain nags at me, and I resist the urge to scratch my neck, still stuck on what I should write back. *Being suicidal feels like rope burn*, is what I want to tell them. The outer layers of your skin get scraped off so everything beneath is raw and weeping, just all the time so you can never forget it. It feels like failure, like the very specific shame that comes with something you have to cover up every time you leave the house so people won't know what you did. Or in my case, what you couldn't manage to do.

In my defense, a lot of very macabre people are eager to be quite helpful on YouTube, but those knots are harder to tie than they look.

After that fiasco, this should be easy. *Write an essay, 500 words or less on why you want to die, please add a clear thesis statement.* It's freshman lit all over again and I wasn't exactly aces at that.

While I think, I snatch up a greasy tub of Bag Balm and dab some onto the scrapes on my neck. Blonde strands of hair stick to the salve so I wrestle my hair up into a clip before I finish treating the wounds. They only have a few hours left in the air before I have to disguise them for my shift as an assistant at a real estate office, which I apparently have to go to now since I am starting to deeply doubt I'll be able to off myself before the next billing cycle. The cover-up is going to be hard to pull off, considering I'm the kind of scarf-wearer that makes strangers reach out to me when I walk into Target. *Here, honey, let me fix that.*

Plus, Phoenix. We're not exactly the land of scarves and mittens.

I close my eyes and force my mind back to what I need to capture in that email: everything I was thinking about when I drove to the forest preserve, then as I tried to slip that rope around my neck. The feelings, yes, but sanitized of the secrets that need to die with me.

When I open my eyes again, the tears have drawn lines all the way down my cheeks, stinging when they reach the raw places on my neck, but my vision is clear. I sit down with my back against the door, because it helps to be a little closer to Cooper's warm weight on the other side. I tell myself it doesn't count if he doesn't know I'm doing it. He's not even my dog, and if he doesn't get too used to having me around, it won't hurt him when I disappear.

I start to type, as fast as my thumbs can fly. I only stop to google and recheck my numbers. Back when I still thought I might manage to graduate from college—state school, at least—I majored in environmental science. The facts are so clear, once you take half a glance in that direction. Humans leave such a scar on this beautiful world. What could any of us do to justify the crater of impact our lives leave? Nothing, that's what. Especially me. Even this sharp, skeptical killer on the other side of my classified ad can't argue with that.

To: FacelessMan00@gmail.com
From: MVictimVolunteer@gmail.com
Date: May 2, 1:59 PM
Subject: My Reason

Dear Faceless,

This is all I think about these days, but I somehow still don't know how to answer your question. Not just because I don't want to talk about it, though of course I don't. It's that no matter what you say about why you want to die, people say that's not a good enough reason. Not because it isn't, but just because that's what you're supposed to say. Well, fuck that.

The truth is, I should already be dead. Everything would make so much more sense if I died six months ago. It made me think, afterward: How do you know you deserve to be alive? How does anyone? But then, it's the same question *you* must be thinking about all the time. Faceless Man and all.

I don't know your criteria, but here's mine.

Name three great figures from history. (Yes, I know the question was why I wanted to die. I'm getting there.) I mean good people, heroes. Here, I'll go first: Jesus, Mother Teresa, Robert Redford.

What do they all have in common? They all did things for other people or the environment. They sacrificed something of their own happiness and comfort and freedom for others. It doesn't even matter which three I could have picked. All good people have that same thing in common. Nobody admires you for saving yourself. To save your own ass is human, to save someone else's ass is divine.

One more point for you, before I get down to my reasoning. The amount of resources needed for a human lifespan is about 70 billion tons right now. That number has tripled in the last forty years. That means, if I live eighty years, it'll probably triple twice more. Basically, 630 billion tons of resources just for little old me. In a lifetime, I'll use 81,585 gallons of gas. More, if I end up with a long commute.

I'll eat about thirty-five tons of food. TONS.

I'm using up all this stuff and for what? What do I add to the world in return? Before I dropped out of college, I had one friend who was more athletic than me, and one friend who got better grades than me. And that's pretty much the story of my life. I'm never going to cure cancer or win the Nobel Prize. I'm absolutely freaking ordinary. All these statistics about the average American are about people just like me. And if there are millions of people just like me, what's the point of me?

Here's the truth, Faceless: I've already done the worst thing a person could do. And there's no taking it back. But even without knowing what I regret, you can't deny this: If I die now, every dollar of health care, every gallon of gas, and every sandwich I will ever use up can go to someone else. Every person I will ever hurt will be saved from me.

No matter how hard you try in life, you can't control everything your actions will set in motion.

If I choose to die, I can control my own impact from this moment forward. I can make it disappear.

So if you want to judge me, then go ahead. You're supposedly the expert. My very own Faceless Man. Do I deserve to live or die?

Sincerely,

Ready to Be Done

P.S. What's with the "Cheers," anyway? Are you British? Are you toasting your emails to a suicidal person? Because that's moderately fucked up.

CHAPTER 4

Dani

BLACK SMOKE SEETHES from under the edges of my car's hood and I glare at the motionless vehicle. If this is another sign, it's a great big middle finger of one, because I'm definitely going to miss my interview at the veterinarian's office. Two vets turned me down before I found one willing to let me shadow them for a few euthanasia appointments.

Shadow.

I like that verb. I'd like to be doing that a whole lot more than I'd like to be scowling at the hood, wondering if I should even bother with the gymnastics to get it propped up. I'm going to have to call him anyway. There's nothing to do with cars and smoke that I know how to fix and getting the stick in the super-high hood is a bitch.

I let out a sigh through my teeth. It was probably pointless anyway, trying out more legal avenues for my gift for death after I already cut someone's throat this week. Not to mention answering the CheepsList ad that could definitely be a cop. I've googled "entrapment" about thirty times since then.

I've just felt *off* since the failed internship interview. Not quite the gut-scraping regret TV claims murderers are supposed to feel, but just a little pang of *oopsie*. Maybe because I've never killed anyone who didn't deserve it before. Or at least asked me for it. And sure, Mr. Funeral Home was kind of a judgy asshole, but not truly bad enough to pull down a death sentence.

It almost scared me.

That I could get caught, sure, but mostly that it's gotten *this* easy. After all, just because I can doesn't mean I should. So I'm taking it slow with this classified ad, and I went ahead with the vet office thing. Just in case. Except then my car died.

It's not just this interview I need the car for: the grocery store's too far to walk, and so is my job. I glance back at the house. When I left, my mom was passed out on the couch in a T-shirt and her underwear, one bare foot slumped off the cushion onto the floor. The bottle of Southern Comfort and the bottle of her pills were both low enough to let me know that the pain was bad yesterday. I should have moved out to my own place and my own life years ago, but she can't make it without me.

I can't keep both of us going without a car, but two weeks ago, I hit the limit of what I was willing to do to keep this thing running. Funny how the world doesn't change its rules even when you're not willing to play anymore.

The metal's hot against my ass when I lean back against the grille of my car and make the call.

"Hey, it's out again. Smoke this time. Can you come over?"

As soon as he agrees, a smile slithering through his voice, I hang up and tip my head back, letting my eyes fall shut. Sometimes the world is so ugly that all I want is darkness.

I keep my lids closed as long as I can. The three blocks from his trailer won't take him long. The sun's already burning my skin red when I open my eyes again to see him walking up the street. Toes wide in that duck-walking swagger, his pants sagging from his chopped-off belt. Even from here I can see how wet his thin lips are. He is the reason I ended up in front of the funeral home.

Looking for any other answer. Any way his life isn't my responsibility to end. If I'm going to keep doing this shit, I want it to be on my terms, but somehow, it never feels like it is.

Eric smiles as he approaches, eyes slitted against the sun.

"More car trouble?" He smells like sweat. Not clean sweat but the kind that festers in your armpits and doesn't come out in the wash. Layered on top of that is body spray made for a man two decades younger than his receding hairline claims him as.

I step back and let him lift the hood. Though I'm not going to fucking ask. "Shitty timing. I'm late for a job interview."

"You get fired?"

"Not yet."

He chuckles. "So, soon then?"

Given that Marilyn just wrote me up for insubordination again last week, and put me on Mondays even though I told her I couldn't work that day? Probably.

I just shrug.

"Ah, shit . . ." He whistles through his teeth, then sidles closer to me as he points into the engine at something that looks like a half-melted belt. "See that?"

I don't lean in. "Can you get parts from the junkyard?"

"Maybe. Desert air means rubber doesn't keep, but if they got in a fresh junker that's the right model, we might be able to do something with that. Wanna ride out there with me?"

"No. I'm busy."

I used to ride with him to the junkyard when we first moved here. Why not? Back before I started to second-guess why he was so eager to help, and this car was just a piece of garbage with beautiful classic lines, abandoned by one of my mom's boyfriends. Eric was the one who dropped a junkyard starter into it and gave me the ability to get farther from my house than my feet could ever take me.

Work. Money. Freedom. I loved the gasoline-scented muscle of that car, the way it drove like every other vehicle on the road would melt like wet tissue paper before it.

Eric's old enough to be my father, but I let him stand closer, look longer, than I would have let anybody else, because of the gift of that car. But I don't let him touch. Not because I can't survive it. I can survive almost anything, unfortunately. I just won't let him make me into a person who will endure things from men.

He reaches into my engine to poke at something, the freckled skin of his arm pallid where it protrudes from the sleeve of his T-shirt. "Can't be that busy right now if you were supposed to be at a job interview."

"I need to call them to reschedule." I'd rather not lose that big open question mark of possibility with the one veterinarian who is willing to let me in the door. Maybe I'm meant for something more than this. Maybe Mr. Funeral Home can be my last one, for real this time.

Eric straightens. "Well, if I gotta go to the salvage yard alone to run your errands, at least walk me back to my house."

"It's only three blocks." I raise an eyebrow at him. "A grown-ass man can't walk three blocks on his own?"

"Gets lonely." He nods to my quiet house. "You oughta know about that. Besides, friends hang out together. We are friends, right?"

It's a test. A punishment, really, since I slapped his hand off my shoulder two weeks ago. An hour later, I saw him at the playground pushing the swings for Aurelio Jimenez, a five-year-old he's definitely not related to.

"Because friends see each other in between fixing each other's cars," Eric presses, his eyes watery and more than a little bloodshot. He's not blinking. "Pretty sure I don't do that shit for strangers."

"Let's walk, then." I don't look away or squirm. Eric nods.

This is why he keeps coming around. It's certainly not because I'm nice to him. He likes me because I'm not afraid of him. Well, and because I've got tits. But he thinks my lack of fear is because I don't know what he wants from me. Probably, he thinks that's why I keep naively asking him over to fix my car.

I look at him for a little longer. His thin nose. Rotting seaweed eyes. Wet lips. *I can kill you*, I think. The knowledge crawls under my skin, like my blood is a different color from everybody else's, and I'm the only one who knows.

I don't mind killing. I know I should. It's messy and exhausting, and in the thick of it, the other person's agony echoes through every nerve in your body, lighting up your internal organs with the atavistic memories of *pain fear run* that seem tattooed on our bones from the days when caves were places of refuge.

All my true-crime podcasts tell me that other murderers thirst for that, that they must thrive on the sadism and adrenaline, but it does nothing for me. I don't crave it, but like surviving, it's just something I can do. Especially when it's a stranger, it's startlingly easy.

But Mr. Funeral Home is still sitting in my gut like a meal I can't quite digest. If I'm going to do this even one more time, it has to be on my terms. My choice, for the *right* reasons, not just because I can. Otherwise, I'm no better than the predators I've made my prey.

I turn toward the street and his hand settles on my back, guiding me around him. His smallest finger slipping under the hem of my shirt. I stop moving, my throat closing so abruptly it's like I've taken a punch. His hand falters awkwardly, the word "friend" hanging in the air between us even though he hasn't said it.

A test. A punishment.

I whirl and grip his wrist, feeling every mile of freedom that car gives me shrinking down until the metal trailers lining the street might as well be bars. I squeeze until his bones grind and he jerks back, fear flaring in his eyes when his arm snaps taut between us like a leash he just hit the end of. I don't let go, and it takes him less than a second to realize he can't make me.

"What the hell?"

"Don't touch."

"Jesus, I thought you might—wasn't trying—wasn't nothing," he sputters. "Thought we were friends!" He shakes out his wrist when I release it, holding it to his chest for a second the way a hurt child clutches a stuffed animal. His lips pooch out. Wounded, almost pouting.

"Friends walk," I instruct him, my blood pumping wildly through my veins until my head spins and reels and I have to work hard not to blink. If I lose my car, we lose our trailer. I lose my whole life. The car's so old, I could never afford to keep it running without him. Wouldn't know how, even if I tried. He knows it, I know it. And I draw the line anyway. "They don't touch."

I pushed his hand away last time, but the car was already fixed then. I didn't say a word, and so he thought maybe this time, I'd let him. He couldn't even wait until we got to his house and he tried to get me inside, that's how excited he was about the idea that he might get away with it.

"Jesus," he mutters. "That mom of yours probably hasn't patted you on the back in ten years. Thought you might—"

"I don't," I cut him off. The only thing that's saved him from me so far is that he's a bigger risk than the others, because he's connected to my real life. The police may be busy, but they're not always stupid.

I start walking toward his house and he jogs to catch up, his stride a little shorter than usual. Wounded, distracted. He's calculating if I'm still worth it, what there is left that I might let him get away with. I let him think it over, hoping his filthy desires will give him false hope enough that I'll get a new serpentine belt and a smoke-free engine out of the deal.

When you don't have what you want, sometimes hope is all you get.

We've only made it a block when a little girl bursts out of her house. She's maybe six or seven and her name is Holly. I know because I've made her lunch a time or two when her parents were working back-to-back shifts and didn't know the babysitter hadn't shown up. I remember how hard it is to be hungry when you're that little.

She pelts up the swept-clean pavement of her driveway, waving to us.

Eric squats down and pulls her into a hug, avoiding my eyes. My pulse jolts as the hand I just slapped off me settles onto her instead. She's so young, his hand is nearly as wide as her whole back.

"Hey, you bored today? Wanna come over?" He gestures to me. "I've got to fix her car, but then I was going to make cookies. You could put frosting on them. You know how bad I am with the frosting."

There's blackness like oil, sliding out from my stomach underneath all my skin. Seeing this, it's like the whole world should come to a boil.

I watch him talk to Holly, just like I watched him push Aurelio's swing two weeks ago. I can keep his hands off me. But I can't keep his hands off everyone, not all the time. Unless . . .

That's the question ticktocking in the back of my brain. If there might be an actual reason for all the ugly situations I've ended up in. If fate exists, it woke me up in time to save my mother. It put Eric in my path. It landed my car outside that funeral home, looking for answers I didn't find. It brought that CheepsList ad to my phone, that desperate woman to my email inbox. It broke my car before I could try to bring death to sick animals in a veterinarian's office instead.

Fate is asking me the same question in so many different bodies.

I'm not ready to answer.

And I don't know how long it will let me keep stalling.

CHAPTER

5

Jeika

WHEN MY EMAIL account finally, finally dings, I race to pull out my phone, even though I'm at work. It's been twenty-two hours since I scraped my heart bare for Faceless Man, and got a big, fat nothing in return. Honestly, I get not always being on top of your email, but if you have a victim just *volunteering* to feed your very illegal compulsion, what do you really have going on that's more interesting?

But when I open my email, it's not from the murderer I've been waiting on.

Seriously? Is Faceless going to ghost me like they have a whole app full of other victims to swipe right on? I nibble on the inside of my cheek, considering. I could have lied, made up a reason so good any logical person would have agreed to assist my suicide. Instead, I told them as much of the truth as I could bear, and for some dumb reason, I thought being honest might be enough. That maybe, they'd even kind of understand.

I swallow and try to refocus on this new response. It's from a legit-looking email address, so maybe it's not yet another bot or scammer. Could I have another chance at this, even if it's not with Faceless Man?

But when I scroll down, the new email is painfully short.

To: CheepsListAd8543493053@
CheepsListserver.com
From: PeterL1978@hotmail.com
Date: May 3, 12:35 PM
Subject: If you're serious . . .
602-555-0126

I'm supposed to be baking cookies for my boss's open house, but the plastic-wrapped sausage of dough just sits on the counter as I stare at my phone. That ad was a last-ditch Hail Mary. I'm not even sure I really thought I'd get a response, but my heart is hammering now like it thinks this one is for real. I don't have much to go on, though, with just a phone number.

Do I dare?

It belongs to a fortysomething man, if the email address is to be believed—and Hotmail accounts don't lie. Anybody who still has one of those probably also has a landline phone and a pager. My head starts to feel too light and I grip the edge of the counter. An adult male is kind of the jackpot, if you're looking to find a serial killer. Which is precisely what I wanted. So why does it feel so much riskier to talk rather than type?

"Jeika!"

I flinch at the sound of my name, even though Renee mispronounced it yet again. Not like we've been working together for the better part of three months or anything.

"*Jay*-ka," I correct automatically.

"Right, right." She waves that away with a flick of French-manicured nails. "Darling, you need to get the cookies in the oven! If the scent doesn't have time to hit the air before the buyers get here, there's hardly any point in doing it at all. You kids need to remember there's a world outside of your phones." She clucks her tongue. "Here, sweetie, don't wrap these so tight or they don't look right." She reaches to adjust the scarf wound too many times around my neck and the fabric grates over raw skin. I twitch back, forcing a smile.

"I, uh, like it this way. Thanks."

"I'm just glad you're stepping outside of your comfort zone a little more." She gives me a too-bright smile, her lipstick bleeding into the fine lines around her mouth.

I glance down at my phone, afraid that means she's seen the screen, but no, it locked when my hand squeezed shut around it. She's talking about my new fashion choices.

"This time in your life is all about taking chances to find out who you really want to be," she starts in.

"Uh-huh." I wave my phone before she gets all the way into one of her boomer lectures about this "golden era" of my twenties. "I just got an important call. Can I call them back real quick?"

I should really wait until I'm off work and have some privacy, but this open house goes from noon to five. There's no way I can hold out that long to find out what this Peter guy has to say. Especially since Faceless Man still hasn't responded, so I have no idea whether they're going to help me or not.

"Of course, hon. Here, I can get the cookies set up myself. I worked my way up in this company just like you're doing, so it's not like I've forgotten how!" Renee trills a shrill little laugh that makes me wonder if she has indeed forgotten how to put premade cookie dough on a tray without an assistant. "You did preheat the oven this time, right?"

"Yup, sure did." I twist the knob on when I pass the stove, hoping she didn't notice. "I'll just take this out back."

I slide the glass door closed behind me and step out onto the stamped-concrete patio—*perfect for al fresco dining!* as Renee always says. As if anyone in Phoenix wants to eat outside in this brain-melting heat. A trio of flies joins the party as soon as I open the door, and I swat at them half-heartedly, one eye still on my phone and that mysterious email. *If you're serious . . .*

I dial before I can talk myself out of it. What do I have to lose, after all? For once, I'm hoping the weirdos on the internet really *are* serial killers. And if this new guy has something creepy in mind before he finishes me off, well . . . hopefully I'll be able to screen that out on the call.

"Hello?" the voice on the other end sounds gruff, but unexpectedly normal. Like a high school social studies teacher or something.

"Um, is this Peter?" It comes out squeaky and I clear my throat so he won't think I'm underage. "You answered my, uh, ad?"

There's a long pause, then he scoffs. "That's for real, then? I wasn't sure anybody would really be that nuts."

"Well, that's pretty much the point, isn't it?" I say tartly. "Not exactly feeling sane and well-adjusted over here."

"Have you gotten any other answers?"

I frown. That was not . . . precisely what I expected a murderer to ask. "Are you worried about *competition*?"

Renee moves past the patio slider, pointedly dusting a table I already dusted when we got here. She gives me a cheery wave and mouths, "*Take your time*," while making a diligent show of all the cleaning she could use help with. All coincidentally centered in front of the glass door.

I turn my back on her. "Listen, I'm at work, so I don't have much time. Are you serious about helping me or not?"

"I am, actually."

His voice sounds different now. Less social studies teacher and more . . . I'm not sure, but goosebumps itch beneath my scarf.

"But I want something in return."

CHAPTER

6

Dani

I SHIFT, TRYING TO get comfortable on the gritty concrete step out back of the restaurant. We've been slammed all morning, and I only get fifteen minutes on my break to clear my head and think about something other than stuffing fried chicken pieces into paper boxes as fast as I can. I take a deep breath, but the air out here is tinged with gasoline from the Sinclair station next door. It reminds me of my old car, and Eric.

I need to find out if my suspicions about him are right. The bloody scalpel has been sitting in my top drawer, staring at me every time I grab a pair of socks. I don't know why I kept it; I never take anything from crime scenes. But maybe I need the reminder this time, if I'm starting to cross the line too impulsively. I don't want to become that person who shoots up a school, spraying bullets over innocent people just because they can. No, I need to be sure Eric is the predator I suspect he is, especially if I'm going to take out someone the police can trace back to me.

First, though, I should decide about the CheepsList girl. I don't know for sure that it's a woman, but most men don't spend much time worrying about rape, and that was front and center in the ad. I've never killed a female, but that's only one small facet of the question facing me now. If death is my purpose, how will *I* choose to wield it?

Her email was a start to answering that, though it's an imperfect test. Her explanation of why she wants to die was a long one, and full of old pain.

I can tell she really believes it—there's a hopelessness to her explanation that speaks of thoughts long recycled. And a defensiveness to everything she says, like it's been a long time since she's had anyone on her side. But there's something about her story that doesn't quite match up. Maybe all that stuff about resources used up, like she was doing the math on her own life. It reeks of bargaining. It's not that strange to care about the environment, but who cares *that* much? If she's doing that math, it's because she already knows an answer she doesn't like and she's trying to get it to add up some other way.

The back door of the restaurant pops open and the assistant manager, Marilyn, sticks her head out.

"Your phone stop keeping time or something?"

This is her asshole way of announcing my break is over.

I rise off the steps and brush the concrete dust off the seat of my Norma Dean's Fried Chicken uniform pants. Fifteen minutes on a crooked concrete step isn't much of a break from anything, but I head into the kitchen and grind back into the routine anyway. Order. Scoop. Box. Slide onto a tray.

I shouldn't be thinking this much about one stupid email. I have my own problems. Making rent. The yellow that's starting to tinge my mom's skin, in the right light. What might have happened when Holly went over to frost sugar cookies at Eric's trailer. The *whys* itching under my skin are growing louder every day. Like they're daring me to reach out and take control of the destiny that's luring me along one step at a time.

One corpse at a time.

Order. Scoop. Box.

OrderScoopBox*OrderScoopBox.*

I move faster than everybody in this kitchen, because they expect me to be slower. And because Jane's being extra methodical today, so I need to push if I don't want Marilyn on my ass about our orders stacking up.

I wonder if this CheepsList girl has talked to anybody about whatever's making her so desperate. It's not really an option in my situation, but when the person you want to kill is yourself, there are all the people in the world just waiting to listen. Hotlines. Support groups. Why isn't she using those instead of online classified ads?

Order. Scoop. Box.

I cut open a bag of chicken pieces and dump it in the fryer basket, the bones rattling against metal.

I've got three more orders waiting, but I jerk out my phone to read her explanation again. *Regret.* The word jumps out at me like it has teeth.

Then Marilyn enters the kitchen, her sharp chin and close-set eyes scanning for an excuse to smack somebody down. I shove my phone back in my pocket and throw away the plastic from the frozen box of chicken.

Marilyn settles on a victim. "Jane! Get a move on!" she snaps. "You don't need to polish every piece of chicken before it goes out, or we'll all still be here come midnight."

Beside me, Jane flinches and jerks back from the counter, staring at Marilyn with wide eyes that quickly slick with tears. Up until last week, she's had state agency support staff with her every day, helping with her job training until she was ready to go independent. I'm guessing she qualified for the help because she's got Down syndrome, but as far as I can tell, her only problem is that she gives far too many fucks to be working for a place like Norma Dean's Fried Chicken.

Her process is impeccable: checking to make sure each box gets an even mix of wings, legs, and breasts, and turning each piece pretty-side up before she stacks the sauces, folds the boxes closed, and tucks in the flaps. For as many times as her trainer gave her the speed-over-perfection pep talk, Jane just doesn't have it in her to do a bad job.

She's starting to huff in these little breaths that make my neck burn with secondhand embarrassment, even though it's got fuck-all to do with me. Marilyn ignores her completely, already turning her back on Jane's stuttered apologies to sneer at me.

"And Dani, don't think I missed you having your phone out in the kitchen when you already had your lunch *and* your afternoon break."

I don't even answer her. Just sink the chicken pieces into the hot oil and let the bubbles roar.

"See, that's why I like you," Marilyn says. "You're as lazy as the rest of them, but at least you don't make excuses."

Jane's still apologizing, and the word "excuses" cuts over the top of her with such contempt it's like Marilyn doesn't even hear her. My gaze sharpens, and every crumb on the steel counter comes into focus. Some people get off on the power trip of having "Manager" on their badge, even if it's got that sad little disclaimer of "Assistant" before it. Even if the only kingdom you rule is filled with trash and cardboard and the cheapest substances that can still qualify as food.

Marilyn's phone beeps with a text, and she pulls it out while she's turning away. I shift my weight, melting to the side. Just enough so she has to shift course to avoid touching me, her hand hits the handle of the fryer, and her phone goes flying into the hot oil. Bullseye.

"What? Oh *shit*!"

I lift the fryer basket up and hook it to the wall so it can drain. "You really should be more careful having your phone out in the kitchen."

I use two fingers to pluck her still-hot phone from atop the chicken and shove it into her palm before she has time to think. My fingers have been burned a thousand times. They're used to heat, and pain is nothing to me. My manager gasps, tears flying to her eyes as the leftover oil sears her soft palm.

"You—you—"

I arch an eyebrow. But we both know I've already called every bluff she had. Besides, everyone saw me touch the phone with my bare fingers first.

Behind her, Jane's gone fish-belly white and her eyes dart between me and Marilyn. She wants to get out of here but doesn't dare break another of Marilyn's rules.

"Jane," I say. "Can you go grab me some napkins to refill our station?"

She loves filling anything back up. It suits her hopeful nature, I think. She darts away from the confrontation storming between me and Marilyn, happy to have an escape route.

The assistant manager's face twists, her mouth opening like she's about to shriek at me. But I turn away, dismissing her.

The phone goes clattering to the floor as Marilyn flees for the office, clutching her hand to her chest in the same petulant way Eric held his, both of them betrayed by a reality where they couldn't have their way against me. Much more hurt by that than anything I did to them physically.

People look at me and think I'll be an easy stepping stone. And they hate me all the more when they find out I'm not.

I shake my hair back and return to my work at a comfortable, leisurely pace.

It says something about you, the victims you choose. Whether you're the sort to go after a Marilyn or a Jane. I close another box of chicken and toss it into a plastic bag. I know which side of that line I land on. The question is, how do I test what sort of person this CheepsList girl is?

CHAPTER 7

To: MVictimVolunteer@gmail.com
From: FacelessMan00@gmail.com
Date: May 4, 5:14 PM
Re: My Reason

Dear Volunteer,

Your reasons are interesting, I'll give you that much. Except in all those words, you never actually answered my question.

Let me be clear: I won't kill someone else's victim. There are some fucked-up men in the world who like to twist you up in shame, so you can't get away because you're caught in your own net, and therefore, theirs. If your desperation comes from guilt, I'd like to know the guilt is truly yours, and that it wasn't imposed on you.

And since you asked, I'm not British. I just don't really think there's any good way to sign emails. "Sincerely" sounds like you mean the opposite. Because if you have to say it, you're really not. "Best" . . . well, what does that even mean? Best wishes? I'm the best? You're the best? Doesn't work. I like "Cheers" because it's like tipping your hat. A small token of electronic respect.

The thing is, we're not here to argue population curves and climate change. The only important part of that story is the piece you don't want to tell me—about what made you decide you deserved to be around less than any other random person picking their nose at a stoplight. Because based on what I know now, my answer is no.

I'm not going to add you to my body count just because you think being ordinary is a capital offense.

If you want me to do it, you're going to have to convince me you really deserve to die.

Cheers,

Faceless

CHAPTER 8

To: FacelessMan00@gmail.com
From: MVictimVolunteer@gmail.com
Date: May 4, 9:06 PM
Re: My Reason

Dear Faceless,

Thing is, I left my ad up, and now I have somebody else interested in the job. Which means I don't need to convince you that I deserve to die—you need to convince *me* you're the murderer I should choose.

If you really don't give a fuck about me, like you said, then you wouldn't care why I'm doing this, or if there's somebody hurting or manipulating me. You also wouldn't have tried to warn me about what could happen if my ad appeals to the wrong kind of person.

This is me calling your bluff. I've got one on the hook and I'm about to find out exactly what might happen. Would I rather do this fast and painless, with an experienced, preferably non-sadistic person? You bet your ass I would. But if I had any other choices left, I wouldn't be here. At this point, I'll take the first person who can end this for me, no matter who they are.

If you don't want to miss your best shot at a willing victim, answer the following questions. I think you'll find them fair.

1. How many murders have you personally committed? How many murders have you contributed to in a supporting role? Please note cause of death in each case.

2. List any criminal or civil charges you've faced in the course of completing your duties, including convictions, plea bargains, and exonerations.

3. What makes you the best candidate to be my murderer?

Cheers,

Hoping You'll Take the Job

To: MVictimVolunteer@gmail.com
From: FacelessMan00@gmail.com
Date: May 4, 9:30 PM
Re: My Reason

Dear Volunteer,

You answered my questions (kind of) so I'll answer yours.

1. How many murders have you personally committed? How many murders have you contributed to in a supporting role? Please note cause of death in each case.

More than you.

2. List any criminal or civil charges you've faced in the course of completing your duties, including convictions, plea bargains, and exonerations.

None.

The people who get caught are the ones who need validation, who leave a signature behind. Who want to show off their cleverness. I don't need that ego shit. That's why I don't get caught.

3. What makes you the best candidate to be my murderer?

I'm not in this to make you suffer. If I kill a woman, it'll be to help you end whatever is making you suffer.

I can do the job fast and mostly painlessly, because I'm not some pervert who's going to get off on it. So if you really want to die, I can make that happen.

If I choose to.

Cheers,

D

P.S. Not that it's my business, but if you don't have good reason to trust whatever other guy answered, you probably shouldn't email him back. Even with a dummy email account, he might know some way to trace you. If he can find you, you won't exactly have your pick of murderers anymore.

To: FacelessMan00@gmail.com
From: MVictimVolunteer@gmail.com
Date: May 5, 7:26 AM
Re: My Reason

Dear D,

You had me at #3. I'll definitely take you over my other option. When do you want to do this?

-J

P.S. What does the D stand for? Is that your name? Or just what you want me to call you?

P.P.S. You're going to be okay, right? If we go through with this, I mean. I assumed since you answered my ad that you do this kind of thing all the time and you're used to it. But the thing you said about having to live with it made me wonder. I just want you to know, if it's going to mess you up or make you sad, you don't have to help me. I've caused enough damage without that.

To: MVictimVolunteer@gmail.com
From: FacelessMan00@gmail.com
Date: May 5, 8:15 AM
Re: My Reason

Dear J,

The D stands for death.

It's like how you don't call your mom by her name, you call her by her role in your life. Before she's a person who hates cornflakes and procrastinates taking out the trash, she's your mom.

You might as well call me by the role I'm going to play in your life, because to you, I don't need to be anything else.

I passed your test, but you still haven't passed mine. You know what you need to tell me if you want this to go any further.

Cheers,

D

CHAPTER

9

Jeika

"FUCK!"

I hurl my phone against the living room wall, fed up with the whole game. Why did I have to get the world's most stubborn criminal? Where are all these impeccably controlled, well-groomed serial killers you always see in the movies? I'd give every dollar left in my bank account for somebody with freshly shined shoes and no personality disorder.

I drop my head back against the cushions of the couch and groan between my teeth.

"Yeah," a voice says sagely. "I've had those days too, girl."

I startle, my eyes coming open to spot my roommate, who I definitely thought had gone to class. Kia leans a shoulder against the door to the kitchen, Cooper at her feet. "Wanna talk about it?"

A semi-hysterical laugh bubbles up out of me. "No, I really do not. That being the current problem."

"Ah." An even more knowing look settles onto Kia's face and she crosses the living room to perch on the couch. Cooper jumps up in between us, making the couch cushions tilt as he turns in circles, trying to find just the right spot. Kia bats his tail away from her face. "Let me guess. You're dating a new guy and you just got to that phase where he wants to know all your dark and dirty, and you aren't here for it."

"Girl," I correct automatically. Not that I can prove it. The tone of the emails is kind of masculine, ruthless and certain. And the email is Faceless Man, after all. But some of the disgusted things they've said about men—not people but *men*—whisper that it's a woman.

Kia's eyebrows tick up slightly, like *that makes sense*. I haven't dated anyone since I moved in here, so she wouldn't exactly know I don't have a gender preference.

"Right, right." She nods, scratching Cooper behind the ears as he finally flops down. "So what are you going to do about her? I kinda think if she can't handle the truth, she shouldn't have asked. If she sticks with you after that, at least you'll know it's for real."

I rub my hands over my face, not looking at her. "Yeah, no. This is the kind of secret you get dumped for, every time."

What I've done is bad enough that even internet crazies would probably agree it's a good reason to check out. But a small, squirmy part of me is afraid that if D hears my past, she'll be so horrified she'll realize killing me would be a mercy. One she has the power to withhold.

Cooper nuzzles my hand worriedly, and I allow myself to pet him this time. Just a little, only so he won't fuss.

I'm not in this to make you suffer. Her words echo in my head. *If I kill a woman, it'll be to help you end whatever is making you suffer.*

But can I really believe that? I put up the ad because even if I hand myself over to a serial killer, I have nothing left to lose. The worst they could do is torture me before they finish me off and while I'd rather skip that part, I probably deserve it. But if I tell her all my secrets, she'll have leverage over me. She could blackmail me for anything she wanted or report me to the police.

Kia pats my knee, looking sympathetic. "Then you don't have to tell her." She shrugs. "There are plenty of other fish in the sea."

She kisses Coop on his head and gets up, swiping her bag from by the door and checking that she has her phone. "Wanna come out with me tonight? Might be a good distraction."

Her dog looks up, watching with perked ears.

"No, maybe next time," I tell her absently. I'm too busy mulling over her words to be offended at the quick flash of relief that crosses her face when I let her off the hook. Can't blame her. I wouldn't want to drag my maudlin ass to a party these days either.

Plenty of fish in the sea.

I wait until she closes the door behind her, and then I retrieve my phone from across the room. The screen didn't crack when I threw it, thank God, and the number I want is still at the top of my recent call list because apparently, I'm so lame that the only people I interact with are killers.

"You going to hang up on me again?" is how he answers. Not promising.

"Yeah, sorry." I try to rein in the sharpness in my tone, because it's not Peter's fault I've had a shit day. "I did email to say I'd call you later, though. My boss walked in on our last call and I didn't want her to overhear. Obviously." I swap hands for the phone. "Listen, I'm in. The other person who answered my ad turned out to be a no-go so you're up. If you help me die, what was the condition you wanted in return?"

"Someone else already answered?" His voice is quick, sharp, like a whip cracking.

I frown. That is not the part I thought he'd be excited about. I honestly thought serial killers would be more interested in, well, *killing*. Shows what I know.

"Sure, but like I said, I'm picking you." I pace across the room, jittery because I really don't want to ask the next question. "So what's the trade?"

"Easy. I want every murderer your ad lures in."

I still, my thumbnail digging into the seam on the edge of my phone case. He wants D? Which . . . I guess I don't owe her anything. She's supposedly a criminal, after all, and I don't know her from Eve. But this doesn't add up. If he's got some kind of vendetta against murderers, would he really . . . be one?

"Why . . ." I try to formulate the exact question, and end up with just, "But why, though?"

"You're kidding me, right?" His voice drips with condescension, and it rams a stiff rod up my spine because it reminds me of the patronizing tone of my old Western Civ professor, who always put the word "sexism" in quotes. As if that wasn't a "real" part of history.

"I asked you for the others because I lost my daughter to an asshole like that," Peter snaps. "You may be asking to die, but anybody sick enough to answer your ad probably doesn't just take willing victims. I can't stand the thought of them out there, acting like they have the right to erase whole people, with lives and families."

"I'm so sorry," I whisper. I sink down on the couch and Cooper whines and licks my free hand. It sucks for Peter to even be talking to me, probably. A woman young enough I could have been his child, who *wants* to throw away the same chance at life that was stolen from his daughter.

Except he still didn't explain why he's willing to switch sides to the enemy camp. Is this an "if you can't beat 'em, join 'em situation"?

"Are you, uh . . ." There is no good way to ask this. I swallow. "Um, sorry, but . . . the deal is to kill? Me?" I cough, and it makes this precisely zero percent easier to say. "Are you going to be good with that?"

"What? Yes, fine, whatever." He dismisses the topic of my life as if I've bothered him at work to ask a favor. "If you'll pass along the one who already answered your ad, and any more you hear from, I'll do whatever I have to do in exchange."

I bite the inside of my lip, my thoughts a stuttering churn. I'm not sure I really believe that. But then, the flippant way he talks about it hints that maybe it wouldn't be that big of a deal for him.

"You still there?"

"Yeah, I am. I, uh—"

"Look," he cuts me off. "If you're worried about how I'll do it, I've got a gun. It'll be as easy as hitting the off switch." A pause, so quick I'm not sure if it's my uneasy imagination. "For you."

What does that mean for what he'll do to D? Will it be . . . not quick?

My stomach gurgles and I find myself wondering all over again if D is really a woman. It makes a difference, somehow, though it shouldn't. *She told you she didn't want you to suffer*, a small voice whispers. Though I guess she's currently leaving me on my own to do just that.

"I don't know why you're asking *me* all these questions," Peter snaps. "I hope you weren't dumb enough to challenge the others this way. They'll say anything to get close to you so they can slaughter you. They're sociopaths and sadists, so messed up that people like us just couldn't understand. They deserve every horrible, humiliating thing that could be done to them, and good riddance."

Humiliating. I don't like that word any more than I liked the idea that it will be quick . . . but only for me. I mean, it's his choice to do those things, not mine. But if I hand a person over to him for whatever sick revenge stuff he has in mind, it kinda does make it my fault. And odds are, it probably wasn't D who hurt his daughter. Phoenix is a big city. There could be any number of murderers out there. I just wish a few more of the saner ones had answered my ad.

I play with Cooper's collar, trying to think. He lays his head down on the couch with a little *huff* of an exhale, like he's frustrated too.

"Of course," I agree a beat late, but my voice sounds weird. "Look, I need to . . . get my affairs in order." *Really, Jeika? Who says that in real life?* "I'll be in touch as soon as I have the other person's location."

I hang up, not sure if I'll really do it or not. D refused to help me, but I don't know if that's enough for her to deserve something "humiliating" at Peter's hands, or for him to take it slow with killing her.

For the first time, I have a little sympathy for her insistence on knowing who she's killing and why.

I have a lot of thinking to do about how far I'm willing to go with all this, because I hate both my options. Telling D the truth risks any freedom I have left to seek my own end, but maybe I could concoct a lie believable enough that she'd help me?

Because if Peter ends up being my only way out, I'm going to have to give her to him. No matter what he does to her.

CHAPTER

10

Dani

I HAVEN'T HAD MANY choices in my life. Frying chicken buys you a few things: socks, ramen. Choices are a little out of the price range. But the consequences of my indecision are mounting every single day. Watching Eric smile at Holly and slip chocolate chip granola bars to Aurelio, not sure what he's doing to them behind closed doors. I warned J that if she doesn't tell me her real story, I'm out, but if I don't help her, she'll turn to that other murderer she mentioned. The one I have a bad feeling about.

It's been like this every time I've killed, except for the first one. Some guy doing ugly shit. An opportunity dangled in front of me, like a flag in a shade of red only I can see. It always seems like it was meant to be me. Well, fuck that.

It doesn't take a genius to figure out why somebody like me doesn't want to believe in fate. I've never liked anybody pulling my strings but me. I definitely don't like that weird, uneasy feeling that still doesn't know if the impulse to kill Mr. Funeral Home came from me, or from something outside of me. Maybe something that knew more than I did, about why he deserved to die. Or maybe some other kind of God, one who doesn't give a flapping fuck about any of this and just likes to mess with us. I don't know any more than anybody else when it comes to naming the wizard behind the curtain, but I know this: I'm nobody's tool.

But it turns out, even once you're trying to make your choices for the right reasons, guilty people aren't that eager to spill their guts so you can make the best call. I can't force J to tell me why she wants to die, but I know where Eric lives. I don't have to wait for him to lie to me—I can just go and find the evidence for myself.

The decision says as much about me as it does them, which is what's brought me to this alley. Hard-packed dirt on the ground, trash cans lined up against the dusty siding of Eric's trailer. Me, staring up at a window I can't quite reach. I need more information if I'm not going to be fate's bitch.

Eric's door was locked when I tried it. But that's fine; better even. The alley that runs along the back accesses several windows that open to a splintery wooden privacy fence and that's what I really need.

Privacy.

The windows are locked too, but I know these cheap, shallow latches. I push at the frame and feel the vinyl bow inward, then I shove up so the latch pops out of its groove with a screech of glass. The latch fingernails a deep scratch up the center of the pane as I force it open wide enough to fit me inside. It'll be evidence, if anyone looks, that I was here.

It's too high to haul myself up and the wind blows my hair across my face as I look for something to climb on. The black strands are a shadow of relief from the relentless blast of the sun, but they tickle my nose, so I swirl them back into the clip I keep on my belt. My vision thus freed up, I spot a dented metal trash can and drag it over, then hop onto its lid with a bang. I don't bother glancing around. This isn't the kind of neighborhood where people investigate strange noises. I step through the window, the sill digging into my ass as I duck my head through, then shoulder the flimsy metal blinds out of my way.

The desert wind follows me inside with a long, lusty howl that skims grit across the surface of an old couch. It's like now that I've broken the sanctity of this home, it's fair game for nature to violate too.

I move further inside, but don't bother with the living room, because even when people live alone, they don't stash their secrets in the front room. Instead, I turn left toward the hallway, but my steps slow without my permission. This kitchen makes my skin crawl.

The vinyl floor is the same sun-bleached pattern of mustard yellow and dog shit brown as my own trailer. There's a dried splotch of ketchup in front of the fridge. Slatted doors fold aside to reveal a washer and dryer across from the sink, and in front of it is heaped a mound of clothes that have encroached far into the space that's supposed to be for cooking and eating. They smell sour.

I let my eyes flick over them, checking for incriminating splashes of red that will have dried to brown. The clothes are all man-sized flannel and jeans, the only stains from grease or food. The shelves above the washer and dryer double as a pantry for the cans of generic SpaghettiOs and canned Spam. A small loaf of bread hunkers in one corner, a fuzz of green mold pressing out against the cellophane wrapper.

On the kitchen table, there are jars.

Fat and rounded, each jar at least two feet high, the sparkling glass enclosing a rainbow carnival of candies. They're brimming full, so the lids push up a little from the bounty within. The counter behind them is lined with a library of colorful boxes. Cake mixes in seven different flavors, cans of ready-made frosting queued up beside them.

When I move, the sole of my shoe peels up with a sticky suck from whatever has been spilled on the floor and never cleaned.

Pictures follow me all the way down the dimly lit hall. They're hung off a string of colorful yarn with plastic clothespins, like you might see at a preschool.

They could be exactly what I came here for, and yet it still takes me a long, choking moment before I can look. They're not family pictures, not evidence of anything that came before. Or evidence of specifically what's going on in the present. Just shots of Eric hanging out with kids from the neighborhood. His eyes the green of something that grows in drains and that self-conscious, lopsided smile. Something like satisfaction lurking behind the shyness.

The metal blinds balloon in a gust of wind, then rattle against the wall with a dry scrape, like teeth on bones. I hurry down the hall, eager to be done with this.

I have to touch his clothes to go through his drawers. I don't even know for sure the shape of the evidence I'm looking for, but I figure evil always gives itself away.

Socks.

Fraying pants.

A musty knee brace.

No loose floorboards in the closet.

No souvenirs hidden inside the vents.

No fucking certainty *anywhere*.

Caught somewhere between relief and frustration, I rip back the crumpled blanket on top of the bed. And the front door opens.

Keys drop against something hard, and footsteps murmur across carpet. Then thump louder as they reach the kitchen linoleum.

I drop the coverlet without trying to recreate its original messy scrump, and I fade two steps back. That's enough to put me almost in the shadow of the door, though the idea of cowering in a hiding place makes me grind my teeth. It's not until a flicker of movement crosses the threshold that I take a final step behind the door.

How sure do I need to be?

A belt jangles and a pair of baggy pants *fwump* to the floor.

My weight eases to the right until I can scan the room. I should stay hidden. I should wait until I'm certain, this time. There are some things you can't take back.

But I know that Holly's eyes are a hazy silver blue, with a startling brown speck in the left one that looks brighter when she cries. I bet Eric knows it too.

His spine is a lumpy line leading down to the waistband of his yellowed underwear. The elastic is so rotten it's begun to ripple, a tassel of tiny white threads exploding out next to the seam that says it won't be long before they give way altogether.

As he rummages for a shirt, I step out from behind the door. My steps are lighter than his, so I'm halfway down the hall before the cheap floor creaks. I don't look back. I skirt the darker patch of kitchen floor layered with textures of different shoe soles that have stuck and sucked free.

Some big, some small.

"Is somebody there?" he calls down the hall, but I'm already in the living room.

On my left is the front door. On my right is the window I now know I can always get in through. I sit down in his recliner.

It sags tiredly along the outline of where a body would rest, the upholstery of the armrests faintly oily against my skin.

It doesn't escape my notice that I didn't bring a weapon. He's strong enough I'll need one.

I listen to the sounds of him moving around the bedroom, then coming down the hall. I've never let him get me alone inside a house. Was never that reckless before. Maybe it flipped a switch in me to kill that mortician, when he wasn't even trying to hurt me. Or maybe that switch is still poised in the center, tension dragging at it from both sides to fall into place because it was only built to go one way or the other.

You're going to be okay, right?

The words of J's email force their way back into my head as I wait. What kind of person asks that of their murderer? I'll survive, is what I should tell her. I'll fry some chicken and cram some napkins into their holder. I'll go home and spray too much Glade to cover the sticky chemical scent of Southern Comfort that rises from Mom's bottles before I dump them in the recycling bin of the apartments down the street. So that guilty clink comes from their trash instead of ours. The difference is, I'll live my ordinary-looking life knowing I've contributed something most people would shy away from.

The decision of life versus death has always been left to groups. Juries and courts and firing squads so you can pretend you don't know if it was your vote or your bullet that made the final call. I won't be allowed that mercy. But if I choose *right* for these people, then I'll have done something for the world a little more important than frying some fucking chicken.

"JESUS CHRIST!" Eric stumbles back and whacks his elbow on the wall when he finds me sitting in his living room. "What are you doing in here?"

"Looking for you."

"Crap," he grumbles, rubbing his elbow. "You scared the shit out of me. How'd you get in?"

I don't answer. I'm remembering how hot and unexpected blood feels when it spills out of a human body. I'm remembering that speck of brown in Holly's eyes.

"Your mom drunk again?" He takes a step closer, his voice dropping like he, too, is remembering that we've never been alone together where no one could see. "You can stay here, if she is. Couch is comfortable enough. I got blankets."

I look him over. If I call the police, all they'll find here is a house. Pictures of fully clothed children and a lot of poor nutritional choices. They're not going to do shit. At a certain point, you have to decide who you're going to be. What you're willing to stand for.

He'll get away with this, if I let him.

I come up against a hard line inside myself as I stare him down, with the jars of candy bright and incongruous in the dingy kitchen beyond. It's not just death I keep being drawn back to. It's *murder*, and so no funeral home or veterinarian's office is going to be enough to quell the dark seethe in me.

I know now that I'm going to kill this man. All I have to decide is how.

CHAPTER

11
Jeika

WHEN THE KNOCK comes at my front door, I'm knee-deep in boxes and sunk even deeper in frustration.

Packing up what little I own was supposed to keep me from thinking. It's something I can *do* while I figure out which of my options I hate the least. I don't love that D is trying to force my secrets out of me, but I'm not exactly pissed enough about it to trade her life for mine. I don't need more on my conscience. Only thing is, I also don't know if I can afford to warn her that Peter's looking for people like her. That would be throwing away my last trump card and I haven't come up with any fresh ideas.

I throw another T-shirt in the trash—a concert tee from a date with a long-ago boyfriend. This feels like procrastination but it's just being considerate; making sure nobody else has to sort through all this stuff when I'm gone. I hesitate over a mood ring my first girlfriend won me out of a claw machine at the mall. Then flick it into the thrift store box with a tiny *thud*.

Ray-Ray always loved helping clean out my room, back when I lived with Mom and he'd spend summers and every other weekend with us. He'd gleefully help me throw tons of stuff away, just to sneak his favorite things back out of the trash to stash at his dad's house or use in his endless pranks at school. Kid was pranking before he even knew the word for it. I almost smile for a second, thinking of his squealing, delighted laughter. Though I suppose he'd hardly want to help if he knew what I was cleaning my room out for this time.

The knock sounds again, long and firm so it rattles the door in its jamb. Not the there-and-gone tap of the Amazon deliveryman. I growl through my teeth at the interruption, wading through a sea of boxes toward the front hallway. It can't be for me—it's got to be one of Kia's friends, though I'm a little surprised they're up so early after how late she was out last night.

I pull open the door, and when I see the dark blue of a police uniform, my hand jerks and I start to slam the door before the female officer stops it with her shoe. She raises an eyebrow, then glances at her partner.

Shit. Shit shit *shit* I should not have done that.

"What did she do now?" I throw out on an impulse. My roommate's more of an every-day-is-a-pool-party type than a bail-her-out-of-the-drunk-tank type, but I need some way to cover the twitchy flush itching up my throat. Can they see the boxes in my room? Does that make me look guiltier, like I'm about to go on the run?

Wait, or are they here because someone reported the ad, just like D warned?

I have a vague notion that suicide might be illegal, or maybe it just used to be? Either way, I doubt advertising to hire a hit man is strictly legal, even if it's just for yourself. Can they have traced an anonymous email account back to my house?

The jingling of tags announces Cooper a second before his soft ear brushes my leg. I haven't let myself pet him all day, even when Kia slept in long enough that I had to take him for his walk. Just this once, though, I let my shaking hand bury itself in the thick fur of his nape. He sits down at my side, not even greeting the police officers.

"Actually, we're here to see you," the female officer says slowly. "Do you recognize me?"

"Kind of? It's been a while," I say, shrugging even though I totally do. There's a scratch in her name tag across the name Diego that makes it look like it reads Biego. I remember staring at it in the hospital while she took my statement, words starting to melt together in my head until everything was just *Biego Biego Biego*, like the whole world was just nonsense syllables. No sense left in it.

"Not that long." She gives me an odd look. Almost sympathetic, but . . . not. There's something else there.

Six months and twelve days. Maybe in cop land that's not so long but for me, it's been an entire new lifetime—one I could have never imagined.

Cooper starts to growl. My eyes startle wide, because I've never heard him make that sound before. "Shh, Coop." I hook a finger in his collar and tug him farther from the door. "It's okay, boy," I say, but I don't even sound convincing to myself.

"We have a few new questions for you."

The words drop like bricks into the space between us, and Cooper lets out a little *woof* of a bark, surging against my hold on his collar. I tug him back and dodge in front of him.

"I told you everything I could remember. You know what happened as well as I do, at this point." I snatch up my purse and give her an odd look right back. "Besides, I'm on my way out to work. I can't be late again or I'll get fired." This isn't exactly a lie, except for the part where I don't actually work today. Cooper tries to follow me out but I close the door on him with a wince before he can make enemies of Phoenix PD's finest.

I push past the two officers on my stoop, fumbling for my keys to lock the door. The sun is blaring out here, ruthlessly bright, endlessly hot despite a stiff wind. My heartbeats race so hard my whole body feels faint, but I have to brazen this out like any innocent person would.

What questions could there be, especially six months later?

"There's been a new development, actually," the male cop says. Without looking, I already know his gleaming name tag reads Matheson. "It's why we're taking a second look at the case."

"New?" I whirl on them, and I don't have to fake the tears hitting my eyes. "How can there be anything new? It's over. It *happened*." And none of us can take it back.

"What's that on your neck?" Officer Diego says.

My hand flies up. My neck is mostly healed now, except for one or two pink smudges to show where the rope bit in before my YouTube noose failed.

"Curling iron burn." I give her a sick, tense smile. "You know how it is." My blonde hair's as straight as a pin, and barely combed to my shoulders, but hopefully she'll believe I put in more effort on other days.

I reach in my purse for the keys I dropped in there, forgetting I'd need them again when I got to the car. My knuckles bump smooth plastic and I try to look like a person who doesn't have emails from two different would-be murderers in her phone.

A cloud crosses in front of the sun as Officer Matheson says, "A witness has come forward."

I'm looking down into my bag as he says it, and everything before my eyes sharpens in that moment. The cracking fake leather of my purse. The browning shoots of lawn under my shoes. The crappy pen with a dry cleaner's logo on it, poking out of the half-unzipped front pocket.

There can't be a witness. There was no one there but us that night. If I'm sure of anything, I'm sure of that.

I turn, my face crinkling with confusion. "A witness to *what*?"

Wrong question. I do not want them to answer that.

"Listen," I say instead. "That night is hard for me to talk about. And I really can't lose this job. So unless I'm under arrest or something . . ." I toss it off like nothing could be more ridiculous.

"You're not," Officer Diego says, but slowly. Like she's not as certain of it as she'd like to be. My legs are so shaky I'm not sure I can make it out of here without visibly wobbling.

"Right." I nod. "Then I'm going. I don't know what else I could tell you about what happened that night anyway."

I open the door to my car and drop inside. They're not stopping me. They're not chasing me, not handcuffing me. Black spots dance at the edges of my eyes as I go dizzy with disbelief.

If I had any sense, I'd hit the gas and not let up until the tank was empty and I was hundreds of miles from this life. Except the consequences I'm really running from would come right along with me—I'd still have to live with what I've done. The only thing the authorities can do to me is take away any chance I have at checking out early: the razor blades, the pills, even my shoelaces, as if I could tie a better knot with those than I managed with the rope.

I fumble to close the door, my mind already racing toward what to do next when Officer Diego catches the outer door handle.

"We still need you to respond to the witness's statement." She hesitates. "We won't force you to miss work, since this is still just an inquiry. But you need to make an appointment and come down to the station as soon as you can."

I nod, but she doesn't let go of the door.

"This week, okay?"

"I understand." And I do.

She lets go of the door, and I back out into the street without even looking behind me.

I was desperate before. But now I'm desperate with a deadline.

CHAPTER 12

To: MVictimVolunteer@gmail.com
From: PeterL1978@hotmail.com
Date: May 7, 3:31 PM
Re: If you're serious . . .

To: Murder Victim

What's our current status? Update me.

-Peter

To: MVictimVolunteer@gmail.com
From: PeterL1978@hotmail.com
Date: May 8, 11:11 AM
Re: If you're serious . . .

To: Murder Victim

Why aren't you answering my calls? Are you talking to them and not me?

-Peter

To: MVictimVolunteer@gmail.com
From: PeterL1978@hotmail.com
Date: May 9, 1:42 AM
Re: If you're serious . . .

To: Murder Victim

You're already dead, aren't you?

-Peter

Serial Killer Wanted

Looking for a specific serial killer.

I know you answered a similar ad for my friend MVictimVolunteer@gmail.com.

I want the same deal you gave her.

CHAPTER

13

To: CheepsListAd948493902@CheepsList server.com
From: FacelessMan00@gmail.com
Date: May 9, 9:04 AM
Subject: Ad

Ad Poster,

Are you fucking crazy? If CheepsList reports that ad to the cops, they can probably get a warrant to get into MVictimVolunteer's email account, where they will find both of us. You may think you want to die, but I promise you want no part of what I will do to you if something happens as a result of your idiotic ad.

Take it down.

Signed,

Faceless

To: FacelessMan00@gmail.com
From: PeterL1978@hotmail.com
Date: May 9, 9:18 AM
Re: Ad

To: Faceless Man

When I first saw her post, I wasn't sure if it was real. I answered the ad to see if she'd gotten any responses, if there was anybody out there who was willing to help people like us. She said she had heard from someone else, and then she stopped answering my calls and emails, so I knew she must have found at least one that was the real deal—you, I'm guessing, since you're still trolling CheepsList for more.

We both know you can't afford to have someone else running around who knows what you did to her. But if you want to ensure my silence, all you have to do is pick a meeting place so you can kill me too.

-Peter

To: PeterL1978@hotmail.com
From: FacelessMan00@gmail.com
Date: May 9, 9:27 AM
Re: Ad

Peter,

She's not dead.

It's amazing, how men can never seem to see any other reason why women wouldn't want to answer their calls.

Especially when it's a sweetheart like yourself who tries to force and manipulate someone into helping them, instead of asking nicely.

One crazy ad can be dismissed as a joke. Two looks like something's going on, especially with an email address attached. Take it down.

Signed,

Faceless

To: FacelessMan00@gmail.com
From: PeterL1978@hotmail.com
Date: May 9, 11:25 AM
Re: Ad

To: Faceless MAN???

Wait, you're a woman? Has there ever been a female serial killer?

Come on, all I want is somebody to kill me, and you don't even like me. We both know what you were on that website for. If you're not going to help me anyway, I don't have to wait for the police to find my ad. I can turn you in myself.

-Peter

CHAPTER

14

To: FacelessMan00@gmail.com
From: MVictimVolunteer@gmail.com
Date: May 9, 3:12 PM
Re: My Reason

Dear D,

Listen, things have changed on my end, and I'm running out of time. If what you need to be willing to help me is my story, then fine. But you have to meet me in person. There are things I don't want to say on the record. I can come tonight, if you want. My number is 602-555-0192 if you need to text to find me when you get there.

Also, if you're going to make me talk about shit I'm not proud of, I want to hear yours too. Who you've murdered, and how, so I know you can really pull this off. You wouldn't believe how many ways there are to mess up and not quite kill a person. It's harder than you'd think.

Cheers,

J

To: MVictimVolunteer@gmail.com
From: FacelessMan00@gmail.com
Date: May 9, 5:05 PM
Re: My Reason

Dear J,

Not for me, it's not.

I can't meet right away though. Some guy saw your ad and tried to force me into helping him, and now I have to figure out how to deal with him. I definitely understand why you ghosted that asshole. You might try your hand at getting him to take that ad down before it lands you in trouble with the cops, since it has your email address in it. I still don't know what your situation is, but I bet you don't need to get arrested on top of it.

Meet me two days from now, the Starbucks across from the library. Four o'clock.

Cheers,

D

To: FacelessMan00@gmail.com
From: MVictimVolunteer@gmail.com
Date: May 9, 5:55 PM
Re: My Reason

Dear D,

Is it a guy named Peter? Are you going to meet up with him? Are you sure it's safe to do that? I mean, what do you really know about this guy?

I took down my ad days ago, but I'll see what I can do about his. Thanks for the heads-up.

Be careful,

J

CHAPTER

15
Dani

I'M STILL THINKING about J's email when I park my car and walk the rest of the way to my target under the cover of darkness. *Be careful.* What a ridiculous thing to say to someone you know is a killer. Especially when I'm going up against an idiot like Peter. Not that she probably knows him well enough to realize how inept he is, since he said she stopped answering his emails.

Peter underestimated me, didn't realize how easily I could find him. Though you don't have to be all that smart to track someone down when their Instagram handle is the same as their email, and their Instagram links to their Facebook. And their Facebook shows location tags for posts with movie theaters and restaurants all clustered around their house, and then they post pictures of said house, with their car right out front. Only took me a few hours to zero in on him.

I wonder if I could find J's Facebook page, if it would have her whole sad story written across it the way Peter's did: with pictures of a pretty, freckle-faced daughter and then consolation posts and funeral information. A relationship status reading "Single" despite the pictures buried deep in his timeline of a shy-looking brunette whose picture stopped showing up not long after the daughter's did. He's not the first one to want to follow a loved one into the grave. But that doesn't mean I'm going to help him do it, especially after he put J and me both at risk trying to force my hand.

Most of his front yard is divided up into raised bed gardens, each neatly framed in stained wood and corrugated tin. They're all grown thick with weeds now, no sign of the plump tomatoes I saw in his old social media photos. That was the only surprising thing: how long it'd been since he lost his daughter.

I check the station wagon against the picture on my phone one more time—don't want to scare an innocent—then stuff the phone back into my pocket, pull a slat of metal out from under my shirt, and slide it down the window. Tilt it and pull, but nothing clicks. Damn it. I pull it out, prop the end of the thin metal against my knee, and push to give it a bit more bend. Most people try to keep it too straight, and it just never catches right. It was one of the first things Eric taught me, one day when I locked my keys in my car.

A darkness rises in my throat and I clench my teeth together, thinking of all the candy in his kitchen. Knowing I want to kill him isn't the hard part. The problem is how to do it quickly enough that I don't get injured in the process, and then what to do with the body and the crime scene so I don't get caught afterward. It's nearly impossible to commit a crime without leaving fiber traces or DNA behind, so the best plan is always to give the cops a reason not to look too closely in the first place. I risked too much at Williams Funeral Home, even though I wiped everything I touched. I can't be sloppy like that again.

Maybe I could set Eric's trailer up like a suicide. Plant pictures or newspaper articles to show that he had an unhealthy interest in children and felt so ashamed he had to end it all. But I'd need a gun to do it fast enough to not risk a struggle, and how can I ensure his cooperation without leaving traces of drugs in his blood?

The long, flat hook goes back into the window of the car I'm working on, and I press my arm into it for more leverage, fishing around.

Clunk.

The lock pops upward and I slip into the driver's seat. The scalpel catches the light from the streetlights; other than the dried smear of blood on the blade, it's bright and gleaming, as if the funeral home bought it brand new. I hold it with my sleeve tugged down over my fingers so I don't leave any traces of me behind. The edge is ruthlessly sharp, but I don't need that, not yet. I tuck it away into the car, where it won't reveal itself until just the right moment.

It was stupid of me to hang on to any piece of evidence that would link me to a crime scene, but that's about to be Peter's problem, not mine. It's a warning, sure, but it's also leverage. If he gives me any trouble, I'll just call an anonymous tip into the police and pin the mortician's murder on him.

I swing my legs out of the car and relock the door, already pleased at how pissed this douchebag is going to be tomorrow when he—

"Hey, what are you doing in Pete's car?"

My head swivels, and the neighbor who just spotted me is hesitating by his trash bins, shoulders as wide as a linebacker. I can try to spin a story, but no, he lives right next door and obviously knows Peter. I run.

"Hey!" he shouts after me.

Average Joe like that, he won't have the guts to do anything but yell, maybe file some paperwork with a bored beat cop when I'm long gone. I have my hair stuffed into a baseball cap to hide the color and the brim pulled low, so I doubt he could pick me out of a lineup. All I need to do is get around the corner and I'll be home free.

Footsteps slap the sidewalk behind me and oh *shit*, he's actually going to chase me? I dodge a glance back and the guy is sprinting like his linebacker days aren't too far behind him after all. He's huge, nearly twice as wide as me at the shoulders and I already know if he tackles me, it's all over. I'll be pinned beneath his weight, unable to even get an arm free. It's not the kind of fight women get to win.

I duck around a streetlight, detour into a yard and vault a low bush, hoping he'll follow me and stumble over the brush.

Every fight I've ever won, I've done it on surprise. On being overprepared, and underestimated, and more ruthless than my opponent is prepared to be. This time, I'm coming up short on two out of the three.

And I've left my only weapon behind.

It wasn't supposed to go down like this, not when I was just here to scare away Peter the balding blackmailer, of all people. I risk a glance and my pursuer didn't follow me over the hedge, just charged around the clear path on the sidewalk. I'm running slow on lumpy lawn and he's *right there*, his hand snatching for the back of my shirt.

"Not in my neighborhood," he growls, not panting as hard as I am. He catches my shirt and I stumble with the jerk against the fabric before I tear free and sprint like a wild animal straight for the street. There's a car coming and I don't have time to gauge the timing, I just *go* right for the oncoming sedan.

They don't hit the brakes, don't see me in the dark. My instincts scream for me to stop, but if I do, he'll have me. And I'll never allow a man's unwanted hands on me, not once while I still draw breath. I hurl myself into the headlights, the car's hood coming so fast I'm already cringing for the impact and then I'm clear.

I can't even breathe, my lungs torched from all the running, but the Good Samaritan behind me will have had to pause for the car and this is my only shot. A horn blares behind me, a door flying open. "Hey, why are you chasing that woman?" an unfamiliar voice challenges.

Jesus, what is it with this neighborhood? Does no one just mind their own business? But this one's in my favor as the linebacker yelps in protest, sputtering explanations to the person who damn near hit me. I disappear between two dark houses. There's a dog in the left yard and I pitch a stick over the fence, catching it in the side so it yelps before exploding into barking.

Very much as if there's someone in his territory.

I shoot for the other yard, leaping and grabbing the top of the fence. I'm spent, but I haul myself up on pure adrenaline, hooking an elbow over the top with my feet scrabbling against the flat boards to push myself up. Then I'm over, my forearm scraped to shit as I land in a thick bush. It's the poofy kind that used to be popular in the nineties; the ones that are all full of spiders. I cram myself under one edge, hidden in the shadows between the bristling branches and the fence, and suck oxygen like I'm going to die in the next ten seconds.

Fuck, running for exercise has nothing on running for your life.

The driver must not have stuck around to play citizen's arrest, because when the linebacker comes around the corner, he does it alone. My heart clatters against my ribs as I fight to quiet my breathing. The dog next door is still barking loud enough to cover what tiny scraps of air I allow myself.

I eye my pursuer between the tiny gaps in the boards. He's wide, like he really might have played football in college. Quick, like he switched to 10Ks after that. But he's got a wild, excited look to him as he peers over the fence into the dog's yard. "Holy shit," he says to himself, apparently impressed by the wild turn his night has taken. "Holy *shit*."

And I smile.

He's already mentally planning how he'll tell the story to his friends. Of how he heroically stopped the car thief. He's still hoping he can corner me and call 911, maybe pictures tying me up with his hoodie string.

This guy may be fast, but he's no predator. He's not capable of what I am.

He turns to the fence I hopped and grabs the top, the boards rattling as he hauls himself up. I press myself in tighter under the bush, the smell of juniper and dust sharp in my nose, twigs dragging at my clothes. He hangs there for a long moment, peering into the dark. My heart thumps in my ears. If he sees me, I'll jump up and slam the heel of my hand into his nose. The pain should be startling enough that he'll lose his grip on the fence and I can get a head start, maybe hop the far side of this fence. I glance toward the house at my back, hoping the neighbor's barking dog hasn't woken up anybody who might interfere.

The fence starts to quake along with the linebacker's arms and he drops back to the ground with a huff.

He's already dialing his phone as he walks away. "Dude, you're not going to believe what happened! I was taking out my trash and . . ." His voice is fading around the corner, but I can still feel his hands closing on the fabric of my shirt. He almost had me.

It's a warning from the universe to me, as sharp as the one I left hidden in Peter's car. I'm vicious, not invincible.

I haul myself to standing, the branches of the bush clawing at me through my thin shirt. I can't win against Eric in a fair fight, so before I come for him, I need to have a damn good plan.

I find the catch on the inside of the gate and walk out like I've lived there my whole life.

CHAPTER

16

To: FacelessMan00@gmail.com
From: PeterL1978@hotmail.com
Date: May 10, 8:18 AM
Re: Ad

HOW IN THE FUCK DID YOU GET INTO MY CAR?

I know it was you, there's no one else in my life who could possibly think a BLOODY SCALPEL was a cute prank.

My neighbor told me someone had broken in, but the door was still locked and nothing was missing, so I didn't know what to think. Then this morning I went to flip down my sun visor and it fell out and cut me! Went right through my shirt and CUT me. I could have lost an eye—or wrecked my car. I hit a curb and barely swerved before I hit a power pole. I could have caused a pileup, hurt other people—are you out of your damn mind?

Why are you doing this? Like I'm not fucking miserable enough? I lost my whole goddamn family, not that you apparently care about anyone but yourself. I have *nothing*, and all I wanted was a way out. I sure didn't know you'd track me down and mindfuck me with some used scalpel rather than just help me.

-Peter

To: FacelessMan00@gmail.com
From: PeterL1978@hotmail.com
Date: May 10, 11:04 AM
Re: Ad

To: Faceless Woman

Seriously? All that and now you're not even going to answer?

-Peter

To: FacelessMan00@gmail.com
From: PeterL1978@hotmail.com
Date: May 10, 7:56 PM
Re: Ad

To: Faceless Woman

Look, I'm sorry I tried to blackmail you into helping me with the ad thing. I understand it was risky to put that out there, but I couldn't think of any other way to track you down without MVictimVolunteer.

How did you even find me that fast? Are you some kind of hacker or computer whiz?

Please give me another chance—I'll meet you wherever, whenever you want. No tricks, I promise.

-Peter

To: PeterL1978@hotmail.com
From: FacelessMan00@gmail.com
Date: May 10, 9:20 PM
Re: Ad

Peter,

I can find you whenever I want and do to you whatever I choose. I'm still deciding if I want to help you. If I do, it'll be on my timeline, not yours.

Signed,

Death

To: FacelessMan00@gmail.com
From: PeterL1978@hotmail.com
Date: May 10, 9:39 PM
Re: Ad

To: Death

I understand. I'll be awaiting your email, and I'm sorry I overstepped. It's your move.

-Peter

CHAPTER

17

To: PeterL1978@hotmail.com
From: MVictimVolunteer@gmail.com
Date: May 9, 10:31 PM
Re: If you're serious . . .

Peter,

Sorry I didn't answer before. It's a lot to think about, but I'm considering your deal.

In the meantime, I need to know if you've contacted somebody named FacelessMan about my ad? Listen, if you have, you need to back off. It'll be a lot better for you if you wait and have me lead you to them rather than trying to pose as a suicidal person yourself. If you scare them off, we're both out of luck.

And you need to take down that ad before the cops see it, if you don't want to put me in danger.

Sincerely,

Hoping You Don't Blow This

To: MVictimVolunteer@gmail.com
From: PeterL1978@hotmail.com
Date: May 10, 9:55 PM
Re: If you're serious . . .

To: Murder Victim

Yeah, I know FacelessMan, though she's no man. We had a little run-in and she's a real bitch. Don't trust a word she says. Just get her name and address for me and I'll handle the rest.

-Peter

To: PeterL1978@hotmail.com
From: MVictimVolunteer@gmail.com
Date: May 11, 10:12 PM
Re: If you're serious . . .

Peter,

I understand. I've decided I'll take your deal—I just need a little more time. I'm in contact with Faceless, but I don't have enough info for you to find her yet.

I need to get her to trust me first.

CHAPTER

18
Jeika

I STAND IN LINE at the Starbucks, the guilt of what I did last night thick and black in my throat. *It was just an email*, I tell myself for the thousandth time. A back door left open a crack, in case I need it. I tell myself a lot of things, but really, it's not like I haven't done worse.

The roar of the coffee grinder makes me jump and I glance around, feeling ridiculous. The woman in front of me has a baby stroller that looks like it was designed by NASA. The hipster in line behind me is sporting a beanie even though the temperature today is nudging triple digits. Everybody else is here for a latte, not to decide between death or failure. Oat milk or soy, decaf or double. Me or her. The disconnect strikes me hard. No one else knows what I'm planning, and it makes me feel like I'm watching all of them from the other side of a pane of existential glass. But which one of us is the prisoner in this zoo, and which is the visitor?

They serve up my iced coffee and I stuff two folded dollars in the tip jar and turn to scan the room again. At four o'clock, only half the room is full and no one inside looks like they might be D, so I head back outside. The idea of waiting at one of the tables is out of the question. I want to see her as soon as she gets here, even more since Peter confirmed my guess that D was a woman. Will she be pretty? Cruel? Athletic? Unhinged?

Besides, she's probably watching from somewhere to make sure this isn't some kind of police sting. I'm guessing that's why she picked the meeting place and didn't give me her description.

I fidget with the buttons on my collared white sleeveless top, trying to decide. Higher, lower . . . The marks on my neck are mostly healed and she's the only one I don't need to hide the evidence of my failed attempt from.

I've had plenty of time to think, but I still haven't decided what I'm going to say. How much of the truth I should tell her.

I'm about to meet a person who is fully capable of killing me. I think it should be a relief, but my pulse is running too high and I don't feel any kind of good. If I don't say exactly the right things today, I'll be left with only Peter's mercy. And so will she.

Just as I reach for my phone to check the time, a car pulls up in front of me. There's not even a second of hesitation because I know her the instant I see her.

The car is broad and solid steel from a different era, with paint the olive green of a WWII uniform and an engine bigger than my whole car. It roars and sputters, and she cuts one glance sideways at me, as if she's already impatient that I haven't gotten in yet.

Like there's no question that this is my ride.

My serial killer has dark, straight eyebrows and a satiny sweep of black hair. A long neck like a black-and-white painting of a ballerina. Tight muscles in her shoulders.

The churning, too-light feeling in my stomach whirls faster and I open the car door. The cracked vinyl of the upholstery scrapes against my legs and goosebumps tingle over my skin. The back of the seat wraps around me and I steal a glance sideways.

My next breath hiccups on its way in. Her right forearm is corded with muscle, tapering to a slim wrist and then . . . nothing.

"Don't worry," D says, and slams the car into gear. "I can still kill you with one hand."

CHAPTER

19
Jeika

THE CAR STREAKS through three blocks, four, and I can't stop watching her drive. It's so graceful and careless and impossible. Her right—what? Wrist? Stump?—slams through the gears without ever needing to grip. When she needs traction, she presses the underside down and works the stick shift with just the pull against her skin on some grippy drawer-liner fabric she has rubber-banded around the shifter. It looks like it hurts, but she never flinches.

She's wearing a black T-shirt with the sleeves ripped out so the edge of her sports bra shows beneath. I feel silly and overdressed in my collared top until I see the slim gray trousers she's wearing. They seem like they belonged to a man's suit once, but they hug the curve of her hips.

Her belt is solid black leather, like a gun holster.

Three tiny jewels arch just under the top rim of her ear. The glint of them feels like a scrape of irony against my tongue. This is my murderer. The one with the power to do everything I was too weak to manage on my own.

"You're being kind of an asshole right now," she says.

I blink, but don't look away. "It's so weird to know what you really look like. Nothing about how I pictured you at first turned out to be right." Now that I've seen her, I can't imagine her any other way. She looks like the only original in a whole museum of forgeries.

"It's not just my face you're staring at."

It's not. But it's not all her arm either, and I think that's what she meant.

"I'm just . . . surprised, that's all."

Her face closes up harder, and I realize she must deal with this all the time—people's reactions to her, because their default is to expect a person with two hands. It must be incredibly annoying to have to explain herself to all of us, easing our discomfort with how she *is*. Because why should she have to? But I don't know how to tell her it's okay because then it sounds like it's up to me to accept or deny her. And it's not.

I fumble, my hands lifting to gesture helplessly as I search for words, then falling with a slap back to my lap. "I don't know the right thing to say. Can we just pretend I already said it?"

A huff of laughter scoffs out of her. "It's fine. This is the part where people either start babbling dumb questions or get all shifty-eyed and pretend they don't want to ask."

"Well, let's skip it then." I lean back into the seat. "I'll give you my best shifty eyes and wait until I get home to google all the questions that aren't really my business anyway."

"Well, that's a first." She shakes her head. "Everybody always wants to know how I tie my shoes, but they never want to hear about the things that are actually hardest."

"Like what?"

"Honestly? Popping a zit."

"Damn." I cock my head, thinking it over, because yeah, it never works the same with one hand. And then flush when I realize I'm talking to a pretty girl about popping zits. I clear my throat and deliberately look out the side window.

It's strange to hear her out loud. Those sharp, spare sentences punching out of her mouth the same way they do off the page of an email. She never says a word more than she needs, but then, she never has to. Every syllable is aimed like something sharp, straight at the heart of the conversation.

"Go ahead," she says, her voice flat again. "Because I know you can't google the one you're really thinking."

I flush deeper, so many things in my head I'd hate for her to read on my face.

"I didn't become a killer because I'm somehow traumatized about being born with one hand." The tires bark as she accelerates. "It's not anything I'd even know how to miss. It just is. It's garbage to think that the reason I am what I am has anything to do with how hard it is to open a goddamn pickle jar."

"That's not what I was thinking." My back jerks straight.

She downshifts, says nothing. Clearly doesn't believe me, basically at all.

So I fold my arms and match her. "Fine. If we're doing it that way, I don't want to die because I'm queer."

She misses the next gear and the engine revs before she catches it. "What?"

"I'm not some gay cliché for well-meaning moms on Facebook to make another awareness poster about," I snap. "I've known I was bi for as long as I can remember. It's maybe the only thing left about myself that I'm okay with, and I was out for years before I wanted to die. Like you said, it just *is*."

She gives me another one of her simmering, quiet looks. Shrugs.

I turn to face forward and we sit through an interminable red light. I can't tell if she's thinking about what I just said, or if she's already sensed all the lies I'm holding in. I hate all of them so much more now that I've met her.

There's no cupholder where I can put down my coffee so I just hold it, the ice freezing my palm and condensation beading clammy between my hand and the plastic. She must not be able to have any drinks in this car, because she's got no cupholders. She couldn't hold a cup and drive, unless it was between her knees, and working the clutch would make that precarious. So many little things I took for granted about having two hands and they're all crowding up my head in the silence.

"You waiting for a red carpet?" She downshifts for a hill and the engine sounds like something that has teeth. "Talk."

I squirm, the plastic of my cup popping under my fingers. The story I came here to tell her sits like a stink on my skin and I want to open a window to let it out of the car before she smells it. I want her face to stay the same kind of hard and indifferent that it is right now. Not twist with disgust like anyone's would if they knew about me.

How ridiculous is it to want your murderer to *like* you?

I need to want the opposite, for her to be so revolted that she's eager to kill me. Her life's at stake now, not just mine. I wish she'd been impressed by my listing of numbers of everything I'd use up, by my readiness to die so better people could live. But then, if she doesn't know about me, no wonder she thought I was saying it to look humble. No wonder she assumed it was a lie.

It's funny that "truth" is such a simple, clean word. When the truth is so rarely either of those things.

"I'm pulling over," she says. "And then you're talking, or you're getting the fuck out."

D cranks the wheel with the palm of her hand and takes a left with a rev of the engine and a weightless unconcern for the flurry of horns and screech of brakes. I flinch and twitch back away from my door, where the impact would come from if we were hit. I remember what broken glass feels like. What was solid and taken for granted a moment ago exploding into points and edges that gnaw you apart.

She looks amused. "For a suicidal person, you sure are jumpy in cars."

"Yeah, well, maybe I'd just rather not end up stuck only halfway to the finish line," I growl, embarrassed in spite of myself. "Kind of why I asked you for help in the first place."

Her lashes are long, untouched by mascara, and her eyes liquid dark when she looks at me. "I'd finish you before the police came. I wouldn't let you suffer."

I fall back against the seat when she accelerates down a side street. It takes so long for the cops to come after you call them. In the movies, there's the crash and then the scene cuts to revolving blue and red lights. In real life, there's unbelievable noise, and movement too fast to track, and nothing makes sense, and everything hurts. It's wrong like nothing has ever been so fucking wrong and there's blood in your mouth. Somehow, you know it's not just your blood.

Nobody should ever have anybody else's blood in their *mouth* and you spit and feel something else in there, a chunk of something solid on your tongue. At first you think it's a tooth—*oh God, my teeth*—but when it comes out it's glass from the side windows.

There's glass inside of you and you don't know what to do and it's so, so long before anyone comes.

"J? Hey . . ." The car lurches to a stop. She's touching my back and I don't understand how because I thought I was sitting up in her passenger seat. "J?" She shakes me, and I realize I'm curled forward, my knees jerking up like I want the fetal position but the seatbelt is tying me down. My plastic cup is crushed in my hands, a puddle of liquid seeping into the floor mat. I stained her *car.* I yank open the door and toss out my mangled coffee cup before I ruin anything else.

"Jeika," I say.

"What?"

I clear my scoured throat. "That's my name." I want her to leap on me and rip me into pieces that fade to invisible as soon as she lets them go. I want to disappear forever and let this car be the last place I ever have to be. I'll tell her anything I have to, to make that happen.

"Jeika . . ." She says it right the first time. The way no one ever fucking does. *Jay-ka.* Her voice isn't gentle, but it's so smooth somehow it feels gentle anyway. Like how the barrel of a gun would slip like velvet over your temple when it's the thing you want most. "What was that all about?"

I had a lie prepared. About a fire in my kitchen, a whole apartment building burning down in a distant, unnamed city. Sure, I stole it from TV. But it seemed dark and specific enough that anybody would buy it—until I met D in person.

She's not exactly someone you can lie to.

"My mom—" I gulp air. "She died in a car crash."

If D's never lost anyone, she won't hear everything crushed within that black hole of a syllable. *Died.* Like the past tense holds within it the million other words you'd have to use to rebuild your current life back into one that *had* a family.

"So what?" she says, all that gun barrel silkiness vanishing into impatience. "I had an uncle. People die. There are graveyards all over the world, and Burger Kings right next to them, and people just keep going to those drive-thrus. Don't tell me you wasted my time to come here with some basic-ass car wreck sob story."

I shrug, the muscles in my shoulders clenching and squirming like screaming fists. "I didn't say I was special."

"Get over it, then. Jesus." D flicks her black hair back. "Cars crash, nobody lives forever. What the fuck do you need me for?"

"I need you to fix it."

I can still see the darkness of the trees where we crashed, feel the scrape of all the cubed safety glass on the seat beneath me when I dragged myself out. How limp Mom's arm was, like a piece of meat that had fallen across the cupholder. The twinkle of the tiny blue stone in the ring she always wore.

"After we wrecked, I just got to keep living my life." It sounds even more wrong put into words. "But my mom . . ."

Hemorrhage. Fractured skull. Catastrophic internal bleeding.

"Her body wasn't even the right shape anymore. We were in the same car, barely a foot apart, but somehow I walked away and she didn't. The doctors at the hospital told me she must have yanked the wheel at the last second, taken all the impact on her side of the car so mine would stay whole."

I can't look at her, so I stare through the windshield. When I blink, the shapes resolve into buildings and signs and I realize I just left my garbage all over the parking lot of a dentist's office. But the plastic of my cup is crumpled and covered with sticky coffee now, and I don't have the energy to pick it back up.

"It was raining that night, and you know how the roads in Phoenix are. All that oil builds up on them, and when it finally rains, everything gets as slick as ice. We were on the way to get my little brother. We have different dads, and while mine was never around, Ray-Ray's was always begging for more custody, more time with him." That shouldn't still sting, after all the other things that have hurt me in between, but it does. "Mom and I were fighting, again. Because I was going to the ASU downtown campus but I wouldn't live at home and she had to keep loaning me money because my part-time job wasn't enough to cover housing. But mostly because I was dating a girl she hated."

I pause, debating whether to admit that was the real reason I'd had to borrow money again. My girlfriend had been a foodie, her whole Instagram full of perfectly arranged plates and I wanted to impress her. The finest restaurants, knock-off designer clothes I scoured all the consignment stores for. It was ridiculous, humiliating. Me, trying so hard for a woman like that. I glance out the window, away from D. That was what I'd really been angry at, that night. Not my mother. But it's too late to tell her that.

"My phone went off right in the middle of our argument and it was her—my girlfriend. Mom was furious, told me to pay attention to my own family for *five minutes* for a change." Oh, how those words hurt now even worse than they did back then. "I went to look at the text anyway and she grabbed it out of my hands."

After that, it's all flashes. Brilliantly, perfectly drawn still images with nothing in between. How we both grabbed the phone, tussling over it for a second. The way that pulled the wheel off center. The way the tires slid sickeningly, the windshield wipers still placidly whisking water off the glass right up until the instant it shattered, like they didn't know what was coming any more than I did.

The crack of her head against the window.

It's the only sound I remember in the whole thing, until I came back to myself, breath shuddering in the car with her slumped-over body hanging in the seatbelt. Part of me expected to hear sirens. Like the world would know immediately that something had gone so wrong. But there was nothing. It was long minutes before I even thought to feel for her pulse, and that's when I found all the places she was bleeding. All the places there was glass in her. Even as the rain started to slash in through the broken windows, I knew, in clear block print, that my life was over. This was a mistake I couldn't take back, and my mother was dead, truly gone in a way I couldn't even fully comprehend.

"Accidents happen. You can't—"

"*Don't.*" I turn on her, and her lashes flare but she doesn't pull back. "Everybody tried that shit on me at the funeral. 'Honey, you can't blame yourself. You weren't driving so it wasn't your fault. Your mom jerked that wheel to take the impact on her side of the car because she loved you.' I know what that means, D. I hear what they're saying. Every fucking time, I hear what they're really saying."

D looks back at me and right now, she's not beautiful. Because I can remember death and how it smelled, and that's her name. It's *her.* I know Death better than either of us thought.

And that means she knows me too.

"You jerked the wheel," she says.

CHAPTER

20

Jeika

"YOU JERKED THE wheel," D says. "Because *you* were driving. But if no one knows, that means . . ."

At first, it was just glass, and blood, and this-is-not-happening. Until it was. There was a moment when I realized that jail was a thing, and that's where you went when you killed people, even if you had no idea five minutes ago that they could ever disappear from this world so fast and completely. But it didn't touch me through the bubble of my shocked numbness.

Nothing did, until I remembered my *brother*.

He was going to know what I'd done. That in one second, I'd ruined our entire family. That I was reckless and stupid, and we'd all be paying for the rest of our lives. He was going to hate me. Everyone was, for every day after this one. Because I was the driver.

I was crying so hard I could barely see when I got out and staggered around the car.

I remember how heavy my mom's body was when I lifted it, and how my injured body screamed with fresh pain. How her hair stuck to my rain-wet face and got in my mouth. How her feet dragged against the grass and one shoe wobbled and started to scrape off over her heel. How I collapsed under her weight, her corpse falling on top of me. I gulped air and waited for the scene to crack along the seams of its own unreality and somehow, it just never fucking did. It went on and on, long after I wanted to black out, or throw up, or rewind my own life into something that made sense again.

I remember how no cars passed on the road above and the trees around the one we'd hit sat so quietly amidst the hiss of the rain. How I worried that the police would see the dampness on her clothes and know I'd moved her, know that I was the one who was guilty and I'd have to shoulder the blame for everything rather than letting it pass away with her.

"There was alcohol in her bloodstream." The words are acrid, somehow even uglier than the ones I don't say. Because now D also knows I must have moved the body. That I scrubbed my own mother's blood off my skin with leaves that shook and tore and smeared dirt along my skin and I lied and lied and lied to everyone who finally showed up to "help" us.

"She'd been watching *The Bachelor* with a glass of Chardonnay before Ray-Ray called saying he missed her and wanted to come home a day early from his dad's." My mouth twists, almost a smirk but too painful to make it all the way. "Really, he left the iPad with his favorite dinosaur game at Mom's, but he always knew how to get her, the little freckle-faced con artist. It's why she called me to drive, that night. But when I moved her—"

"They all thought she was driving drunk."

I nod, once. When really, it was the phone that did it. Me fighting her for it, over a girl who I never called again after that night. With her stupid expensive tastes, and her stupid beautiful face that I wanted so much I couldn't take five damn minutes away from my phone to keep my own family safe.

D stares at me. "You think you can't live with yourself once you've killed someone? Grow the fuck up."

My eyes flare. What the hell does she know? If she's answering ads for serial killers, she must have picked this life for herself, chosen her victims. But what I've become was never the person I wanted to be.

The cops never even came until I called them. And when they saw the smashed-in driver's side of the hood, they didn't ask why I lived and she died. Because they didn't know that demolished side was mine. They didn't understand I should have been the one who died.

And I know, after all the endless months in between, that the answer to that question is nowhere in any of the corners of whatever I am. There's no story that covers the taste of your dead mother's hair in your mouth. That fixes the people whispering at her funeral about her "secret drinking problem," and the way the skid marks started in the wrong lane on the road above. About how lucky *I* was to have survived my mom's reckless driving.

My voice is as dark as D's when I answer.

"It's not just that, not anymore. Now the cops know."

D jerks at that, sitting straighter in her seat. "You came to meet *me*, you put up that ad, when the police are already watching you?"

"They don't know about the thing on CheepsList. They only showed up this week, and I had already taken the ad down by then." My fingers twist in my lap. The road was so quiet that night. How could anyone have been close enough to see the crash, but not come over to help? "They say they have a witness. Somebody saw . . . something. So they're reopening the case."

"If it was a car accident, DUI, it'd be open-shut. Barely a case to open. If they've got a witness, somebody must have seen when you—"

I flinch, and she stops before she says the words. But we both know, if somebody'd seen me, they would have come forward six months ago. Officer Diego would have shown up with handcuffs, not requests. I remember the odd way she looked at me, questions in her eyes. They know something, but they don't have the whole story. Not yet.

I look up at D. "I've got one last chance to get out. If I die now, they'll have no reason to pursue the case, and no one ever has to know the truth."

"But you put up that ad even before the cops came."

It's not a question. Seeing her now, in person, the darkness in her tells me this woman *knows* the answer to what she keeps asking me in those emails. It makes me wonder if there's anything I could have said to change her mind. What she was hoping for when she agreed to meet me.

This new silence is a squirmy thing, slithering between the seats and under our clothes. It's touching me in places

I don't want to be touched and I don't know how to make it stop.

"It's not just about the jail time, though, is it?" She picks at the lacing on the steering wheel. "What happened is bad. It would be some ugly shit, no matter what. But not knowing why." She flicks away the piece of threading she ripped out of the leather. "That's what starts to rot inside you."

Air no longer exists in this car. Nobody's ever known me this way and I didn't know how awful it could be. How plucked-bare the last six months of my life could sound in her voice.

"Well, now you know my story." I arch an eyebrow, feeling cold or numb, or maybe none of those things. "Who'd you kill?"

"Says the one probably wearing a wire." Her lips take on a sardonic twist. "Smooth, Jeika. Super smooth."

The way she says my name flushes heat up my legs. It's sharp, like a supermodel's jaw. And I don't know if it's that or the unnamed challenge flaring between us that's to blame for what I do next.

I yank down my shirt, the center band of my frayed old bra exposed and I hold her eyes like a dare when I do it. "See? No wire."

She flicks a glance over me. Then sweeps her hair back over her shoulder with that slim, strong wrist. "My uncle. And a kid from my neighborhood. Two more after that. No, I guess it's three, now." She pauses, then shrugs. "He pissed me off."

Her voice is different when she says the last one, but I can't focus on that because I'm still stuck on the first thing she said. *Family*. She killed family too. Sickness uncurls tendrils in my belly as I think about all the terrible things that might mean.

"Did he hurt you?"

"Uncle Ricky?" She laughs, achingly. "No. When I was little, he used to put a sock over his hand, try to learn how to do things one-handed so he could teach me. Half the time I ended up teaching him." Her fingers drift over the smooth skin where her right arm ends. "There's no word for this part of me, you know that? Only *stump*. A word for what's missing, except I never lost anything because this is the body I was born with."

I tug at my shorts, upset for her about all the people who always seem to want a whole world that's just like them. As if they have the right to claim a normal that doesn't include the rest of us. I take a breath to tell her I know how bullshitty that feels, but she's still looking down at her right arm.

"My uncle used to call it my lightsaber. We'd have battles all over the living room; him with a stick and me with my arm. He said because my lightsaber was part of my body, I got to choose what color mine would be. Red or green. Evil or good."

"But then why . . ." I don't want to say it, but it feels cowardly to shy away from the words, when I know she never would. "Why'd you kill him?"

She puts the car in gear.

"I'm still answering that."

She drives us back to the Starbucks without asking if that's where I want to go. I can't tell if this means she's going to help me, or if that's off the table for good. I'm still looking for clues when she stops right in the street in front of the coffee shop and shifts into neutral.

"I don't think you want to die."

My teeth clench. "I don't think you get to tell me how I fucking feel." I *knew* she was going to bail on me. That something about me or my story wouldn't be good enough. "I think you're just making excuses because you're too chickenshit to do it." If she murdered somebody not long ago simply because he pissed her off, maybe all I need to do is get her riled up.

Her gaze shifts my way. Dark eyes, dark lashes. She's thoughtful, not angry. "I *don't* want to kill you, actually. But I could."

Headlights flash in our back window and D doesn't turn to look. A horn blows and it might as well be in a different universe. I love how unimpressed she is by the rest of the world. Except now, when I need her to help me and I don't know how to make her.

"I think you want me to punish you for your dead mom."

I flinch, my breath stuttering.

"Here's the thing, though—death isn't a punishment," she says. "Because you're not there to bear it. It doesn't change anything, redeem anything. It can never make up for anything that's already been done." She looks away, her hair flickering against her cheeks with the recycled air from the vents. She's tense like she's talking about something else entirely, and it's impossible to hate her when she looks so tormented. "Even the most justified death ruins new things," she says, very quietly.

The light outside is hitting the windshield just right to mirror us back to ourselves; light hair beside dark. She's not what I thought a murderer would be. But then again, am I?

I try to picture what Peter would be like, if I were meeting him today instead. How he might plan on killing D, if I turn her over to him. He said he had a gun, that "for me" it would be quick. Something harsh and lumpy rises in my throat and I swallow, trying to force it back down. She's done things, yes. Wrong, illegal things.

But does she deserve *that*?

"Nothing feels like it's supposed to, since the crash," I whisper. "So many things would make more sense if I'd died along with her."

I didn't mean to admit it, not that much, but somehow D's honesty draws it out of me.

"I didn't have any sort of grand epiphany or turn over a new leaf after the accident. I didn't even quit college. I flunked out of my scholarship. And after that, I just sort of kept getting up and doing the bare minimum—losing one job after another and cramming dry toast in my mouth when I bothered to eat at all. Like I was just a placeholder for a real person. Everybody told me it would get better as time passed but it just never *did*. And then I realized it has been months and I haven't done a single thing that's worth me having lived when she didn't. It was like a slap in the face to stop fucking around. Can you be somebody that's worth all the food and water you're using up, or are you going to call it for good?"

I glance at her, because even though we just met, she knows better than anyone in my life what an impossible question that is for me.

"So I tried to commit suicide. A whole bunch of different ways. And I couldn't even manage that."

"Fuck." The quiet obscenity is the first clue I have of how closely she's listening.

"I put out that ad like I was shaking a Magic 8 Ball, you know? Like, just tell me yes or no. Live or die. Am I supposed to still be here, and if so, what the hell *for*?" I tug at a stray thread from the hem of my shorts, staring at the windshield. "I don't think I really believed there was anybody out there who would reply. But you did. It hadn't even been up long—only a few days. And I thought, okay, there's my answer. It was like one of those slides at a water park, the really steep ones where it drops out from under you and you're flying. You're weightless and free and at the same time, it's going way too damn fast. It was such a fucking relief, you know?"

I look at her and I think her head twitches but I can't tell if it's a nod or a denial because the words are still tumbling out of me.

"Not to have to figure out how to live with myself for the next sixty years or whatever. It's just . . . easy." I close my eyes. "Since you showed up, it's like the first right thing that's happened since those tires started to slip."

I'm waiting for the lecture, I think. For her to tell me to stop being such a fucking baby and taking the simple way out. Or for her to say I have a thousand things to live for.

Instead, she says, "I wasn't sure I wanted to be a killer. When I saw your ad."

Her voice is so quiet it doesn't even sound like her. It makes my heart throb in my chest, a pain echoed that I know too damn well.

"But your uncle," I say. "The kid." Somehow the other three she mentioned don't bother me the way they should, but those first ones do. The uncle must have done something terrible, I can guess that much, but I can't imagine what would have happened to make her willing to kill a child. Not this strict, unbending woman drawn in shades of white and black. But I already know she'll only tell me as much as she wants to, so I don't ask.

Her face shutters.

"I didn't know if I wanted to *keep* killing," D clarifies precisely. "If that's what I wanted to be, not just something I did a few times. I can walk away with no consequences, right now. There's no evidence left. No one knows. Knew, I guess. Before you."

I swallow. That makes me a loose end. Which helps my cause, but it also feels a bit like that water slide, dropping out from under me.

"But you answered the ad . . ." I say. "It wasn't me who made you consider it again, was it?"

"Not just you." She doesn't look away. "There are others."

Does she mean Peter? Is he still trying to con her, even after I warned him to let me take the lead? Or are there other potential victims? Unwilling ones.

I want to ask a million things, but it feels like an invasion and I would never. Not without her permission. "So have you decided, now?" is all that feels safe to request of her.

She shrugs, the brake pedal making an odd little swooshing sound as her leg begins to twitch. "It's the only thing that sets me apart. Something I can do that most people can't. But it's harder than I thought, being a Faceless Man with no Faceless God."

"Drawing your own lines."

She nods, a single dip of her chin that looks like it costs her.

I squeeze my hands in my lap against the fresh onslaught of guilt. Cars have been lining up behind us and the first few break free and start to flow around us. I should be using this first wisp of vulnerability against her, forcing her to believe that helping me is the right thing to do. It's even protecting her, in a way, because of Peter. But the woman sitting next to me has spilled blood against her will, and played lightsabers with her favorite uncle, and before today, there was only one thing I was desperate for.

And what I hear myself say is, "It doesn't seem right that I know how many people you've killed, but I still don't even know your real name."

She looks at me, and I don't know how I can read the surprise in her without the smallest flicker in her expression. Maybe it's just in the way she looks an instant too long before she blinks.

"Dani," she says.

Satisfaction rises in me, giddy and true. The D was real, but it wasn't for Death.

"Short for Danielle?" It hardly matters, and it bounds out of my mouth too eagerly, giving me away.

It takes her an instant too long to answer, long enough that I know she thought about lying.

"Danìella."

I inhale quickly, as if I can snatch the sound of the word right out of the air and keep it in me.

I tell myself I asked because I wanted to hear her name, in her voice. I tell myself she trusted me with that precious bit of truth, and I won't ever say it aloud to another person. That no matter how desperate I get, I won't trade her to Peter for my own freedom.

I tell myself a lot of things.

CHAPTER

21

Dani

I TEASE MY FINGERS across the scratched glass of the display case, avoiding the thin butterfly knives and gaudy old earrings. Looking for something with the smallest price tag and the largest caliber.

Across the pawnshop counter appears a slouchy polo shirt and chipped nail polish, enveloped in the scent of White Diamond perfume from the dollar store, the kind that comes in bottles as big as hairspray. I don't look up.

"I need to buy a gun."

I haven't decided about Jeika yet, or Peter, but I know the world will be better off without Eric. And a bullet will be the easiest way to end his evil.

"I'm gonna need to see some ID." A stack of papers hits the counter, then a Bic with a plume of frayed fabric feathers taped onto the top. "Here's the registration and background check forms."

The clerk has red hair, parting at the center with fine rake lines left by her comb, the strands too greasy not to cling to each other.

I nod to the thick stack of papers. "I need to buy a gun, not apply to commit a crime."

"According to our nanny state government, those are pretty much the same thing." She looks me over. "You want a revolver or a semi-auto?"

"Revolver," I say. That's what my uncle had. With a semi-auto, I'd probably have to brace it against something to rack the slide, and a revolver looks easier to operate one-handed. But then I glance at the paperwork again and reconsider. I can't afford to have a paper trail tying my name to any of this. Plus, I can see the prices on the top rack of guns and they've got too many digits for me. "Do you have anything that comes without all the homework?"

She bends to reach under the counter, her name tag, reading "Debbie," catching on the edge and straining the cotton of her polo. The holes left by the pins stretch a little bigger. "If there's a man giving you trouble, this'll do the trick better than a gun."

She slaps down a taser, old and scraped. But when she hits the button, the electricity bolting between its two prongs comes out clean and strong.

I flip over the paper price tag, then flick the taser back across the counter to Debbie.

I wish Jeika would have had greasy hair, and dirty fingernails, and Eric's rotting seaweed eyes. Not because it's necessarily harder to kill someone when they're attractive. But when your subject is already an innocent, it doesn't make anything easier for her to have soft blonde hair and angel blue eyes.

I lean on the counter, suddenly tired as I stare down at the weapons I can't afford. If you're up against a man who's bigger, and stronger, and older than you, surprise gives you one free shot. Even if you have a gun, it can be a liability. If your aim isn't impeccable, or if adrenaline overrides his injuries, then your weapon becomes his. But still, a pistol would have evened our odds.

"I don't see anything like what I need," I lie, and Debbie nods and puts the registration papers away. She works at a pawnshop, so she knows all the ways people avoid saying they're going to have to wait for their next paycheck. Or a lotto win.

I walk out and the sun blasts my skin, like I can feel my individual cells starting to curl at the edges and shrivel. The heat from the parking lot rises to suffocate my ankles. I can't stand here too long or I'll just be meat, cooking away.

Why does Jeika think she deserves to die, when she obviously never would have killed her mother on purpose? If she'd been in my place and she realized what she was doing after the second stab, she would have dropped the knife in horror, not driven it in a third time. She wouldn't have survived, the way I did. She would have died innocent, with those blue eyes wide and full of misplaced faith.

Why does she trust *me*? She knows what I've done, and it's not like she doesn't understand what that really means. She's tried to live in a house pressed silent by loss. She knows as well as I do that a family is like a smile—one missing tooth can turn it ugly. Especially when you're the one who ripped it out.

I get in my car and leave the pawnshop without anyone knowing I came for a murder weapon but I couldn't afford it. The kids in my neighborhood will be in danger until I can find a cheaper way to stop Eric, because frying chicken is a service to society that no one values, not even me. But if I try to do this without a better weapon, his next victim is going to be me.

CHAPTER 22

To: FacelessMan00@gmail.com
From: MVictimVolunteer@gmail.com
Date: May 12, 3:14 PM
Subject: Tired of waiting

Dani,

You said there were others that you're going to kill. So if you want me to convince you, tell me who managed to meet your criteria.

-Jeika

To: MVictimVolunteer@gmail.com
From: FacelessMan00@gmail.com
Date: May 12, 10:39 PM
Re: Tired of waiting

Jeika,

Fine. You want to see someone who actually deserves to die? I'll show you. Tomorrow, same time, same Starbucks.

-Dani

CHAPTER

23

To: MVictimVolunteer@gmail.com
From: PeterL1978@hotmail.com
Date: May 13, 9:22 AM
Re: If you're serious . . .

To: Murder Victim,

Have you been able to ID Faceless yet? Have there been other people answering your ad? I'm not going to wait around for you forever.

I have other ways of getting what I want.

-Peter

CHAPTER

24

Jeika

I'VE GOT TO tell her today.

As I slide into the wide passenger seat of Dani's car, the warm vinyl embraces me and an ache throbs in my throat. Peter is starting to make threats, and he might already be trying to get to her without waiting for me. Also, she might figure out anytime that he's not really suicidal, that he's a would-be vigilante killer. I don't have much time left to convince her to help me so I can cut him loose.

This secret about Peter is no longer a trump card slipped up my sleeve. Instead it feels like a scarlet letter, hidden from her sight but burning into me all the time. Just because no one knows your sins doesn't mean they're not there.

I swallow, struggling not to fidget. I spent a long time googling suspicious deaths in Phoenix after I saw her last, trying to corroborate her story. No one died recently by the name of Ricky, but there was a Richard who was stabbed to death in a burglary attempt, though it was quite a few years ago. Could that have been her uncle? As for her most recent kill, there have been two murders in the last couple of weeks—a carjacking and a business owner who had his throat slit at work. That one caught media attention because in a twist of ironic convenience, he died at a funeral home. Not to mention the subsequent juicy scandal when his wife's lover got cuffed for the crime. So neither of those was probably Dani, but who knows what "recent" means to a murderer? Since I don't have evidence to back up her kill count, she could be making them up, but my gut says that what she shared with me is more true than anything I could read in a newspaper.

"Where, um, are we going?"

Dani doesn't answer me, just takes a turn down an unfamiliar street, headed deeper into a part of the city I've never been to, and the blood in my veins goes cold and thick.

Peter told me not to trust her. She's taking me who knows where, to see some godawful kind of person. I wore sneakers, in case . . . I don't know what. Running probably won't be enough to protect me, if this all turns wrong.

It's not long before she turns into a trailer park. Dani's jaw is tense now too, as if she doesn't like it here any more than I do. My hands clench as she parks next to an overgrown hedge that straggles up nearly as high as the car. I consider the double-wide we're parked in front of. The yard is scattered with sun-faded concrete gnomes and frogs and a tiny garden flag. It doesn't look as ominous as the atmosphere in the car suddenly feels, and it certainly doesn't look like the kind of destination I was expecting. Dani stays in the car, so maybe we're still waiting for someone to show up.

I glance around, because I'm going out of my head here and she doesn't seem the type you make small talk with. Through the top branches of the bush, I spot a playground next door, patchy brown grass giving way to a couple of swings and a crooked old merry-go-round. The jungle gym stands bare like a skeleton, a lone little boy playing on the merry-go-round. His balding dad watches from nearby, the kid hopping off the toy to pelt running circles around him. The man laughs and digs into the backpack sitting next to him, offering up a brightly wrapped granola bar. The scene is so wholesome compared to our reason for being here that I have to avert my eyes, scrubbing at my hand as if to rub away an itch.

"That's sweet," I say, unable to stand the silence for a second longer.

Dani looks over at me sharply. "What?"

"The dad bringing snacks to the park."

"That's not his dad."

I take a second look. The little boy's skin is a shade darker than the man with the thinning hair, but not so much that they couldn't be related.

"That's who I'm going to kill."

For an instant, I think she means the child. When I realize what she's actually saying, I still have to resist the urge to jump out of the car and tug him away.

"Did that guy . . . I mean, to that little boy . . ."

"I think so."

I inhale abruptly, because whatever I was expecting, that's worse. If that kind of cruelty is the bar for what it takes for Dani to agree to kill a person, then I just . . . can't. My eyes follow the child's every movement. I only found out what kind of danger he was in seconds ago, but somehow it feels like if no one is watching, anything could happen.

"Can't you call social services?" I twist the edge of my shirt, embarrassed to look at Dani, like she might be amused at how shocked I am.

"Have you ever called social services on someone?"

I swallow. "No."

"If you had, you wouldn't ask me that. A guy like that has to commit a hundred crimes before there's enough evidence to prove to the authorities that he's committed one." Dani doesn't fidget, and somehow her stillness is more unsettling. "I'm not going to wait for ninety-nine more."

I drop my head. If that skinny guy and his well-stocked backpack were going to do something, it probably wouldn't be in plain daylight in the middle of a playground. Also, if he's been doing this long enough that Dani's found out, this probably isn't his first victim. The realization echoes ever darker and deeper inside my head and I try to force myself to think past it, to refocus on why I'm here.

My fingers rise to my mostly healed throat, fingering the last scuff mark where it's sore. I need this to work, with her.

"You only kill people who hurt other people." I state it like it's nothing. Like I can handle this. "So what? You know what I did to my mom."

Dani makes a dismissive sound. "Accidents happen. The car did all the dirty work. By the time you realized what would happen, it was all already over. Moving the body so nobody would blame you is dark, I'll grant you that, but I doubt you would have been charged either way."

The cops who've started calling daily would probably disagree. I never showed up to talk to them at the station, and they've clearly noticed.

"You don't know what I've done." It scrapes out of my throat, but even now, I don't want to tell her all of it.

"Do you mean Peter?"

I stiffen so fast the vinyl seat squeaks under my legs. My fingers twitch toward the door handle, but it's already too late to run.

"Whaa—t?" I stammer out.

Dani's eyebrows arch darkly. "What'd you do? Make a suicide pact and then ghost him? He was all bent out of shape about it. How many people answered that crazy ad of yours, anyway?"

"How . . . how do you know that?" I'm putting the pieces together as fast as I can, terrified to blurt out the wrong thing. From what they've both said, I know they must be aware of each other, but I'm not sure how much she's figured out, or what cover story he might have given her. I tuck my trembling hands between my knees before she can see them. I was going to tell her about the deal today, but if she found out I went behind her back before I have the chance to confess, this could go a thousand terrible ways.

I'm here because she's dangerous. I can't forget that.

"He thought you were dead," she says. "Made an online classified ad to find me, tried to blackmail me into helping him kill himself."

That wasn't who he intended to kill, not at all. I hold my breath. Should I tell her now? But I can't predict which way that would make her fall on my case.

"So, are you going to?" I venture. "Help him, I mean?"

"Seems like you know him better than I do. Should I?"

"How much has he told you?"

"Not much." She laughs, staccato and short. "He tried to manipulate me instead."

I can just imagine how that went.

"I know he used to have a daughter," I say softly. "I mean, I get it. It was so hard to lose a parent, I can't imagine how bad it would be if it was your child."

"So you think I *should* kill him?"

"I don't know," I hedge, still too scared to tell her he was the other murderer. Besides, this might be a good opportunity to feel out what *would* convince Dani, if my past hasn't done it. "I mean, what else does he have in his life now that his daughter's gone? Does he have a job or other kids? Is he married? Could he be the one who finds the cure for cancer someday?"

"So that's your scoreboard." She gives me a contemptuous look, and I squirm because I know how shallow it sounds when you lay it out like that. "Two points for a spouse, one point if you're employed, two if you're a medical researcher. How many points for whoever you're going to leave behind? Do we count extra if they've already lost someone else?"

"I don't *know*!" She's so unimpressed, but it's bullshit. Just because pain doesn't seem to touch her doesn't mean the rest of us don't feel it. "Maybe this doesn't matter to someone like you, but what if I just don't *want* to be here anymore? In a world where one fight over a phone can ruin a life and a family, just like that? A world so fucked up *that guy* runs free and nobody even notices?" I flip a hand out at the playground. "I mean, have you ever tried to get out of bed in the morning and just couldn't? Because even walking to the bathroom is too fucking much. Everything out there is just—" I cough into silence, my lips twisting as I try to hold back a sob.

"You're miserable." Her words are quiet now. "I get it. So you're saying it's cruel of me to make a person keep suffering, when I could release them from that."

We were supposed to be talking about Peter, but I don't correct her. Instead, I swipe at tears, the skin around my eyes always a little raw from the last time.

"But what if they'll get better?" Her voice is dark like manacles, locking us together in this conversation neither of us want to be in.

I try to speak and a keening thread is all that comes out. I can't keep doing this long enough to get better. I can't feel like *this* for another year, or even another month, even before that supposed "witness" came out of the woodwork to make the whole situation worse. Fuck Peter, fuck her, fuck values and scoreboards and promises. I want out. But she's still talking.

"Everybody loses somebody in their life. Grief is temporary. So what if I kill someone when the hardest part is about to be over?"

"What if the hardest part is never over?" I whisper. "What if it just gets worse, the longer it goes on?"

My insides are a bruise and with every snatched breath, the whole world crushes them further down. On the playground, the little boy's smiling, and the man reaches for him. I flinch, my hand flying to the door handle again. But the older guy just pats his back, sending the kid on his way while he watches with a small smile that ferments inside my heart.

Dani's not looking, her head tipped back against the seat and her gaze on the ceiling. A small huff of breath escapes her, almost like a laugh but not quite.

I'm almost afraid to ask. "What?"

"My uncle," she says. "Everybody always thinks life is too bad, that they'll be better off on the other side." She looks so tired. "But none of us really know, do we? If it's any different. Any easier. If it's anything at all."

"Is that what your uncle said to you? You told me that lightsaber story, about him playing with you, but those are just the good parts that are nice to remember after somebody's gone. If that was all he was, you wouldn't have killed him."

"You didn't know him. He was trying to help us."

"Okay . . ." That doesn't sound right to me, especially if he really was the Richard who died in a burglary, but I don't want to do anything to stop her from confiding in me.

"He had a shitty life, okay? When I was little, he'd always play games with me. Jacks, pick-up sticks. All the stuff my mom figured I couldn't do. He lived with us until I was five, then took off, chasing some woman out to L.A. But from there, his life pretty much went to shit. Even worse than my mom's. In the end, he lost his job, his latest girlfriend kicked him out, he went to jail for a while, and then he was crashing on our couch. He decided life was bullshit and he wanted out." She glances at me, almost tentative. "What he did. It's because he loved us. I didn't get that in the moment, but afterward, it was so clear. He didn't want us to suffer. He wanted us to pass peacefully in our sleep."

This does not sound like it's going anywhere good. "How old were you?"

"Fourteen."

I'm pretty sure there's no reason a fourteen-year-old ever needs to die, peacefully in their sleep or otherwise, but I let her tell her story the way she sees it.

"Uh, how was that supposed to work, exactly?"

She glances away. "He was acting all different one day. Said he was going to start doing his share of the cooking, so he made these smoothies for me and Mom. Mine tasted weird so I pretended it was really good and dumped the rest down the toilet when he wasn't looking so I wouldn't hurt his feelings. He put liquor in Mom's, so she chugged it right down and passed out. She didn't drink as much back then, it was more of a just-on-the-weekends thing, so it was weird to see her conk out like that. I drank enough of the smoothie to be sleepy, so I was almost dozing on the couch, but I woke up enough at one point to see him get the box of bullets out."

My skin tightens around my bones. I don't think I want to hear this.

"When I saw him loading the gun and going for my mom, I grabbed a knife off the kitchen counter and that was it. Over in a second. No thinking, no decision. Once I realized what I'd done, and it sunk in what he'd planned to do, I freaked out. Panicked. But there was blood just all over the floor, and a body. No way to hide it and Mom was still sleeping away."

Glass in my mouth. Blood. I gulp air, remembering my own mother's body and how desperately I never wanted anyone to see what I'd done.

"I thought I'd go to prison for the rest of my life, so I decided to cover it up."

This time, I can't help my small inhale, but I can't tell her what I'm thinking, so I just nod for her to go on.

"I made it look like a robbery. Hit my mom in the head with a pan from the sink like she got knocked out instead of drugged, put her on the floor. Left my uncle's pistol near him as if he'd been running away from the burglar to get to his gun and defend us. I'd always loved CSI shows and true-crime podcasts, so I knew how to set up the scene just right, and how to explain away the things I couldn't change, like the blood spatter. I told the police the robber came in the front door, and I was in my room and went out the window. I told them that's why I lived."

At fourteen, she was trying to figure out how to stage a crime scene. No wonder she's hardened as iron now, so many years later. But somehow, it's not how I pictured this all starting for her.

"That's not what I th . . ." I battle with what I want to say, at wanting to share how much I hate what she's gone through, but afraid it'll hurt my case. "I mean, that's super messed up. I guess I just don't get how that made you *want* to kill. To ever go through that again."

She glares down at her lap. "I mean, for weeks after that I was just all alone in my head, trying to figure out why it happened. My mom imploded, started drinking hardcore, and it wasn't like I could talk to anybody about how it all played out or if I'd done the right thing. I only went after him so he wouldn't hurt us, but afterward, I couldn't stop thinking . . ."

"Why you," I finish softly, reaching for her, my whole body aching with the pain of this story. She jerks away and I realize I reached for her right side, the one she always seems to hold a little away from everyone else. I don't push it, but I keep my hand on the console between us. "Why you were the one who lived when he didn't."

"No," she says, shifting further away. "Just . . . why. Why I could do what I did. Why it happened that way at all. What the fuck was the *point*? It felt like there was one that I was just missing. And then I remembered the animals."

My hand goes cold and I draw it back to my lap. Serial killers tortured animals sometimes; I'd read that somewhere. That was expected. Exactly what I'd hired her to be, in a way. "What animals?" I force myself to say.

"We've always lived at the edges of town, out near the desert. Animals got into the house sometimes. Rats, mice, once a snake." She gazes out toward the chain-link fence at the end of the playground.

This place is pretty far on the edge of town too, with some crooked cactus on the far side of the fence with shreds of old grocery bags blown across their spines.

"The cheap traps my mom used injured more animals than they killed. She said if we just left them there, they'd eventually die, but I couldn't stand their scrabbling and writhing all around. Not when they were in so much pain. So once when I was really young, I took one outside and finished it off. One clean stroke and it was at rest. After that, it became my responsibility. Mom set the traps, and I finished the job. I hated it the first time I had to chop one, but when I saw its little body relax . . . It was something my mom couldn't do, but I could."

A car zooms by, its shocks bucking and rattling when it hits the crumbling old speed bump. Neither of us look up.

"I remembered that one day, when I was thinking about how bad off my uncle had been. He wanted out, and he genuinely thought this world was so terrible that the best thing he could do was take us with him. I thought . . . maybe it was like the animals. That he was the one who was suffering, and I made it stop, like he wanted. My mom would have never been able to do it, even if she was awake. She would have cried," Dani says, her face hard. "And she wouldn't have done shit."

I'm thinking of her saying "a kid from my neighborhood" and I'm wondering when she made her second kill. It hasn't escaped my notice that she hasn't exactly volunteered the details. Or that the three more she mentioned were just numbers, like they weren't even people to her. She must have killed them so easily, so why not me?

"And that's why you answered my ad?" I ask slowly, fishing.

"I thought . . . there are things no one should have to live with."

My back jerks straight. "And now, what? You think I'm not suffering *enough*?" I think of the rope, the little brother I never see anymore. All the nights when it feels like I'm coming out of my skin and I can't make my own thoughts stop.

She tilts her head, studying me.

"The cute dad who brought snacks . . ." she muses. "When you look at yourself, you see all the bad parts. But when you look at other people, you assume they're good. I don't know if that's sweet or nuts."

"You don't know shit about me." All the different memories of my sins seethe under my sleeves. I don't know how I ever thought we had anything in common, she and I.

We've both stood over the graves of our family, nobody knowing what we've done while people cried all around us. I'll remember how that felt until my last breath. If she can live through that and feel no guilt, I don't understand her at all.

There's only one place people like us deserve to go.

"You know what? Fuck it. If you don't think what I've been through is bad enough, fine. You think I've got my whole life ahead of me and I'll get over it, whatever. But if you're really here to ease suffering, then you owe Peter a chance to convince you too."

She snorts. "Peter's an asshole."

"What, because you don't *like* him you don't care what he's going through?" My temper's flaring now and I don't care what she thinks of me. "If you're going to play Faceless God, you've got to suck it up and sit in judgment sometimes." I jerk my chin toward the playground, even though the man is long gone. "Newsflash: The people who deserve to die aren't always going to be the ones you'd like to have a beer with."

Her eyes are black flames, but I don't back down. I'm already burning. I'm not going to tell her Peter's not who she thinks: that he's the murderer I didn't trust, not another person clamoring for her help to opt out. If she's going to screw me over, I'll screw her over right back.

"All right," she says abruptly. "Set up a meeting with him, for tomorrow. I'll listen to what he has to say, but beyond that, I'm not promising shit." She starts the car without waiting for my answer. Without questioning if there might be any other reason Peter and I would want to get her alone.

I know what I've done.

And for once, I just don't care.

CHAPTER

25

To: PeterL1978@hotmail.com
From: MVictimVolunteer@gmail.com
Date: May 13, 9:50 PM
Subject: Let's do this

Peter,

I'm bringing you the murderer. We can meet tomorrow night. She's going to send me a dropped pin on Google Maps, far enough out in the desert we won't be disturbed. But if I turn her over to you, you have to promise you *will* kill me.

To: MVictimVolunteer@gmail.com
From: PeterL1978@hotmail.com
Date: May 13, 10:32 PM
Re: Let's do this

To Murder Victim,

You're doing the right thing. Bitches like her deserve to die.

-Peter

CHAPTER 26
Dani

I WAKE UP TO the sound of sizzling meat. It's so unfamiliar that I jerk upright, coming half out of my bed with the sheets dragging at my ankles as I try to orient myself. It's been so long since anyone else cooked for me it feels like I've somehow woken in the middle of my childhood, but my body's too tall.

I blink and shake my tangled hair back from my face, rising out of the grogginess. It's already evening, edging toward sunset. I fell asleep right after work, knowing I'd be out late because today, I'm probably going to be making my next kill. Did my mom sense that something was different about me? Is that why she's up and cooking at an hour when she's usually too drunk to change the channel on the TV?

Maybe she didn't drink today . . .

I throw the sheets back, kicking my way into my jeans. Fuck it, even drunks get hungry. Doesn't mean anything. I snatch up my hairbrush and jerk it through my hair, the tingle of hairs being ripped loose waking up my scalp. It clatters when it hits the warped surface of my dresser.

The reek of meat turns my stomach. It's hamburger, the pack that's been going brown in the fridge all week. I don't want to smell like hamburger when I see Jeika.

My mom glances quickly at me from beneath her hair when I stalk through the kitchen. Twice, like she's checking on something. "You hungry? I'm making burgers."

"We don't have buns." I sit down to pull my black sneakers on, but they're my work shoes. Can't get blood on these. To get another set, I have to pass her again, my front nearly brushing her back in the narrow kitchen. She smells like Suave shower gel, her T-shirt musty with back-of-the-closet scent.

"I thought I could do them with ketchup and macaroni, the way you used to like."

"Haven't eaten it like that in years." I duck back into my room, but the only other shoes I have are a pair of boots with a broken lace. I sit down and begin the laborious process of knotting it together so I can re-lace it. As I work, my sleeve nags at my peripheral vision. The tiny, uneven stitches on the wrist of my shirt, where Mom hemmed the sleeve shorter for me so the extra fabric wouldn't flap. I ignore it.

"Is, uh, work going okay?" She comes to stand in the doorway, her hands hanging at her sides. She doesn't even lean on the doorway, like this is too much my space for her to touch it. Behind her, the meat sizzles too loudly, starting to burn. "How's Madeline treating you?"

"Marilyn." I get the knot done, but it's too far up the lace, and it jams against the hole. The boots won't lace tight this way, but I don't care. I stuff them onto my feet anyway. I don't have time for this shit.

"Right, Marilyn. She still being a bitch?" Mom gives a shaky laugh and I look up at her. She even put on mascara, but it's so old and dry that it's already starting to flake off on her cheeks.

"She's a bitch, but she's a bitch who shows up for work."

Mom flinches and her gaze falls to the carpet, the wrinkles in her T-shirt shifting and coming into sharper relief as she fidgets her weight from side to side. We both know how long it's been since she was able to hold a job.

I jerk to my feet, my body getting that hollow, too-small feeling it does sometimes when Mom's actually sober and looking at me. Especially now, when I know what Jeika would give to be standing face to face with her mother again.

I don't need this uncertainty today. If I call off everything and sit down to the dinner she's currently burning, then that pull from her darting, uncertain eyes will just haul me off center. Tomorrow, she'll be at the bottom of another bottle and I'll be alone, grasping for a reason to bother putting on my shoes for one more day.

Right now, I'm doing what I have to do. Showing up for my one fucked-up purpose that this fucked-up world seems to need me for. People are relying on me. I grab my keys.

She follows me to the door. "You're not staying for dinner?"

I meet her gaze, the flecks of mascara laying like black freckles in the hollows under her sunken eyes. From the kitchen, I can already smell the first hint of smoke. There's not going to be any dinner. "I have plans."

Gnats whirl around me in an irritating cloud as I shut the door, heading the long way around our trailer to the old shed so I won't pass the kitchen window. She won't remember later once she gets drunk, but it's better no one sees me. It takes me two tries to remember the combination on the sun-faded padlock. I dig past spiderweb-strewn boxes and an old, broken microwave, and then my palm closes around a shovel. I carry it to my car and toss it in the trunk, on top of the other supplies I already gathered there. All I know about Peter is that he lost his daughter, and that's far from enough for me to agree to help him die. But I have a feeling about him, and it tells me I'm going to need this.

We only own one shovel, and I can't imagine Jeika's going to be in any shape to help me dig afterward. Still, it'd go a lot faster with two. Digging's not the easiest thing for me, since I can only grip the shovel with one hand and press down on the handle to steady it with my short arm. It's a splintery, slow process, nearly impossible in hard ground, and I've only tried to do it once, during Mom's short attempt at planting our flowerbeds when I was in middle school. I've never had to bury my own bodies before. The police took the first one, the hospital the second. The other two I chose because they were so easy. Right there, doing bad shit I wasn't supposed to see, and so unconnected from my life that I could walk away afterward and just leave them all behind.

I wanted to know if it would be different if I didn't know them. And it was and it wasn't. Mostly, I didn't like feeling that fate was calling the shots instead of me. But with the guy at the funeral home . . . that wasn't really me or fate. It was a whim, not truly a choice, and then it was just over. And he meant nothing.

It's that nothing that grinds at me. The gravity of meaninglessness threatening to tug me under like it did my uncle.

I already know I can kill. If there's a little tug of mystery to it, a shadow to my destiny I don't quite understand, there's no better way to sort it out than with a woman who's literally begging me to murder her.

Because if that's not what I'm for, what else do I have?

One of the gnats made it into the car with me and it buzzes around my head as I start the engine and turn out in the direction of Starbucks, where I'm meeting Jeika.

I probably wouldn't have even agreed to this meeting if it weren't for her. I don't give two fucks about Peter, but if I do decide to kill him, it might just save Jeika. She thinks she understands death because she saw her mother's body, but a car accident is nothing like a murder.

Except now, I'm wondering how she's going to handle it while it's happening. If she'll go quiet or hysterical. If I should take her phone in case she freaks and tries to call the cops. I've never had to worry about a witness before. Will she turn me in, days after this, once the memory of seeing what I did to Peter has twisted ever uglier in her mind? I know all too well how the images can consume you.

The GPS on my phone chimes the next turn and I take it automatically without paying any attention to where I'm going. If I do this right in front of her, and she decides she does want to live, will we keep emailing each other? Will she be afraid of me?

I've always preferred people fear me, when compared to any of the other things they might think about me. Funny how today, the thought of it sits as poorly as that old hamburger would have.

CHAPTER 27
Jeika

WHAT DO YOU wear to watch someone be murdered? I reach for a black T-shirt—dark, to hide the stains—then realize it won't matter because my own blood will be joining it, and who knows where my body will end up by morning. A shallow grave, dug by one or the other of them, or just left on the ground.

It's one thing to know you're going to die before morning. Another to not be sure how, or who's going to do it.

Deep down, I don't believe that Peter intends to kill me—I think he's capable of it, for her. And it's not like I think he's totally logical or anything. I just have trouble believing anybody with a grudge against murderers would be chill about assisting with a suicide. Given that, tonight's deal with him is my riskiest play yet. The thing I'm counting on, the only thing I'm sure of, is that if he attacks Dani, none of us will live through the night except for her.

I stomp into a pair of sneakers too white to match my outfit and look around. There must be something else I can do to prepare myself.

Nothing in my apartment can make me feel ready for this, though, because I don't know what's going to happen. I mean, maybe Peter will fulfill his promise, or maybe he'll just be as unhinged as he sounds on the phone and who knows what he'll do to either of us? But really, I think he's no match for Dani, even with surprise on his side. I think she's going to take him out, and after she does, I won't have to beg her to kill me. Once she realizes what I've done, she'll do it for free.

I pace into the kitchen, ripping open a packet of ramen. It makes sense to eat to steady my stomach, but underneath the black of my clothes, I'm quivering.

I used to think all the time about what it would be like if I were the one lying in my mother's coffin. How dark and quiet it would be inside. My head on a satin pillow. Some days, every cell in me felt like it was yearning toward that. But now, instead of relief, all I feel is doubt. Not about my death, but Dani's. I was so angry yesterday, so sure that if she could stand on her uncle's grave and feel no guilt, then she deserved anything Peter could do to her.

Bitches like her deserve to die.

When he says it, it doesn't sound true anymore.

If she really didn't feel anything, why did she go searching for reasons? So that so many years later, she's still trying to find an answer she can live with for why she murdered her uncle? To me, it's so clear. She wanted to live, to save her unconscious mother. Maybe she doesn't call it guilt, but it's not indifference.

Things happen so fast sometimes and when you catch up, the blood is already spilled and you can't put it back. So what do you do?

You can try to rebalance the world, the way Peter and Dani have both done, in their own way. To kill the right people. To find the tiny threads of justice and pull them out of the crazy complicated weaving of fate so they don't get lost to mere randomness.

Or you can admit it's impossible to know the "why" behind anything and you just opt out, like me. Before you can hurt anyone else.

The microwave beeps and I startle from my thoughts. I carry the bowl to the table and drop it just as the heat begins to burn my fingers through the plastic.

Except somebody's going to get hurt tonight, not just me. Him, or her. Not that it should matter, because they're both murderers.

Murderersmurderersmurderersmurderersmurderersmurderersmurderersmurderersmurderersmurderers

I try to eat, repeating my own justification in my head until the word itself loses its black and white crispness and goes every shade of gray. No matter how I match up their situations, they don't seem the same.

Let me be clear: I won't kill someone else's victim. There are some fucked-up men in the world who like to twist you up in shame, so you can't get away because you're caught in your own net, and therefore, theirs.

One of the first things Dani ever emailed was about if someone was abusing or manipulating me. Even then, she was worrying if I was safe. The ramen in my bowl suddenly looks like the twists of guts.

I toss it into the sink and head for the door to meet her, even though I'm early. I snatch up my purse, then hesitate. I won't need my keys to get back in, won't need my phone to call anyone after today, but it seems wrong to leave without it. Briefly, I consider texting what's left of my family one last time, but no. There's no bigger apology I can offer than my death, so that's what I'm doing. Even if they never know what I'm sorry for.

I drive to Starbucks in a haze, and the first thing I see is the army-green steel of Dani's car waiting at the curb. The ramen already in my belly writhes like intestines that belong to someone else.

Is it wrong that I want her to survive him?

I put all this in motion with Peter because she refused to help me, then because her sins were too much like my own and I couldn't forgive that. And yet, I still want her to be the one to do it, even if I have to force her hand.

I close my eyes so I won't have to see her as I open the door and slide into her car. Thinking about all the terrible things we do to escape the terrible things we've done.

We don't speak all the way to the desert. As the dusk light wanes in long shadows, darkness drapes the ground and stretches like it's growing. More and more of it all the time. I swear I can feel my heartbeat all the way into my stomach because *this*. This moment feels like a line I'm crossing, just the same as the white line at the edge of the road when my family's car flew across it—gone before I even saw it, and still, somehow, it's come to define my whole life.

Dani parks at a spot that looks like any other: just dust and bushes, far enough out that no one would come here unless they had to do things they didn't want anyone to see. There are acres of dirt that belong to no one and I can't help but wonder how many bones are already moldering under our feet. Forgotten, like I will be.

I close my eyes, sinking exhaustedly into the idea of that. Her voice snaps me back into this excruciating moment with words I didn't expect to hear.

"Get out."

"What?"

"And give me your phone."

My pulse bleats. Does she know about my deal with Peter? My thoughts race, trying to decipher her, but I dig the phone out of my purse without protesting because we both know she can make me.

Dani turns the device off and sticks it in the glove box, then she gets out without a word.

My door creaks, slow like a horror movie, when I obey and follow her out. She unlocks the trunk and shoves a tarp to the side, a shovel clanking underneath. My stomach burbles greasily. Somehow, nothing in my life has ever seemed as real as seeing a tarp and shovel in a serial killer's trunk. I swallow back saliva and pray I won't throw up.

Does she want me to help her get things ready, in case Peter's argument is good enough to convince her? Somehow, with all her resistance to helping me, I forgot that this is what she does. That wielding death is what has given her enough purpose to pull her through all the years since her own uncle turned on her.

Dani pulls out a roll of duct tape. "Hold out your hands."

I jerk a step back, my eyes flaring wide. She knows. She must. Oh fuck, how much is this going to hurt?

She clears her throat. "It's just insurance." There's something in her voice that's almost soft. "I need you out of sight when he gets here, because I want him to think I'm you."

"But why . . . I mean, I told him we were meeting so he could make his case, tell you why he wants to die. That won't make sense if there's just one of us."

"If he thinks I'm the murderer, he's going to tell me what he thinks I want to hear," Dani says. "If he thinks I'm you, he won't have any reason to hide the truth. I'll tell him the killer is still on the way, get him talking while we wait."

"I mean, but you don't need to tie me up—" I stutter, trying to buy time. They both think they're meeting for different reasons, and without me, I have no idea which way that could go. "I could help, I could—"

"I'm sorry, did it sound like I was asking?" She drops the roll of duct tape over her wrist and pulls out a strip. "It was your introduction, but this is not your party."

I hold out my hands, telling myself there's no sense in struggling. She's stronger than me, tougher. But as the tape winds tight around my wrists, it feels like relief.

"Please, be careful." As soon as I say it, I realize exactly how much I had to lie to myself to get us all here today. I don't hate her for what she did. And without that, I don't think I can stand whatever's coming next. "He's— Dani, he's—" I begin to blurt.

Her fingers brush my cheek as she presses the strip over my mouth, the stickiness cold over my lips.

"I can't risk you losing your nerve and trying to interfere," she says. "It's my call now, whether he deserves to die or not. And if he does, it's not the kind of thing where you can change your mind partway through."

My face feels stiff with tape now, my voice sealed in, and tears fill my eyes. Not because I feel guilty that I didn't get to speak, but because I'm glad. If I save her, I'm saving myself, and I don't want to be saved.

Without waiting for her to insist, I use my bound hands to steady myself, balancing my fingertips against her taillight as I climb into the trunk. As she starts to close the lid, the darkness hides me, and it feels safer than any coffin. The tape is secure where it holds my wrists and I wriggle a little, just to feel its strength. In here, none of my choices can be wrong, because I don't have any.

I can't hurt anyone.

No matter which way this goes out there, I'm going to die tonight. I can't worry about who either of them might be leaving behind, who might be devastated by their deaths the way I was by my mother's. The ripple effects just keep going, but I'm not God, and I can't smooth the surface of water back into place with only my hands.

It'll all be over soon, and it doesn't matter how bad it'll get before then, because I'll never have to think about anything again.

CHAPTER

28

Dani

I LEAVE THE TRUNK open just a crack, so Jeika can watch. It's why I really let her come today. I've known enough guys like Peter to know—if that dick thinks he deserves to die, he's probably right. There's probably more to his story than I saw on his Facebook page. He won't be like Jeika, wracked with guilt for something she couldn't have changed. Always trying to be better than a human is capable of being. And if she has to watch me do it, she'll realize.

She doesn't want what she's asking for.

The hood of my car is warm against my ass as I watch for approaching vehicles. It's always the desert where I feel most at home, with its clean heat and miles of open air. You can see everything coming at you, out here.

Right now, the only things within striking distance of me are the twilight-lit silhouettes of sharp cactus and low, lumpy bushes. One set of parallel curves I immediately recognize as a rib cage. It might not even be human, but my gaze lingers on it anyway.

Every desert is a boneyard, skeletons laid bare and crumpling under the weight of sun and time and animals' teeth. There's an honesty to it that doesn't exist in a funeral home's basement where bodies are embalmed with chemicals or vaporized in the unnatural fire of a crematorium. Keeping the dead out of sight so we can pretend the world only belongs to the living.

I look out across the land and almost imagine I can see the gentle rounding of the earth. The one true curve underneath all the artificial ripples of landscaping and bridges and buzzing, discontented cities. Underneath sin and guilt and all the other human inventions.

It's long, quiet heartbeats spent until Peter appears. This is the time when a good person would be having second thoughts about the role I've come here to play. But now death is so near I feel nothing at all.

It's not until Peter parks in front of me that I remember he drives a station wagon. In his subdivision it fit in, but out here it's vaguely ridiculous.

I hunch my shoulders and take a hesitant step forward, trying to match what he might expect for Jeika. "Um, Peter?"

He gets out of the car, scanning behind me and peering in the windows of my car. He looks older than his pictures on Facebook, more haggard. One ear is slightly smaller than the other, making his face seem a little off-balance. His eyes narrow, flicking over my right arm, my shortened sleeve. I watch the crease in his forehead as he tries to reconcile the reality of me with all the conclusions he drew before he ever saw me.

"Murder Victim?"

I only barely catch an eye roll. Right. That's her email address, and she probably never gave her real name to him. My smile comes out fierce, and I have to add a wobble before he notices. "That's me. Faceless Man should be here any minute. I wanted to get here first, make sure, you know . . ." I scrub my toe uncertainly in the dirt, and hope it looks more natural than it feels. "That you really want to go through with this."

"Never been more sure of anything."

There's a thirst in his eyes, and it creeps ugly gooseflesh over my skin. I've never seen anyone crave their own death with such enthusiasm. Not even Jeika, at her most despondent. It seems unnatural, and something about it makes the numbness creep deeper in me.

I move closer to him. "Why." I sound like me again, not her, so I try for more tentative when I offer, "I mean, how do you know it's what you really want? Sometimes, I'm not totally sure, you know?"

"My daughter belonged to a cult, did I ever tell you that?" His lip curled. "They were sure. All of them. That this world was ending and only the pure of faith would make it to the beyond. They had to prove their faith that the end was coming by being willing to step off the cliff before it came."

As he speaks, I see the father in him. In the dusty station wagon and the way his cheeks droop a little more than they should for a man his age. In the sagging, vacant seat of his khakis, like he's lost weight and hasn't gone shopping since he was still showing up for soccer matches and PTA meetings. It fits a little oddly with the asshole he's been in his emails.

"She and her boyfriend had a secret pact," Peter says. "Read it all in their texts after she was gone. They'd beat the rest of the group to proving their faith and go on to be their leaders in the afterlife." His face twists and the loving father in him disappears in a blink. "Her fucking cult boyfriend said he was going to *help* her, isn't that disgusting? They were supposed to do it together. But he killed her first, and then he lost his nerve. That sick, selfish asshole killed my beautiful little girl for a better world it turned out he didn't even believe in. Then skipped town so he never had to pay for what he did."

His eyes start to water and they reflect the shine from where I left my headlights on.

"That's why I'm going to do it," he says hoarsely.

I open my mouth to try for something that Jeika would say, but he's already turned his back on me, heading for the rear hatch of his wagon and throwing it open. I follow him, my steps measured. Jeika mentioned a daughter, and his Facebook page hinted at the rest—probably the wife left after the daughter died—but none of that really matches with the way he was to me in the emails. His cockiness, the way he didn't seem defeated or depressed so much as determined.

He rummages inside the station wagon, throwing a glance toward the dirt road we took to get to this nothing spot in the desert. "How long's she going to be?"

I shrug, considering him. He has an ordinary face, flabby nose. The skin is dingy, like something vital has leached out of him as the years have passed. I know he's not lying about losing his family, but something's still not quite right here. I can feel Jeika's gaze on my back. I think she'd see some good left in him, if she were really the one standing here.

"Should I use the pistol or the crowbar?" he asks me, and I look over to see him opening a plastic Smith & Wesson case. A flush of odd electricity goes through me at the sight of the gun. I brought my own weapons but figured I wouldn't bother to get them out of the car until I'd made my decision. Somehow, it tracks that a control freak like him would bring his own. But then, why would he ask *Jeika* her opinion on which method he should die by?

The hairs on the back of my neck rise, and my eyes fall on the third item inside the hatch. He supposedly came here to die, but he brought a shovel.

I go very still.

He finishes loading the revolver and snaps the cylinder back into place, gesturing toward the access road with a flick of the barrel. "So what'd you tell the bitch? To get her here?" He tucks the gun in the back of his khakis.

Now I feel Jeika's eyes boring into my back for a whole other reason. She *knew*.

I dive for his gun. He twists away with a shout at my abrupt movement but I don't have time to look up because I've got my fingers on the grip and—

CHAPTER

29

Dani

I DON'T KNOW IF that explosion was pain, or sound, but now there's dirt under my knees and my head shrieks with an agony that hasn't settled enough yet for me to know if my face is the same shape it used to be.

"It's *you*," Peter hisses. "The crazy scalpel bitch."

I throw myself toward my car, things happening too fast for anything but gut-deep instinct. But my body's too heavy, off-balance in a way I don't recognize and fresh pain shrieks through my side as he kicks me in the ribs. I hit the ground, gravel scraping my cheek and I gasp in the desolate scent of dust.

"Stop!" Peter barks and I sag back, blinking until his outline fuzzes into two, then slowly sinks back into a single man. And a crowbar. He hit me with the crowbar. I try to think what to do next, but everything hurts so much and there's no room for thoughts. "I can't believe how many of you there are in this fucked-up world," he says, and he's anguished now, shocked with bombed-out eyes.

"Many of us?" I try to say as I sit up, but it comes out not quite right.

"You don't even have a cult, do you? No reason, no religion or excuse. You just . . . do this. To innocent people." He shakes his head.

I try to shake my head too. No cult. But that hurts so much I fall back on my elbow, the skin scraping open against the grit of small stones and hard-packed dirt.

There's a muffled squeaking from nearby and it takes me a second to realize it's Jeika, screaming through her duct tape gag. Probably trying to get his attention so he'll untie her. But she sounds scared. I wonder if she realizes how far in over her head she is with him.

He tosses the crowbar down and pulls the revolver out of the back of his pants, pointing it at me.

I grit my teeth against the stomping pain in my head as something wet and warm drips down my cheek. "What do you want?"

"I want people to be able to live their lives," he spits at me. "For no sick-minded sociopaths like you to be preying on them. Answering their ads when they're vulnerable, filling their heads full of nonsense. Where is the girl who posted the ad? Or did you already kill her?" His eyes glitter, and if he starts to cry, I might be able to get the gun away from him. "You're just like *him*. Cult or not."

"I didn't kill her."

I pull my legs to the side, shift my shorter arm on the ground so I can push off with it. I could open the trunk and show her to him as evidence, but I doubt that would change what he came here to do. This was all bullshit. He never wanted my help so he could die—he schemed with Jeika somehow to get me here, and I just threw him off by posing as her. The pieces are falling into place one after another. The anguish on her face, the warnings she was stuttering over when I pushed her into the trunk, the way she ghosted him for so long that he posted his own ad trying to find me. I thought Peter was another suicidal person she knew, but she also told me there was another murderer that answered her ad. They must be the same guy, and she stopped answering his emails because she didn't like his deal, but after I shut her down again, she took it. Me for her.

If she thinks I'm hers to trade, she doesn't know me at all.

"It's not just about her. The world doesn't need sick freaks like you," Peter rants, "who just fucking ruin people's lives."

"What do you think you'll be, if you shoot me?" I rise to my feet.

"Don't!" he snaps, and I *see* his finger tightening on the trigger. My heart jolts, so hard my vision goes white and then black. I stomp my foot down to catch my own dizziness, and then realize he hasn't cocked the gun yet, or that single finger twitch would have been the end of me.

Fuck, it felt like that was it. It's never seemed real before that death could touch *me*.

"I think if I do this, there'll be one less criminal running loose in the world like they can do whatever they want, hurt whoever they please. And that sounds pretty good to me." Peter's face twists, and I can see all the years of pain that have chewed on him until he's ruined like a carcass, even though he's still breathing.

He's going to do it.

This man wasn't always a killer, I don't think, but I can sense the desperation in the air between us. It feels like the third stab, when the knife went all the way in on my own strength and nothing else. The point of no return.

"Get down on your knees."

Something in me comes up against a hard wall at his order. He absolutely *can* kill me. I'm not faster than a gun, no one is. But he can't make me kneel. No man ever has.

The pistol is pointed right at my face now. Big enough caliber to kill me with one shot, if the hole at the end of the barrel is any indication.

Is this what everything was actually leading up to? The ad, Jeika, Uncle Ricky. Am I supposed to die tonight rather than kill? It doesn't feel quite real, even though I know in my gut he *is* going to do it.

"Get down on your knees!" He lunges toward me so I have to back up or take his gun barrel to my eye. "Her name was Hannah. Her eyes were light brown. Her whole room was covered in angel dolls when she was a little girl, and all she wanted was to get to a better world than this one." His thumb lifts, and he cocks the hammer. My mind is dead quiet, and I move like I'm in a play I've been rehearsing for all my life.

I bend one leg, and the hard ground grinds into my kneecap. In my car, I have a knife, a hatchet, a syringe. Everything I need to end this man's life as quickly and easily as possible. But right here, in the only moment that matters, all I have is a single empty hand. I can hear faint sounds from far away now, like someone's crying. Jeika could kick the trunk the rest of the way open any time she wanted, but she hasn't. She's too afraid, and I'm glad, because we both know she can't handle him. He hasn't looked that way, so maybe he hasn't yet picked up on the tiny noises. He may act like he's angry about what I might have done to her, but I'm not certain she'd be safe with him either, if he knew we weren't alone.

He moves around behind me—he's an amateur, of course he wouldn't want to look me in the face when he does it. Execution style, they call it. It's harder to get the drop on someone when you're starting on your knees and you can't see what they're doing. The idea is that most likely if you jump for it, they'll shoot and you just end up dying slower, from more wounds.

"You're just like him," he whispers. "Hurting innocent people. So what if they're sad, so what if they want to die? Without you, they'd live. You're the problem, just like he was."

The barrel of the gun is harder than anything I've ever felt when it nuzzles into my hair and grinds into the back of my head, almost pushing enough to tip me off balance. Will it snap Jeika out of wanting to die, if she sees me being shot? Or will it sink her even more deeply into despair?

For a second, I wonder if I can just let him do it. If that can be it for me, so I never have to do anything else ever again. Worry, ever again.

"What was his name?" I ask. "The guy who killed your daughter."

"What the hell does—"

I drop back, the coldness of the gun barrel and the roughness of his knuckles skimming my cheek. As soon as I register warmer flesh, I turn my head and bite.

The scream I hear next could have come from Jeika or Peter, and I don't care which because I'm sinking my teeth all the way to the bone, my jaw flexing with the effort. Blood fills my mouth and I have to fight against the urge to spit.

A shot explodes, the gun bucking and shaking me loose of the hand I'm biting. My ears ring so loudly, I can't hear a thing, but there's no fresh pain so the bullet must have gone into the dirt instead of into me. Peter staggers and I grab his ankle and yank upward, sending him all the way onto the ground. The pistol bounces away under the car, so I leap to my feet and sweep up the crowbar. When I turn to Peter, he throws his arms up to protect his face, and I just stare down at him.

I survive, and I kill. It's what I've always done, whether I liked it or not. A pang of disappointment drops down through me, and I brush it aside. That moment of wishing it was otherwise was just delusion. If I ever thought I could fight my nature, or that my purpose was something other than death, this is my answer.

The terror in his eyes shifts and he rolls, lunging for the gun. I don't react. I should have killed him already, but I'm so fucking tired. Both sides of the scales in my head weighing heavy. It would be so easy to just stand here and let him do all the weighing.

But Jeika's tied up and helpless in my trunk and she doesn't deserve to die at the hands of this misguided asshole. I have to finish this for both of us.

I'm already moving before I complete the thought, my survival instinct faster than any morals I pretend I still have. My boot catches Peter under the chin just as his hand slaps down on the gun. A choking gargle coughs out of him as my boot buries itself in the soft flesh of his palette, kicking him over onto his back in a puff of dust. I breathe in the grit from the air as I hammer the crowbar down on him. Once, twice, the thuds like dull meat before he starts screaming, and once more after I've already heard the crack of bone. That last rib was for making me kneel.

He's choking on the pain but he still manages to glare at me, tears leaking from his eyes. "You're just like him," he rasps.

I raise an eyebrow. "If you're the good guy here, why'd you bring a shovel?"

He doesn't know it, but the shiny newness of that shovel is the only reason he's still alive. I drop his crowbar through the belt loop of my jeans. I'm not leaving this asshole a weapon, or one of my fingerprints.

"Your daughter is dead," I say to him. "But you don't have to be."

I kick him in his broken ribs and he howls, curling into himself like a dying spider. I sweep up the gun, and stuff it in the back of my pants. His keys and phone, I pluck from his pockets. He'll have a hell of a time walking out on the web of desert tracks with no GPS, but if he dies out here, it'll be his own goddamn fault, not mine.

He's rolling on the ground as I walk away, his shoes scuffing up dust as he writhes in pain. Behind my eyes, I see sprung traps and broken legs and bits of fur, the years of my life spooling out like an ugly motion picture.

I stride around the back of my car and slap the trunk closed, which has my own shovel and a tied-up girl inside, and I take off in a billowing cloud of dust.

One off the scales, two to go. My night is far from over.

CHAPTER 30
Dani

ALL THE ROADS out here are unmarked, but I know the whole maze like it's a map of my own blood vessels. Pulsing through darkness as I take one turn away from Peter, then another and another. I don't hear anything from the trunk, and I wonder if I imagined Jeika's weeping.

She knew.

The thought makes me tired, and I thrust my foot against the brake because dealing with her is just another task that needs to be done, and fate has never given a single fuck how I felt about any of it. My skull feels like it's webbed with invisible cracks, pain radiating out through them from the point where the crowbar came down on me. Peter's gun flips over on the passenger seat as the car jerks to a stop. I've never killed anyone with a gun. It seems unnaturally easy, like that alone makes it wrong.

The keys bite into my palm as I get out of the car, the light from the city faded by the distance until it's so weak it barely exists by the time it gets to me. I unlock the trunk, and the girl inside just keeps crying. She's curled into herself, small and hopeless. Her blonde hair trembles as she shakes with the sobs that are caught behind the wide strip of duct tape.

My numbness thickens, cementing into place like black bricks between me and her. I feel nothing.

"Get out."

She flinches at the invasion of my voice, and I don't care. I want this done and I still have the whole ride home stretching out in front of me. Long, accusing minutes and no other paths in sight. This is what I am.

I survive, and I kill. The binary of me leaves no room for her pain.

She reaches out, her fingers pale as they wrap over the edge of the trunk to steady herself. She has such pretty hands, long and slim. The kind that never look dirty. But I don't have patience for her hesitation. I grab her wrists, the sticky edges of the duct tape clinging to my hand, and yank her out onto her feet. She's still crying, her eyes fixed wide on mine like they're trying to see something that's probably not there. Tears pool at the top edge of the duct tape, and then spill over, sheeting down the slick gray.

I pinch the edge of the duct tape, catching the soft skin of her cheek in the bargain, and rip the tape off in one unflinching pull. She gasps, fresh tears trickling into the quickly reddening skin around her lips, and the first thing she says is "I'm sorry, oh my God I'm so sorry. Please . . ."

Begging. Behind the black bricks, I grow ten degrees colder in an instant. I should have expected she'd be afraid, that she'd assume I was like Peter. That after his attack, my shame and rage would build until I lashed out at whoever was nearest, just like he did after losing his daughter. Hurt like a too-sharp knife passed from person to person until everyone is left bleeding.

We barely know each other. A few emails, a few weeks. It was stupid to think she'd understand me better than that.

"Quit with the crying already. How many fucking times do I have to tell you I'm not going to kill you?"

I jerk my chin toward the car and turn, hardened dirt grinding beneath my heel and reminding me of the dust still fresh on the knees of my pants. No matter who came out on top in the end, I'm always going to know he made me kneel. And she watched.

I stalk toward the driver's seat, leaving her hands bound because I don't care.

"I was wrong!" she blurts and I stop.

"I thought . . ." Her fingers brush the back of my shirt, fabric transmitting the whisper of a touch that never quite reaches me. "I thought you felt nothing after you had to stop your uncle. I couldn't . . . I told myself that you were just as bad as me." Her voice is quiet, as limp as her body was when she was curled in my trunk. "I wanted to believe it so I could justify trading you to Peter so he'd help me. I hated myself even more for doing it, and that made it even easier, since I needed him to kill me so it would all end, the guilt and . . ." She takes a breath. "But I knew. I think I knew the whole time that you felt *everything* when you killed your uncle."

I stare out across the dead black of the desert, an ache growing like a tumor in my throat. I think nothing, feel nothing, say nothing.

"He's all you thought about, ever since you were a kid. You built your purpose around him, around making that into a way to help . . . not even just people, but animals too. I knew that but I couldn't admit it because I had to hate you to get what I wanted. But then I was watching you and Peter tonight and I realized you two were nothing alike."

A scoff breaks free of my throat, jarring pain loose as it escapes. It hasn't exactly always been about helping people, not that she needs to know that. I rip open the car door, snatch up a folding knife from the supply of weapons I never got a chance to use on Peter.

She gulps down a breath, but her eyes draw shakily back up from the weapon to my face even as I flick open the blade with my thumb. "He was so sure," she says achingly. "And you were always questioning. The whole time, testing, wondering. Trying to divide right from wrong. That's when I realized how terribly wrong I was to give *you* to *him*."

I hook her arms and pull them up and she doesn't cringe away even though I used my short side. The part of me everyone always avoids, as if my arm is an alien thing they can't relate to, just because it doesn't end in a hand. I slit the duct tape holding her wrists together without responding, as if I don't care what she might say next.

"Dani?"

Her voice is soft, too vulnerable for this flat-out desert full of sharp and dead things. I pocket the knife and pull the duct tape off her wrists myself, because I know if I left it to her, she'd do it slow and hesitantly, drawing out the pain and stretching the delicate skin underneath.

"Why didn't you kill him?" she presses. "Even after he attacked you like that, you left him alive. But . . . why?"

I flick the wad of sticky tape into my trunk and slam it with an elbow. "He brought a shovel."

She bites her lip, glancing away at this fresh evidence of the con they tried to pull on me. "It was for me too," she offers, as if that makes it any better. "The deal was, if I traded you to him, he'd kill me, after." She hesitates. "Though I wasn't ever sure . . ."

"That he was lying about helping you? You think?" My sarcasm slices, but I'm not sure if I'm punishing her naivety or my own. "But the shovel still had a sticker on it, from the hardware store. Brand fucking new. This was going to be his first time." I shrug, so sharply a muscle in my neck twangs. "It's not mine. So, I gave him one more chance to think over who he wants to fucking be when he grows up."

She moves forward all in a rush and I jerk back, going for the knife, before I realize she's not attacking me. She's hugging me.

"I should have helped you," she says, her breath warm against my throat, her forehead pressing tight against my ear. "I realized, even while I was still watching, that I was wrong. I wanted to come out of the trunk, I was just so scared, I couldn't even—I just . . . Dani, he had a gun, but he still brought a *crowbar*."

Goosebumps crawl across my skin at her words, because even though my head's still throbbing from that crowbar, I didn't think about the depth of cruelty in his intent until she said it like that. He could have killed me cleanly with the gun, but he brought a separate weapon because he wanted to beat me to death. So he could make it last.

I shift my weight to my heels, my body pulling against the clasp of her embrace like gravity spinning, tugging me away, always away.

"It's not your fault." It comes out more like a growl than a murmur. "I was stupid. I should have known a guy like that wouldn't ask a woman for help."

"He could have *killed* you. Your head, the pistol . . ." Jeika says. I can barely understand her now, she's sobbing so hard. "All because of my stupid ad. Because I lied to you and brought you here and— God. My God."

I grip her tighter now, and I don't worry about which arm I'm using anymore, just squeeze her into my chest like I can press the quaking fear out of her.

"He was never going to kill me," I tell her, and I can hear the echo of sadness slipping into my voice. "I'm the one who survives."

She clutches at the back of my shirt, crumpling it in her hands. "You're not invincible! He could have—he could have—"

"Shh."

She's nearly hysterical now, and I stroke her back to still her shaking. It should feel more awkward, considering how long it's been since I was willing to hold another person. Briefly, I think of my mother and wonder if she ate the dinner she made for us. Or if she scraped it into the trash when I turned away from her.

I squeeze my eyes closed, refusing to think about her. The thin skin at the inside of my right wrist is cradling the back of Jeika's head and her hair is so soft that I let it rest there a little longer while she gulps for air. Holding her is steadying me faster than I thought anything could after this tornado of a night. She feels just as graceful as she looks, and I wonder if she takes after the dad she never mentions or the mom she can't stop thinking about. Her mother whose death she thinks she's responsible for, just like she thought she was going to be responsible for mine tonight.

Maybe that's why she's crying so hard. Simple guilt. Not really over me, who she scarcely knows. I don't mind either way, and my touch is gentle when I brush the damp strands of hair back from her face. Her weight is starting to sag into me, relaxing except for the occasional shudder.

"I get it now, you know." I don't realize I'm going to tell her until I hear the words in the stillness between us.

She sniffles and looks up at me, her eyes wide and shiny.

"For just a second, I thought, wouldn't it just be fucking easier to let him do it?" My skin itches restlessly at the thought of giving in like that, and I clench the muscles of my legs just to feel their strength. I shake my head, the tips of my hair wet from her tears and swinging heavy with the movement. "That draw . . ." Maybe it's what my mother feels, when she tries to set down a bottle. "I get why it's hard."

And I understand why she'd lie. To me, to him, to anybody, if it would let her out of all this. It's impossible to blame her for that, with bruises throbbing over my whole body and the kind of weariness behind my eyes that sleep has never scrubbed away.

She swallows and shifts back, her hands slipping down my arms. I feel too light without her, like I'm going to drift up, up and straight into the wide-open sky. Lost like a balloon nobody cared to hold on to.

Suddenly, my head hurts like screaming hell. Jeika's hands fuss at wiping her cheeks and I move to the passenger side of the car and hit the button to pop the glove box open. Eric changed it out from the old lever for me, so it would be easier to open one-handed.

Eric.

I stare at the gun and the crowbar sitting on the passenger seat for just an instant before I remember to grab a napkin out of the glove box. She blows her nose, stealing those little glances at me again. Awareness scabs across my skin, and this is the part I was dreading about tonight. The way she'd look at me, once she saw firsthand what I am capable of. I look away. "Let's go. It's late."

"Are you okay?" she asks instead. "Really."

Her glances brush gently over my neck, my jaw, my chest, and understanding falls into place with a tingle. It's not disgust or fear, why she's always looking at me. Instead, it's the same reason I'm always *not* looking at her. Shit.

"Jeika . . ." For the first time tonight, guilt seeps in under the black bricks of the wall between me and the rest of the world.

The woman who is obsessed with the idea of her own end—of course she would think she was attracted to me, because I'm the only one who can deliver it to her. She's in love with Death, not with me. But I don't say a thing to spoil the moment, even though I probably should. No one on earth has ever known everything I've done and still looked at me the way she just did. Looked at me like they didn't want to look away.

She reaches over and her hand slides over my skin. I twitch back, because it's my short side and she glances up at me. "Is this okay? You only ever reach with your left, but I—you don't have to. Not with me."

Her fingernails skim lightly over the smooth curve where other people have a hand and a thrill tingles along my skin. She's looking down and I know she sees the telltale goosebumps, but I let her keep touching me because it's washing all the pain out of my head.

It's worth it. The crowbar, the tiny rocks grinding under my knees when I had to kneel to him in order to buy time. The taste of his blood still lingering on the back of my tongue and the ringing in my ears from the shot that could easily have torn through my body. Because of tonight, she wants *something* other than death. Even if the thing she wants is only to comfort me.

It's my life's purpose, twisted into its own negative image. Light, defined by darkness, but this time I'm on the unfamiliar side.

What does it mean that *I* could bring her to that?

C H A P T E R

31

Jeika

When Dani drops me off, her headlights glow warm on my back. I'll have to pick up my car tomorrow, and there's no one waiting for me inside my house, but I don't feel alone even after she drives away. She let me hold her the whole way back, her forearm flexing under my palm as she shifted. I could scarcely catch my breath the whole time.

I toss my keys down under the calendar that sits by my bedroom door, the one with its last seven months torn out and every square before today checked off like a duty, endured. I never intended to make it this far into this cursed year. I pick up the marker but instead of a check mark, I find myself drawing a rounded D, with a swish at the end of the curve. Graceful and quick, like she is. She didn't stumble or scrabble or even rush when she picked up that crowbar. Just brought it down on him like she'd already won.

No one ever told me that violence could look beautiful.

I guess I should feel sorry for Peter. His daughter and her terrible cult-follower boyfriend and the way Peter thought he was saving the world from Dani. But the sickness still gurgles in my belly from how close she was to dying tonight.

When it was him on the ground, she didn't choose to pull the trigger, that's what gets me. Even after he cracked her across the face, called her a bitch, and put the gun to her head. She came out to the desert fully intending to help him die if his reasons were good enough, but her intention changed without discussion once she knew why he was doing what he was doing. According to Dani's justice, his crimes cost him a few broken ribs, a phone she tossed in a sewer drain on the way to my house, and a long, painful walk back to town. Not death, even though she so easily could have finished him off with the weapons he brought to use on her.

It's late, but my body's full of too much twitchy energy for sleep. I head for the door to go for a walk but catch sight of my reflection in the dark glass of the kitchen window and stop. I should hate Dani, should hate anyone who can do what she does, when I know how terrible that truly is. I thought I did, and then watching her show mercy to Peter after what he did to her . . . I just *can't*. I want to hold her and tell her she doesn't have to do any of this. I want to trace her lips with my finger and inhale the air that's scented like her. She's probably having none of the fantasies I am. Honestly, she's most likely straight.

But God, when was the last time she was touched before tonight? She's so rigid, her body used to being a weapon, and she doesn't deserve to be set on a shelf like an old bayonet—left behind once the war is over.

I clench my teeth and turn away from the door. None of these urges matter. What I need is to convince her it's right to let me go, to release me from this life and everything I've messed up with it. But all the reasons I know I've earned that sentence sit inside me all sticky black like bog mud, and I don't want to stain her with them. There has to be an argument that will work, though. She's so sharp and certain, but still full of questions. She sees too many sides in the world to believe in simple answers.

I sink down on the couch, staring into the empty kitchen a few steps away. She must have killed her uncle in a kitchen, because she said she hit her mom with a pan out of the sink to fake the robbery angle. I picture his blood pooling on the floor. Dani realizing he had no pulse, that she was stuck with the body of what used to be her family, and a mom who was going to wake up any minute to see what she'd done. Then arranging the room—the *corpse*—to fake a new crime and holding the lie inside of her against the eyes of all those police officers. I know all too well what that sinking feeling is like, of knowing you're going to ruin every good thing your family has ever thought about you. That you're going to make them regret, probably, ever being related to you at all.

How did Dani not just collapse into despair and self-hatred after that night? How did she come back from it, far enough to be able to show compassion to a cruel stranger in the desert?

But then, her uncle wasn't her only victim.

I fumble my phone out of my bag and almost drop it when I see the smudge of blood that must have come from Dani's fingers when she gave it back to me. Insurance, she said, because she didn't trust me not to turn her in. An empty pang drops down through my belly and I shove it aside, dialing her number as I move toward my room so I won't wake up my sleeping roommate or her dog. It rings long enough that I'm not sure she's going to answer, but then her voice comes across the line. Sharp and sure, like always.

"What's wrong?"

"The people you killed . . . after your uncle, I mean. The kid you knew from your neighborhood, and the others. Why them?"

I grip the phone, the sticky bit of blood clinging to my fingers. It seems crucial, somehow, that I know this. Like it'll change everything I know about myself, because it's how she found *her* way through the aftermath.

You think you can't live with yourself once you've killed someone? Grow the fuck up.

Dani came back from that, enough to want to help me, and even Peter. I don't know how to come back, and suddenly, I want to.

"You call me before I'm even home to ask about my other murders? I guess you're not worried if I'm okay anymore."

I frown. "Shit, are you still in the car? How's your head? I probably should have driven us back."

The bleeding had stopped by the time we left the desert, because it had only come from a scrape on her scalp where the crowbar broke the skin. But she could still have a concussion.

"I pulled over before I answered. Stick shift, you know. A girl's only got so many hands." Her voice is dry, almost light. "You didn't need to take over. Head hurts like fucking crazy, but the day I can't drive with a headache is the day I slash my own tires."

"I guess going to the hospital creates a trail of evidence, but I still think it'd be better to get it checked out."

"Why do you care about the other ones all of a sudden? You didn't ask, before."

I curl my knees up onto the bed with me. Her voice sounds so close, like she's right here, and it's impossible not to feel safer when I can hear her.

"I just . . . there must have been years in between. It's been what, ten years or so? And only five of . . . them." I hesitate on the word. It seems offensive to call them "victims" to her face, but I don't know how she sees them. "You were fourteen when everything happened with your uncle, and I assume he came first, but I don't understand how you got from one to the other."

"It was just like you, actually." The line is quiet, and I don't hear the engine of her car, so she must still be pulled over. "Not with a classified ad, obviously, but he kind of dropped into my lap, like fate didn't know how to be subtle. He lived just one street over, and everybody heard when he got the diagnosis. He was super young, always seemed healthy like he'd have a fighting chance, but he got sick really fast. When he got bad, I think I was the only one of our neighbors who went to see him in the hospital."

She pauses, and I swap ears with the phone.

"Not because we were close, but just . . . everybody was treating him like he was contagious, like they didn't know how to talk to him anymore. So I went. The doctors had told him he wasn't going to make it, and he was in a lot of pain, and he was mad at the whole world. His family had literally just put down the family dog. After it went through about a week of the suffering he'd been going through for months at that point. He was probably just upset, wanted to complain to somebody who wasn't his mom, you know? But he was so small, lying in that bed, and I could tell he didn't know how to bear that kind of pain." She goes quiet for a second. "So I asked him, what if there was another way?"

"How did you do it without people finding out? You couldn't fake a robbery in a hospital."

"Air bubble into a vein. Went right to the heart and he finally got to sleep. That time it felt peaceful, momentous. Nothing like it was with my uncle. Afterward, his face looked totally different and I realized I'd never seen him relaxed before."

It's not what I wanted to know, not really. "What made you offer in the first place? I mean, with your uncle it sounded like you were really upset. And years had gone by."

"Sure, but it wasn't really over for me."

My whole body zings when she says it. I know what that's like, for six months to feel like yesterday, and at the same time, to stretch out into a whole lifetime where I'm a girl with no mother.

"It didn't feel like years, and the whole time . . ." Dani paused. "I was thinking that if what happened with my uncle had happened for a reason, then maybe this was happening for a reason too. But then I was sitting in that hospital room, watching him die so damn slowly, and I realized it was still happening, all around me. Suffering. And I could fix it." She stops, and I can't hear her breathing. I'm holding my breath too.

"Is that what happened with the others?" A sharp jerk tugs in my chest, and I realize I want to hear that it is. That it was simple, forgivable. That she helped people who were already suffering, already going to die. That she's not like me.

But my fingers have gone cold, waiting for her to speak again. Because if she only does it for the right reasons, will she help me?

"No," she says.

Like a door closing. Simple, just like that, even though it's anything but.

"I thought, if I *could* kill, then maybe that's what I was supposed to be doing. A couple of times over the years, I ran across people doing some real nasty shit, and I took care of them. It seemed obvious, like I'd been there for precisely that reason. Then, just a few weeks ago, there was this guy. Kind of sexist, kind of an asshole." She makes an irritated sound. "Saw that I was missing a hand and told me I couldn't have a job because of it. Garden variety jerk. I killed him, but then after . . ." Her voice wavers a little, and for the first time, I wonder if she's waiting for me to say it's okay. "Every time, I thought it was the last time. But it's like once you open your eyes, there are chances everywhere."

My lungs start to burn, but it feels wrong to relieve that small discomfort when I can hear everything strung so tight behind her voice.

"A few weeks ago, before I saw your ad, I realized this guy in my neighborhood, Eric, was nice to a lot of younger people, not just me. Little kids. Patting them on the back, telling them they were good at stuff, asking them over to his house and promising movies, candy, games. I don't even know how long he'd been doing it before I started to fucking *notice*."

Her breathing is harsh in my ear and I can't take it. I gasp in a breath and immediately feel weak that I didn't hold out longer. For her, somehow.

"I knew I could stop him, even if no one else would. It felt like death was following me, using me for its own ends. And I decided, if I was going to kill, it would be on my terms, nobody else's. When I answered your ad, that was me trying to decide what they were."

Her voice sounds different when she talks about this. Less sharp, less certain. It makes me shift in my seat on the bed and I'm glad when she keeps talking so I have something else to focus on.

"By then I had started to look for other things it could mean, the way death didn't bother me. Like if I was supposed to be a mortician who prepared bodies, or a veterinarian who puts animals to sleep. Except instead of helping sick animals, I found myself slitting the throat of a stranger just because he pissed me off." She pauses, her voice changing. "I didn't know him. Could have been a good guy or a shitty one or anything in between. I realized it had gotten too easy and I needed to hold myself to some kind of code, take it slower with the choices and be sure. That's when your ad popped up. And not long after, Peter's. Even though I didn't know what he really intended until tonight."

Air whispers over the speaker as she exhales.

"Jesus," she says. "It's lucky he didn't go after some religious leader, thinking he needed to revenge himself on cults. Hopefully I knocked some sense back into him and he'll lay off the vigilante shit and get himself a grief counselor."

Can she hear herself? How can she say that so easily for him and not even apply it to herself? I try to shut up, because I don't think she wants to hear it, but I can't help myself. "What about you?"

"What about me?"

"Why didn't you get a grief counselor?"

"You can't tell a counselor you stabbed your uncle and covered it up, Jeika. They're not that fucking confidential. I could have lied about what I was there for but getting therapy for a lie . . . I don't really think it works that way."

I hold the phone a little farther away, even though she can't see me. I'm a hypocrite, and I can't argue. She's right. You can't fix a lie with advice that feels just as false.

"I was wrong," I whisper. "Before tonight, I thought no murderer could ever deserve to live but I didn't see how many shades of right and wrong existed. I didn't see how much you care."

"So?"

I jerk a little, nearly dropping the phone at the lash of her voice.

"Peter cared. Didn't stop him from doing some terrible fucking shit because of it."

She's right. I cared about my mom, so much more than I thought I did all those times we fought, all those times I couldn't wait to move out and get out from under her thumb. Caring hasn't fixed a thing and neither has guilt. It's what you *do* with all that emotion blasting through you once the person you love is gone. Dani's the only one I know who has found how to pull something meaningful out of all that darkness. And oh, how it's cost her.

"Hey, I have to go," she says, her voice sharp.

"Right. Take care of your head," I say, but she's already hung up.

Rain is starting to patter on the roof, the sound only emphasizing the silence inside my apartment. I let the phone fall to my lap. She has places to be, and I don't. But then, I guess I got the answer I called for. The way Dani got through was because all of this has been a part of her greater purpose.

The problem is, my mom died from an accident, caused because I was stupid. I don't know how that can mean anything except that I should have been the one who died. I could see how it would release me, if I thought it was all for the best and she somehow died for a reason, to thrust me along to some greater purpose in my life. But even in my head, that sounds like bullshit.

Dani was put in an impossible position with her uncle and she made it through to become this uncompromising person dispensing her own brand of ruthless mercy. That's something for her to live for, in all the tiny squares waiting to be checked off my calendar and beyond, into the months I've long since ripped off and threw away. All *I* have in all those empty boxes is a single, beautiful D.

I should be focusing on my own purpose, scrambling for some key that will unlock the mess of my life so I'll stop ending up where I was again tonight: trapped in a car and watching someone I care about being hurt because of my own reckless bullshit.

But all I can think about is how it could possibly be okay to kiss her before she kills me. Like, maybe just a little goodbye thing. Ceremonial, like the "Cheers" at the end of every email. A respectful tip of the hat to each other before you sign off.

I close my eyes and picture Dani's hand, and her strong fingers that never reach for anyone. If there's anything I could do, anyone I could be that would make me the person she wants to touch, even once in the time I have left.

I want it with a thirst that makes death feel a distant fiction, as impossible to see as the air I can't seem to stop breathing.

CHAPTER

32

Dani

LAST NIGHT, I fell asleep to the pop and rattle of heavy rain on the metal roof. I wake up to quiet and light through the sagging shades that tells me I've already used up most of the time before my afternoon shift. My blankets fall to the floor with a tired *swush* and I bend to pick them up even though it makes bruises pull all across my back. Fuck Peter, that lying asshole. Hope he enjoyed his rainy walk home from the desert and those ribs I broke.

I throw the blankets on the bed in a heap and turn toward the kitchen with a wince. But the lumpy covers nag at the back of my mind and I go back to smooth them over the bed, so it doesn't look quite so much like I slept in my clothes after a long night that got entirely out of my control.

What the hell is wrong with me that I just assumed Peter was telling the truth in his emails? Or that Jeika wouldn't lie to get what she wanted? I haven't been that naive about people since the first time my uncle borrowed my lunch money to buy "groceries." Before I had to ask my mom where rehab was, and if it was like heaven because people couldn't come back to visit once they went there. I messed up with Peter because I got too distracted by Jeika's wide blue eyes and sad, downturned lips. Hands that twitch and fidget and are always smoothing at her clothes—not jerking at them like she's nervous, but more like she's savoring the feel of the fabric. Hands that smoothed over my skin last night in exactly the same way.

I lean my arm on the door to my room without opening it, letting my forehead fall to the bare skin that's still gritty with desert dust. It's not that I never date. It's just that sometime after that little boy's funeral, I stopped having girlfriends and started having hook-ups. The parts of me they touch aren't the same as what Jeika touched last night.

I never even told her I'm queer, but I saw the shift in her eyes last night when she figured it out. Would it have made this easier if I'd pretended I wasn't?

I need to call her, see where she's at. Last night didn't scare her off her plan the way I meant it to. It *did* scare her—I've got the tear stains stiffening the fabric of my shirt to prove it. But Peter was a wild card and I don't know how that changes the hand she's holding. It seemed to refocus her on me, for some reason, make her start asking about my other victims. Her voice sounded awed on the phone, almost impressed. My fingers curl against the door, an odd inflated sensation rising in my chest. What makes her respect me as a murderer are the same things that should repel her from me as a woman. The fact that they don't is like a flare of brightness against the filth of the rest of my life. I want to stretch out and soak it in. But that's a small, selfish desire only a tiny sliver as important as fulfilling the purpose I'm uniquely qualified to provide for the world.

And no, this time it won't be an assisted suicide. But now that I have a gun, I can make Eric's death look like one.

I pull open the door and head for the shower. The lump of hamburger from last night is burnt onto the bottom of the pan, a dry crust cracking across the top. Flies alight back into the air as I pick up the skillet and empty it in the trash, knocking it against the side of the can to shock the meat loose. I toss it in the sink to deal with after my shower and glance at the open door to Mom's room. She's gone, for once, which might mean a new boyfriend, or a new job. Which would also explain the guilt and sobriety from last night, even if it didn't last all the way through dinner. It's better this way, though, because I'll have the trailer to myself to gather the clues I'll seed into Eric's crime scene so that the detectives won't question that it's a suicide.

Three days, I think, is what it'll take to get everything together. I can let him live for three more days. Urgency thrums under my skin as I undress and step into the shower.

Thirty-six hours. It feels wrong, hairs-petted-backward unsettling, to wait. Doubts have flickered through my head for all the years since I killed my uncle, despite all the clues that have lined up to tell me what my purpose is. But last night was bullhorn-loud and clear. I can still feel the gun pressed to the back of my head, with the round eye of its barrel and the scratch of the front site against my scalp. And yet here I am, alive and reaching for the shampoo. I'm the one who survives. I'm the one who kills.

Even if I misjudged Peter's motives, I may still have been what he needed. Bringing him close enough to death to wake him up and make him rethink his grief-stricken plan to track down killers. His soft, middle-aged hands aren't a match for any criminal he might find. Especially not me. I did the right thing last night, and I can feel that rightness propelling me forward toward my next goal.

Thirty-six hours.

As soon as I'm dressed, I snatch my keys and head out to lay the first step of my plan. I don't even pause to let my hair dry or wash the hamburger-crusted skillet. The patchy brown of our front lawn sags in puddles of dirty rainwater, disguised by the reflection of pure blue sky above.

Gravel scrapes under the soles of my black work shoes as I hop over the still-flooded gutter and walk down the high middle at the center of the street. It's only a few blocks to Eric's trailer, and his car's there, but he doesn't answer my knock.

The scrape on my cheekbone burns as I wait, listening for footsteps within. He's not home, but that won't slow down my plan much. I can call him this afternoon and feed him the lie about Mom having a guy over later this week, ask if I can crash on his couch that night. Our neighborhood's small and if he's seen her running around with some new boyfriend, it'll sound all the more believable. After all, it's not like he hasn't tried for a sleepover before.

I turn to walk home, but then I think of one more place he might be. The playground's only a block out of my way. My steps hesitate, something in my belly shrinking away from the *why* of him being there again. But I'm used to that sinking knowledge now, and I push forward, still plotting.

The Peter fiasco was good for one thing—I now have a free gun that's not registered in my own name. Which means I can move forward with Eric without worrying if he might overpower me. He won't tell anyone I'm staying over, because I may be well into my twenties now, but he's known me since I was a minor and if he's still interested in me, it's because I'm young enough to be forbidden in his messed-up head. His perversion will deliver him right into my hands, so I'll already be in the house and I won't have to worry about waking him with the scrape of the window when I break in.

I can place the suicide note and other evidence while he sleeps, and if he wakes up during that, I can turn the element of surprise into the element of seduction. That'll get me close enough to put the bullet in his head at an angle he could have done himself. Then out the back before anybody has time to respond to the sound. Pull the window down closed, the wobbly latch making it look like it was locked the whole time. Simple, clean. The authorities will bury the body for me, so I won't even have to wield my own shovel. And if they get suspicious enough to check the gun's registration, it'll lead straight back to Peter, who will then have two murder weapons tied to him that I can leverage if he ever gives me any trouble.

If this intoxicating certainty is how I'll feel after each time I fulfill my purpose, I can't wait. It's almost as solid as I used to feel when I was a kid, before I had done anything I needed to doubt.

I turn the corner and pass Mrs. Chao's hedge and then the playground comes into sight. Everything's speckled from last night's rain, the sky dotted with clouds that are slowing down the sun's drying heat. The playground's deserted other than two figures. One tall, with his shoulders curled ever-inward as if they're ashamed to be seen in public, leaning down to dry the seat of the swing for Holly with the sleeve of his shirt. He couldn't even wait until the playground dried out to get his fix. Something oily and revolting cringes in the base of my stomach, one more thing I can't digest.

Swings are his favorite, I've noticed. The monkey bars and slides encourage kids to run and jump and bound away. But with the swings, his hands can make contact with their little bodies every time they pendulum back toward him, gravity betraying the children as it brings them back within his reach, over and over again.

Holly grins up at him as he lifts her over the puddle stretching beneath the swings and sets her on the seat he just prepared for her. His sleeve is dark with rainwater now, and he gives her a mild push to get her started before he takes a step back. I hesitate, wondering if I should interrupt them so I can ask to stay the night. It's unlikely Holly would remember the interaction, even more unlikely the cops will think to question all the neighborhood kids after Eric's "suicide," but it's best not to leave witnesses of any kind. I stay mostly hidden behind the hedge, figuring I can catch him on his walk home.

Holly swings her legs, attempting to keep them high enough so her scrupulously wiped sneakers won't skim the water, but still trying for more momentum. She kicks her legs gleefully and that's when it happens.

Her hands slip on the wet swing chains, the seat tilts under her bottom, and she falls out backward, landing with a splash on her back. I jolt forward, then hesitate, not wanting to reveal myself. But it looked like she hit as much with her head as she did her spine and I don't know if Eric'll stick around to help now that his game's been thwarted. Or worse, if he'll use the excuse of checking for injuries to put his hands on even more of her.

The patchy grass of the park squishes beneath my sneakers as I break into a run. I can lay the groundwork for his death anytime in the next three days. For now, I need to check on Holly. Her parents work so many shifts that sometimes she's home for an hour or two alone before her aunt or grandma can get there to babysit. She's supposed to stay inside and keep the door locked, but I know she's snuck out to the playground before, because she's begged me not to tell.

I skid to a stop in the rotting wood chips of the playground just as Holly manages to roll over onto her knees, crying as she crawls out of the puddle.

"Are you okay, honey?" Eric says, reaching to awkwardly lift her to her feet. He hangs out with the kids almost daily, but when he actually touches them it always looks like they're alien creatures. There's an innate self-consciousness to the way he reaches for them, like he's always afraid someone might be watching. That they'll try to stop him.

She shrieks, her shaking hands reaching to try to brush mud off the back of her pink shorts. The mud's all the way up into her ponytail and caked in gobs around the hair elastic, so she must have hit her head at least a little. Though maybe the mud softened the fall.

I squat down. "Does your head hurt, Holly?"

"I'm all dirty!" She doesn't answer, too busy thrashing at the mud on her back, her movements just rubbing it deeper into the fabric. "I was supposed to stay inside and watch my movie, and now it's gonna stain, and it's never going to come out, and it'll be ruined!"

"Here, I'll take you home." I hold out my hand. "I won't tell your mom you went outside. We'll just say you were watching that movie, okay?"

She wails, shoving a hand across her face and leaving a streak of mud behind. "She'll know! She'll know because it'll stain and it won't ever come out and I won't have no clothes because I ruin them all."

My heart gives a big, painful thump. I know the sound of an oft-repeated lecture when I hear one. Her parents always keep the peeling clear-coat of their car scrupulously waxed, and their crabgrass lawn mowed twice a week, even when they have to do it in the weak light of early dawn before they go to work. They work so hard for Holly's clothes; of course they don't want them ruined. But she's a little kid. Kids get dirty.

"I'll take her," Eric says. "You don't know what her ma's like. I know just how to fix this." He gives Holly a smile. "Nobody'll ever know but me and you, right, kitten?"

She stops crying and looks up at him hopefully. "Promise?"

"Holly, you're not supposed to let anybody into your house when your parents are gone," I remind her.

She glares at me. "You said you wouldn't tell."

"C'mon, let's go before the stain has a chance to sink in." Eric bustles her off and I hesitate, weighing my options. If I fight with him now to stop him from going inside her house, it's not going to be believable when I ask to stay the night at his place. If I'm not already inside the house, there's a chance he'll wake up and I'll have to kill him right away. That will lose me the safety of surprise and risk him dying from a wound wherever I hit him, not carefully and unsuspiciously placed in his temple. I'll have to leave right after the shot rings out and won't be able to plant more suspicious pictures of neighborhood kids as evidence of his supposed fixation—ones taken through windows or from behind bushes. Or the suicide note texted to his brother from his phone about how he realized the error of his ways and wanted to save all those kids from his evil urges.

I start after them, slowly, as I try to formulate a friendly excuse for why I should go inside with him to get Holly cleaned up and checked over. One he can't refuse. Eric's moving fast now that he has an excuse to get her alone, his eager steps so long Holly's almost jogging to keep up. But when they reach the sidewalk, they turn left for his house, not right for hers, and I know. To clean her up, he'll have to take her clothes off.

I no longer have three days.

My brain clicks over, all the whirling thoughts and considerations clarifying into simple, laser-focused bullet points that I complete one at a time. Nothing else matters.

- Back to house.
- Get gun.
- Hide it under shirt.
- Move fast but look bored.
- Enter alley at the far end, grab trash can you'll need to stand on.
- Push in on the pane of the window to pop the latch out of its groove.

I'm back at his house within minutes, my feet moving as fast as my thoughts. I won't have any time to formulate a new cover up to make this look like an accident or a suicide. I *really* don't want to do this in front of Holly, but he may not give me a choice.

As soon as the window scrapes open a little, I can hear them in the kitchen. Too close, shit. They're going to see the window move. As soon as I confront him, this will become the only chance I have to kill him. But I can't leave Holly in there alone, with mud caking her curly ponytail, and her parents thinking she's curled up safe at home, watching Pixar movies.

"Don't cry, kitten," he says. "We're going to make sure your ma never finds out about what happened. That you snuck out to the playground, or got your britches dirty, or any of it. It'll be a secret, just for you and me to know, okay?"

"They won't be ruined?" she whimpers.

"Nope. I know how to get stains out real good. Better than anybody. Your ma won't have any reason to get mad, promise."

I flatten my back against the wall, trying to slow my breathing. They were too distracted to hear the window when I gave it the first push, so I've got time. It'll need one more push before it's open high enough for me to fit through. Once I'm in, I'll need to shoot him before he shakes off his surprise.

"Hold on," he says. "Let me get some stuff and then we'll get you out of those clothes."

My pulse explodes in a burst that feels like a dry heave, and I have to blink back the dizziness before I can peek through the window. Eric's back is a flicker of movement before he disappears down the hallway. Holly's still in the kitchen, wrapped up in a towel over her clothes and shivering, mud already staining the pale green fabric.

If I choose my moment, is there any way I can kill him without her seeing? Even if I can do it in another room, she's going to hear the whole thing, and that's a secret too big for me to ask any kid to carry. If I wait until tonight, I can get away with it. But that won't save Holly right now. *Fuck*, I don't want to go prison.

Possible scenarios rack up in my head, so fast they're one on top of the other. The clear, bullet-point thinking of my journey to my house and back here is gone. If power is preparation, then right now I'm weak.

He returns from the bedroom with a clean towel and what looks like a folded shirt. I fade as far to the edge of the window as I can get, just one eye peeking past the edge of the curtain. I can't wait. He's going to tell her to take her clothes off and I don't want to kill him in front of a child but I can't—

I pull out the pistol. I haven't handled many in my life, but I've seen enough movies to know I need to thumb the hammer down before I can fire it. It fits oddly in my hand, probably designed for right-handed people, and it nearly slips out of my fingers before I get enough leverage to cock it. I stuff it into the back of my pants and pray it doesn't fire because I need my hand to grip the edge of the window and pull myself inside, and I won't have time to pull it out and cock it once I get there.

"Ow!" Holly squeaks and I jump forward, nearly smashing my face into the windowpane in my haste to see. But Eric's just working her ponytail holder out, using two hands to try not to pull her hair and doing a horribly clumsy job of it anyway.

"I want you to go in the bathroom and change out of your wet clothes," Eric says. "Then toss them out in the hall so I can wash them. There's soap in there, and a fresh towel. Once you're all clean, you can get dressed up in that shirt and robe I left in there. They'll be too long for you, but they can drag on the ground like, um, one of those things on a dress. Right?"

"A train?" She tilts her head. "Like a princess?"

"Uh, yup. Just like a princess."

Pain burns in a straight line across my fingers and I realize I'm already gripping the bottom of the windowsill, standing in plain view. I let go and edge more out of view again, trying to make sense of this. This is the perfect opportunity for him. He's got her alone. But why would he tell her to get changed in the bathroom with the door closed? Maybe he's going to peek when she's in the shower.

"Wait, do you know how to turn on a shower?" He shifts, looking out of his depth with the ruffles of her tiny, muddy scrunchy stretched over his too-big wrist.

"Turn the knob," she says. "Then pull up the stick! But Mommy doesn't let me take showers without her."

"Uh . . ."

This is it. This is when he pretends to be reluctant about giving her a bath.

"Well, there's a mat in there so you won't slip, so be real careful and only stand on the mat, okay? I'll set the water for you so it's not too hot."

He's out of the kitchen again before I can fully register that he just turned down the opportunity to help her in the bath. Holly waits for a second, then tiptoes over to his table and slowly works the lid off a jar of candy, snatching out a piece and popping it in her mouth. She chews with careful movements so it doesn't crackle and make a sound, but when Eric finally returns, she looks up at him, horrified and guilty. "I didn't touch nothing!"

He chuckles, looking a little less stressed and scratching above his ear. "It's okay if you had a candy, kitten. Want one more?" He passes one over and she drops the towel to grab it. Under it, she's still fully dressed. "Okay, go get in the shower now. Don't forget to throw your clothes and shoes out into the hall."

If he tries to follow her into the bathroom, that will be my cue to go in. But I'm no longer certain that what's going on in there is what I feared. When she traipses up the hall, I move back in front of the window and coil my weight in my legs, preparing in case he goes after her. But he stays in the laundry nook off the kitchen, pulling laundry detergent and bottles of various kinds of soap out, frowning over them hurriedly. Something thumps in the hallway, then Holly shouts, "There they are!"

"Okay! Good girl," he calls back, but doesn't look up from where he appears to be searching something on his phone. "Let the mud dry?" he mutters. "Fuck."

He heads up the hall and I grip the edge of the window.

"Holly, what time's your sitter coming today?" he calls through the door, then listens for her answer. "Okay, good. You doing okay in there?" I hear her say something, but I can't make it out. He comes back to the kitchen and I have to sit down on the ground under his window because the dizziness is just getting worse.

How could I have been wrong all this time? Maybe it's just me he's creepy with, and he's just being friendly with the kids. I think back to every hour we've spent together. He's invited me to his house a bunch of times, after he found out I don't live alone, that my mom's just holed up drunk so often that people rarely see her. And he's touched me a few times, on my arm or elbow. But now that I think about it, I don't think he's ever touched me in a sexual way. It's more like he's always trying to act like we're closer friends than we are. But why would he be spending so much time with kids if he's not a pervert?

I push myself back up to my feet, the still-cocked pistol grinding against my spine, and for one guilty second,

I remember the awe in Jeika's voice when she called me last night. I watch, lurking at the edge of the window, as Holly comes out of the bathroom swaddled in Eric's shirt, his robe dragging behind her, and prances around the kitchen in her princess fashion show while he laughs. I watch while he scrambles her an egg to go with the three more pieces of candy she wheedled out of him. I watch as he sends her back to the bathroom with her clean clothes to get dressed, and then while he takes her hand and leads her out the front door.

I don't watch as he walks her home. I stay in the alley and drag the window shut, and I let tears slide down my face like slug trails, disgusting and wet. Their shame punishes me, so I don't wipe them away.

I'm the one who survives. I've been wrong so many times lately, and that's the only thing left I know that's true.

It feels more and more like a curse all the time.

CHAPTER

33

Dani

I STARE AT THE frozen leg. The wide curve of the thigh, the whiteness of the bone. I've fried thousands of pieces of chicken and I've never thought so much about how they're really chunks of flesh. The insides of a living creature, skinned clean and dismembered. I drop the leg into the fryer basket with the rest of them and try to work up to dipping the basket into the oil.

Every time I do it today, all I smell is cooking muscle. When I got even a tiny bit of oil on my fingers, the skin crawled with the remembered burn of ruining Marilyn's phone. How much would it hurt to be fully submerged? Every part of your body changing color and texture as it cooked, loosening from the bone until your thigh could be easily torn off by the bite of children's dull teeth.

"What are you doing, building a religion to the damn things?" Marilyn's voice snaps out because of course she's behind me. She's always behind me. I reach for the basket handle but my fingers won't clasp. I can't force myself to drop the dead bodies into the oil to fry.

Hannah. Hannah Hannah Hannah.

It's the name of Peter's dead, not my own, that echoes the loudest. His daughter's name is a palindrome, the same backward as forward. Like a mantra, a chant of magic that's not exactly real, but holds power nonetheless.

"Hey!" Marilyn's louder now. "Are you high? Let me see your eyes."

A little further down the counter, Jane cringes away, but for once, she's not the target of our assistant manager's wrath. I am.

I turn and Marilyn draws back a little, the tight lines around her mouth going loose with surprise. That's when I remember the puffy-feeling itch in my eyelids and realize my eyes must be red from crying. It's not something Marilyn's ever seen, in all the time I've worked here. I harden my face, drawing up a scowl to hide behind.

But she's quicker than I am, coldness snapping back down over her face and the lines guarding her mouth again. She has a frown line between her eyebrows that's so deep it looks like a wound. Something about it reminds me of a tally mark, and I remember how many people have been hired and fired here since I came. Dozens. So many I don't remember. I'm sure that she doesn't either.

"I don't have time for any emo shit today." She braces her fists on her hips, her phone clutched too hard in her hand that's farthest from me. "The district manager is supposed to do a 'drop-in' sometime this week, and you know what that means. She's a psycho and it's all our asses if we fail inspection."

She snaps her fingers in front of my face and my arm flies up. I barely catch myself before I knock her into the griddle. *Fuck.* That violence is in me, even now, set like the spring of a trap. Anyone who touches the bait gets crushed before I can stop long enough to wish I hadn't been built this way.

"So help me, I'd send you home without pay if I had anybody else who wasn't too lazy to get the job done," she says through her teeth. "Get your shit together. We've all got problems."

She's right. Fuck me, but she's always been right. Underneath it all, Marilyn and I are struggling against the same mundane tide. Lashing out because without a fight to distract us, we might notice that this is our real life. That this is probably all we'll ever be. Cardboard and garbage and the ticking of that grease-skimmed clock watching over us all.

"I'm sor—sorry," I stutter.

She's been doing her best this whole time. Trying to help us all keep our jobs the only way she knew how. And all I saw was the worst in her.

Marilyn blinks once, the breath she'd pulled in for her next rebuke going still on her lips. Apologies aren't part of our playbook.

I turn away. Maybe I was just deluding myself that I could have a greater purpose, trying to feel important like I was somehow better than minimum wage. That my uncle's death had a meaning beyond one miserable person trying to exit a fucked-up world and fucking up his family on his way out. Maybe I'm just a mouth, gobbling up seventy billion tons of resources, and for what?

Maybe this is all there is.

I pick up the fryer basket and sink it into the oil. Today, the boiling of flesh shakes me more deeply than any murder I've ever committed.

I try to ignore it, to focus on the drone of my coworkers gossiping behind me, but they're talking about the Medicaid cuts, the eggs that are twenty dollars a carton, the constant evictions. Everything that's messed up in our world from the whims of one rich, corrupt idiot. Everybody working here was already skirting the edge and this is going to tip some of us over. On a normal day, I might even care that this time, it'll probably be me.

A gentle touch brushes my right elbow and I only tense this time, my spring coiling without lashing out.

"Sometimes I forget too," Jane says. "Even though I've done it before. It helps to make up little stories. C'mon, I'll help you."

She pulls down a box, grabs the tongs to take a piece of chicken from the mound waiting for our stacked-up orders.

"First, you put the chickens in the coop." She lays a three-piece meal into the box. "Then you put in a dish of water, in case they get thirsty." She adds the little tubs of dipping sauce. "You close up the roof so it doesn't leak when it rains." She folds the box and tucks in the flaps, then places it in a take-out bag. "Don't forget a couple of blankets, in case they get cold from the rain." She adds napkins, then smiles at me. "See? The stories help you keep track."

I manage a nod. I want to say I don't need help, but when I look back at my station, it's all just shapes and I can't focus enough to tell food apart from cardboard. Jane reaches and gingerly lifts the fryer basket out of the oil, which is when I realize the bleating I hear in my ears is the timer alarm.

She hands me a box. "I can help you, if you want."

"Th—" I have to force the words out past my knee-jerk impulse of wrongness. It feels like stripping out of my bra, right here in the kitchen next to the griddle. It feels like admitting I'm too weak to do something for myself, which is a low I've never let myself descend to, not once in my whole shitty life. I make myself say it anyway. "Thank you."

Jane smiles, that light that's never far from her eyes glowing out of her whole round face. "You're welcome."

"I just need to get something out of my car first." I check for Marilyn, then dart out the door and scuttle to my car, ducking below the level of the windows to unscrew the top of the bottle I took from my mother's room this morning. Sickly cherry floats up from the neck of it. It smells red and chemically and I don't want to drink it. But Southern Comfort is the only thing that keeps her going, keeps her numb, and I need that numbness.

How can I feel nothing when I kill, and so much when I don't?

I slug it down, but every painful swallow carries a name. *Eric. Peter. Jeika.*

There were three tests, and I failed two. Jeika's the last one left.

You're the expert, she told me once. *My very own Faceless Man. Do I deserve to live or die?*

Without a Faceless God, you have to draw your own lines. I choke down more liquor instead. It hasn't helped at all yet, but I stagger back to the kitchen anyway. The heat from the fryer singes the air, but Jane's smile is gentle, and it pulls my eyes away from the boiling corpses.

"It's okay," she says. "We'll do it together."

For the rest of the day, I move only when her voice tells me to. She's quicker than she's ever been, even on tasks that have always been my job, never hers. She's right—the stories really do help. They make simple sense out of disconnected movements, remind me what to do next. But they also emphasize the one thing I don't want to think about.

I don't know my own story anymore. And I have to find it, because Jeika needs me.

CHAPTER

34
Jeika

THE POUNDING ON the door is starting to throb through my temples with the stress of it. I'm curled up with my back against the sink, in the farthest corner of the kitchen because it's the only place you can't be seen from any of the windows. I thought if they knocked and I didn't answer, they'd go away. Leave another five voicemails like all the ones I've been ignoring.

Cooper keeps pacing between checking on me with tiny, wet presses of his nose and then going back to stare anxiously at the door. He doesn't understand why I'm not answering it. The people outside aren't shouting, "Police! Open up!" the way they do in the movies, but who knocks this long if they don't know there's someone inside, ignoring them?

My car's in the driveway, but so what? I could have walked somewhere, be out for a jog, for all they know. I grip the legs of my jeans, rough denim scouring my knuckles as I fist it just for something to hang on to.

It's been three days since Peter tried to kill Dani in the desert and she hasn't contacted me once. Neither has he, which is a little weird after everything that happened.

He didn't actually care about me, though. Didn't even email me afterward to see if I was okay, if Dani was lying about not having killed me. It was all about his revenge. He can't find the guy who killed his daughter and somehow in his mind, Dani is the same as that cult guy, taking advantage of vulnerable people. If it was my daughter, I'd have been pissed too, but I don't see how that gives him the right to go around killing other women.

A fresh volley of knocks rattles the cabinet behind me, the impact of fist on door traveling through the thin walls. Whatever their new witness told them, it's not some little pedantic detail that will get buried under their pile of new cases if I ignore them. The week they gave me to come down to the station has come and gone, and I've been sending their calls to voicemail. I probably look even guiltier for not answering their questions but I have no confidence in my ability to lie to an officer's face, especially not Officer Diego.

Biego Biego Biego

Even the thought of her name tag sends my head swimming back through that endless, horrible night in the hospital when I kept expecting them to tell me they brought Mom back. That she gasped to life on the table after enough CPR, like people always do on TV. Whatever they have on me, I doubt I could lie my way out of it. They've had months while my injuries healed to analyze the crime scene, look at the injuries on Mom's body and realize they're not consistent with being in the driver's seat. I'm hardly a master at setting up forensic evidence. My only way out of this now is prison or death. I need Dani, but she's not answering my emails.

Cooper comes back and lies down at my side with an unhappy whine. I stroke his fur, giving him scritches between his shoulder blades like he usually likes. "Shh, boy. Just a little longer. They'll go away."

Someone calls my name through the front door and somewhere deeper in the apartment, a knob squeaks.

Shit. My roommate! She was out super late again, some kind of house party or maybe a parade? There was glitter in her hair when she came in, catching the low red gleam of sunrise. No one could sleep through this racket, though.

"Are you going to answer the damn door?" she mutters, shuffling sleepily along the hallway. Cooper lifts his head when he sees his owner but doesn't leave my side.

I scrabble across the kitchen floor, doing an awkward crab walk to stay below the level of the window and stick my head out into the hall just as she's reaching for the lock.

"Don't!" I hiss.

She blinks down at me, confused to find me on the floor. "Seriously? Is this an ex or something?"

The knocks stop, as if they heard her and they're listening.

"*Power company,*" I mouth to her, then point at the corner of the kitchen where we toss bills. We're not late on this month's bill yet, but she wouldn't know that. She

Venmos me when she gets paid, and the automatic bill pay comes out of my account. Which means it's on my credit when we run late. Bitterness twinges through me but now is not the time to argue how to best split up utility bills.

She nods, pulling an oversized sweatshirt closer around her, and turns back for her room. A breath of relief falls out of me, but my muscles haven't even relaxed yet before the knocking starts again. Will they break down the door if I don't answer? They clearly know I'm in here. Cooper paces past me and stares at the door. When the door rattles under the next knock, he starts barking.

I just let it happen, and Kia doesn't come back out to shush him. Maybe if there's a barking dog, the cops will think the house is empty?

"Dani . . ." I whisper her name like a mantra of protection. Where has she been, these past three days? I'm worried her concussion might be bad, and that she won't have anyone to take care of her if she falls unconscious. But then, I don't truly believe anything could take Dani down, not even a head injury.

Maybe she's been wrapped up with the other person she told me about, the guy from the playground. I'm worried about things going sideways with him, about her maybe needing backup. I wasn't much help with Peter, but that was just the shock of it all, and after all, I was tied up. I wouldn't freeze up a second time, if I were prepared. I mean, it's not like I'd actually *kill* anyone myself. I just want her to be safe, that's all.

Mostly, I want to see her again. There's something about the pure, dedicated purpose in her. It's simple, not like all the doubts and insecurities clogging up my own mind. I just want to be as close as I can to that feeling, to see what it's like to *know* what you're here for.

The knocking stops, Cooper subsides a second later, and I hear frustrated voices arguing through the thin wood, then feet retreating down the front steps.

I let out a breath I feel like I've been holding forever, and Cooper comes over to sniff worriedly at my face. I hug him tight, burying my face in his furry ruff as if he really can protect me from the police. He whuffs, licking my ear.

I squeeze my eyes closed. They're going to get a warrant, if they don't have one already. I can't be here when they come back or I'll be going with them in cuffs, the idea of "questioning" a quaint memory.

"Coopie!" Kia calls from down the hall. "C'mere, baby."

He pulls away from me, running to obey his mistress and I swallow back the knot that tries to rise in my throat. *Not my dog*, I remind myself. There's nothing here that I'll truly be leaving behind, other than a soon-to-be-late power bill.

I pull my phone out of my pocket to email Dani again.

She's my only way out that can come in time, and even if it weren't for that, I want to see her again. Want to be chosen by someone like her.

But if I'm going to change her mind, I need a hook to make me stand out from all the other potential victims she could choose. So I say the one thing that might make her listen.

To: FacelessMan00@gmail.com
From: MVictimVolunteer@gmail.com
Date: May 17, 3:48 PM
Subject: I want to help

Dear Dani,

Hey, how are you doing? How's your head? Have you heard from Peter again, or do you think he's gone for good?

I figure you've probably been working on your next project. The guy you showed me, at that playground. I guess what I'm trying to say is, can I help?

Cheers,

Jeika

CHAPTER

35
Dani

THUMP.

The time clock slams down on my timecard hard enough to dent the thick paper. We've got a computerized system, but Marilyn doesn't trust computers, so she makes us clock out in both. Though, of course, she always uses the earlier of the two clock-out times, so apparently she trusts technology only as long as it saves her money out of our paychecks.

"Want me to put your apron in the bin for you?" Jane smiles, holding out a hand with her apron already balled in it.

"Yeah, uh, sure." I pull it off, trying to act as if I hadn't forgotten I was wearing the thing. It's been five days since the standoff with Peter in the desert, two since Jeika's fucked-up email that I still haven't answered. Every hour is as exhausting as dragging my body through peanut butter, but at least I've gotten back to where I can do my job again, however mechanically. Though sometimes the gentle brush of Jane's elbow reminds me that I've fallen into ruminating and forgotten to move again. If we hadn't been scheduled on the same shifts all week, I'd probably have been fired by now. "Thanks," I call after her.

The word comes easier than it used to. Jane's given me plenty of practice. She beams and waves in acknowledgement, though we're only a few feet apart.

"You're welcome."

I give her a nod and head for the back door, my thoughts already swallowing me back up. Jeika's going to start worrying if I don't answer her soon. But that email stuck in my throat like trying to swallow chunks of ice.

I guess what I'm trying to say is, can I help?

I forced her out into the desert with me to watch a man die, to scare her into trying to live, and now she wants to help me kill? There seems to be no limit to how deeply I can fuck things up. If Jeika's my third test, I'm cruising to find a grade somewhere south of F. It makes sense, though. The phone call, only minutes after I left her house, asking about my other murders. A chill crawls down my back, thinking of it. She's searching for a purpose, and she's starting to lean toward mine.

What would I do, if I could go back to that first time? When I was dozing on the couch from the drugs in the smoothie and blinked my eyes open to see my uncle loading that gun. I could have let him shoot us. Or tried to fight him for the gun. What was the way out that would have left my soul clean?

I still don't know, but the awful crossroads I found myself hung on that day, Jeika's there now. I want to help her find her way out, even if I still haven't found mine. The sun beats on the back of my neck as I cross the parking lot, shoulders hunched as I think.

This all started because Jeika felt guilty for crashing her car and wasn't sure how to pick up the pieces of the life she has left. All she's really asked for is a direction, somewhere to point herself so she doesn't get lost. Like me and Marilyn, turning mean so at least we have a fight to look forward to in the meaninglessness of our days. Jeika needs something to fix her eyes on, and I can feel how much possibility there is brimming inside her. There has to be something, and I'm going to find it for her.

All the way back at the beginning, she told me good people are the ones who help others, who save someone else's ass, but she seemed to think she was too ordinary to be of any use to anyone. She was looking at it in terms of being the best at something, though, not simply being of service. Maybe if I could find her someplace where people were even worse off than her . . . but it can't be a career. She needs something *now*, not something that only materializes on the other side of another college degree or a stack of applications and interviews. Nothing abstract either. Just one specific person who needs her who she can look in the face. Like those Big Sister mentoring groups or the charities that grant wishes for cancer kids.

I fumble my keys, still thinking, and forget to shield my hand with the hem of my shirt when I open the car door.

"Fuck . . ." My breath hisses in as I let go of the scorching metal and shake my burned fingers out, dropping the keys in the process. It's so hot in this hellhole you can't even touch your own car without paying the price. I nudge the door open and the scent hits me before my eyes register the change.

Death. Blood.

It's so old, the memory of this, that I almost fall to my fourteen-year-old knees before I remember where I am. Who I am now. This parking lot will blister my skin if I fall but as I stare at the scene before me, my legs waver.

My driver's seat has been mutilated. The original vinyl slashed deeply so the blood splashed all over the seat has sunk down inside. The yellow of the foam cushioning has turned all brownish red like old meat, the blood already going rancid in the heat. I blink, wondering if I'm losing my mind. Is this a hallucination? Some kind of guilt-induced flashback, maybe?

"Is everything okay?" Jane calls. She's waiting in the scrap of shade on the back step for her ride, the way she always does. Something about my hesitation has her stepping out into the brutal heat, shading her eyes with one hand.

I could ask her if she sees it too. But then she'll know how fucked my head is right now. And what if it's real? How will I explain a car full of bloodstains?

Flies alight on the edges of the slashed seat, hungry at the scent of blood. It has to be real. The flies wouldn't be this interested in a hallucination.

It's just the driver's seat, though, none of the rest of the car besmirched. *My* seat.

Jane's halfway across the parking lot now, and I slam the door before she can see the damage.

I snatch up my dropped keys and start walking back toward the kitchen. "Left a soda on my seat and it tipped over." I grimace. "What a mess. I'm going to grab a garbage bag to sit on for the ride home."

"Bummer," Jane says, returning my grimace. "I forget sodas sometimes too."

She doesn't. Jane loves soda, and she slurps them away to the last drop every time she has one. But she's too kind to say she'd never be dumb enough to leave a soda balanced on her seat.

My heart is pounding as I pass Jane, thinking of what a cop would do if they pulled me over. Is it human blood? Is it *Jeika's*?

I rip out my phone, one foot already into the kitchen. It's the cruelest message Peter could send, to kill Jeika in my car. He could have lured her out with a single call. What if she tried to go back and take revenge on him in the two days since she sent me that email? It would be just like her to try to protect me in some overly brave and totally reckless way. This is the girl who job interviewed her own serial killer, after all.

It rings once.

"You're letting the air conditioning out!" Marilyn yells across the kitchen. "You want to pay the power bill out of your paycheck this month?"

"Hello?" Jeika answers. "Dani?"

I step inside and let the door fall closed behind me. I close my eyes and don't answer, just so she'll speak again. And she does. God, of course she does.

"Dani? Are you okay?"

No one has asked me that, not for years. Not until Jane and now, Jeika. I swallow.

"Hey." I pinch the phone against my shoulder and swipe a big black garbage bag off the roll, letting myself outside before Marilyn can take that out of my paycheck too. "Hit your number by accident. I'll email you later."

I hang up before she can hear it in my voice. The new shakiness I never want her to see. I wonder if I still sound like myself to her.

Jane's waiting in the oasis of the shade, and she takes a step back to let me by, offering a sympathetic smile. I try to return it, but it doesn't feel like it's shaped right.

Before I open the car door, I take a deep breath, not sure whether to hope that the mess will still be there, or that it'll have been a hallucination, slipping back out of the cracks of my reality. Both options have dark implications.

It's real, though. The splashes of dirty red, the ruined car seat. I flap the garbage bag to wave the flies out, then lay it over the seat, tucking it into the crease of the headrest so it won't fall down when I sit. I brace myself against the thought. The blood is going to squish out of the foam, pooling up over the plastic and soaking into my pants anyway. It's not that dry, and there's so much of it.

I glance around. The back lot behind the restaurant is surrounded by a chain link fence with sun-faded plastic strips woven through it for privacy. There are just a few employee parking spaces and a dumpster. The drive-thru snakes around the back of the building and up the far side, but if no one was waiting in the drive-thru, you could pull back here and do whatever you wanted with no witnesses. Butcher whatever creature you needed to in order to get this much blood.

When I used to finish off the mice in the traps, it only ever left a little splash of red to wash off the hatchet. Whatever this was, it was so much bigger than a mouse.

Is there any chance this is just random vandalism, some kids playing a prank? I thought this was a threat, a very physical reminder that the revenge he wants to exact from me has become personal. But if Jeika doesn't know anything about it, it might not have been Peter. Maybe there's still a chance he hasn't been able to track me down.

I consider the evidence. The car door was still locked when I got here. I left the window cracked for the heat this morning, but the lock buttons on my car go straight up and down, no flared-out piece to grab with a coat hanger to unlock it that way. Whoever did this must have learned the same slim-jim trick Eric taught me, but that's no clue to who it was.

My back goes straight, pain pulsing up the vertebra. If it was Peter, there's one thing I know for sure he'd do.

Slowly, I reach for the sun visor above my driver's seat. I flip it down, and a folded paper flutters out, and silver flashes past as something heavier falls. I flinch back before it can cut me, and it bounces off the seat and lies gleaming on the impeccably vacuumed floor mat.

A scalpel.

CHAPTER

36

Dani

I POCKET THE NOTE before I pick up the scalpel with a torn-off corner of the trash bag, in case it was used to slice up whoever or whatever is currently soaking my seat. He just turned my murder-weapon insurance policy back around on me. I can't call in a tip to the police and frame him for my crime, but now he can definitely do that to me. The blade has a dried smear of maroon on it, but I can't tell by the shape if that's the blood from my victim, or Peter's, or both.

I leave the scalpel on the passenger's seat, wrapped in the ripped bit of black plastic, and pull out the note, dropping it twice while trying to unfold it.

You'll never guess whose car I saw yesterday, when I was visiting my sister at her restaurant. I waited a long time, but you weren't eating at any of the tables, and I didn't see you at the counter, so you must work back in the kitchen. Too bad. I would have liked to say hello. So I left you a little surprise, instead.

I know how to find you. It's my move now, bitch.

-P

I whip my head around, but the back parking lot is empty except for Jane's mom's sedan pulling out as Jane waves from the passenger side window. I lift my hand, but it's too late because they've already turned the corner and she didn't see. I jump in the car and crank the ignition. If Peter's waiting somewhere nearby, I'll be safer on the move.

I pull out with a shriek of tires. My eyes jump from windshield to rearview mirror then my side mirrors, over and over again. I take the long way, with lots of sharp turns that leave the seat squelching wetly every time my weight shifts. I drive around, watching, for forty-five minutes before I turn for home, once I'm certain no one is following me.

But then, why would he bother? He knows where I work. *My sister's restaurant.* He has to be talking about Marilyn. Our general manager is a sixtysomething snorefest named Harry, and Peter wouldn't say it was "hers" if his sister was just another employee, right? If he tells her who I am, what I've done, going to the police is only the simplest form of revenge they can take. She has my Social Security number, the address where my mother lives. Everything a person would need to ruin my life, or to take it.

A vague memory tugs at the back of my mind. Marilyn abruptly taking several days off, a few years back. A funeral. The way her face sagged for weeks when she returned, like she'd aged a decade. *Her niece. Peter's daughter.* Was she as brittle, as cruel, before that funeral? I can no longer remember. But what I am sure of? She won't be any more sympathetic toward murderers than her brother is, even if I wasn't the one responsible for her niece.

I miss the turn for my own house and have to circle the block, because my thoughts are racing with everything he can do to me now in payment for his broken ribs. He can find me any time he wants, take my mother as a hostage, or call a tip into the authorities about the scalpel murder weapon he just planted in my car. Rent's due next week but I'm going to have to quit anyway. To find the money to move somehow. He has our emails. There's no evidence of a crime, but the emails are probably enough to charge me with something. Intent to commit homicide, or whatever the lawyers would call it. The assault on him, at the very least.

Can he get Jeika arrested too? *Would* he?

I'm still shaken when I get home, and I drive straight up onto the curb, the sturdy frame of the car barely bucking at the jump. I leave it there, crookedly parked with the right side higher than the left, and hurry up to my house. Tonight, I can boil the scalpel clean of DNA and bury it somewhere far out in the desert. But first, I need to deal with my car, which is currently a crime scene that's not so easy to bury. There's a garden hose tangled by our trailer and I yank it out, straightening coils and knots until it reaches to my wounded car. The hose is sun-faded and cracked, so when I turn it on, as much water leaks out into the dry lawn as makes it to the end of the hose. My neighbors aren't the type to give a fuck about anything but themselves, but I glance around anyway to make sure no one's watching.

It's too hot for anyone to be out, and the shades are all pulled to keep the sun from beating in the windows. I'll just have to hope no one is peeking through the cracks. I yank the plastic trash bag off the seat, then pull out the floor mats and stash them safely atop the car. At least some part of my property will go untouched by today's carnage.

The water pours red as it washes across my driver's seat and tips out into the street, the tilt of how it's parked creating a waterfall into the gutter. After a moment, it runs pink instead, but all the foam showing through the slits is still stained dark. I press the liquid out of the foam, my throat shrinking at the thought of where Peter might have gotten the blood. A stray dog, maybe? Blood has never bothered me when I was the one spilling it, but this is something that died *for* me. A memory flashes before my eyes, the pool of dark red spreading across our kitchen floor. The way I edged away from the puddle of it when I was setting up the crime scene, so it wouldn't touch my shoes. Maybe blood did bother me once.

"What the hell is this?"

I blink back to myself and Eric's standing just to the other side of my car's door, his chapped mouth fallen slightly open. It's too late to hide the pink in the waterfall of water coming from the driver's seat.

I can't believe he'd walk right up to me like this, after everything that happened. But then, I guess he never saw me watching through his window. He has no idea how close I came to killing him before I realized he wasn't hurting Holly—that he was being kind. Something that's so foreign to me, I still can't quite wrap my mind around it.

Everything I thought about Eric was wrong, the blood in my car is no longer a secret, and I'm still not sure I can help Jeika before she ends up like me. So I just say it, all pretenses as far gone as my good intentions.

"If you weren't trying to fuck me, why did you help me?"

"What?" His face crinkles and he jerks a step back.

"Why'd you fix my car all those times, for free? Invite me over. Offer me dinner."

Eric flushes. It doesn't suit him. The red goes all mottled in his neck, like something contagious, and it makes his freckles and birthmarks look even darker and more blemished.

He glances down. "Folks don't usually talk to me much. I knew you were just putting up with me so I'd work on your car, but . . ." He shrugs.

I stare at him. He *was* creepy and awkward. He was lonely and maybe trying to act like we were closer friends than we were. But he wasn't going to push it further than that. And without him, I never would have had the freedom this car gave me. My mom and I would have been evicted when she wrecked her Honda and stopped going to work, because without my own ride, I couldn't have gotten to Norma's. But I can't—I just can't have been so far off about him.

"The kids," I say abruptly, not blinking as I batter him with my gaze. "What's with all the candy and pushing kids on the swings? Making cupcakes with them. You think Holly's pretty, is that it? You like the attention of pretty girls?"

His teeth clench and the mottled blotches of red on his neck darken to almost purple.

"Fuck you. You think I'm one of those crazies, preys on little kids? You think it's wrong to be *nice* to them?" He explodes out in a laugh that's as bitter of a sound as I've ever heard. "My dad sure thought so. He always said I was a pussy, didn't want to throw the first punch, so I'd be the one who got the beat down, every time. Wanted me to grow up tough, so he'd send me out to beat up the other kids, to prove I could. All of 'em. It wasn't enough to take after the bullies, even after they stomped my ass into the ground so many times. I had to go after the small ones too. He didn't want a son who couldn't win a fight, he said, and whenever he sent me out, he wouldn't let me back inside if I didn't do it. Or he'd give me the whupping I wouldn't give them."

Eric stuffs his hands into his pockets, glaring at me.

"Asshole's dead now. I don't have to do what he says no more. I never wanted to be . . ." He pauses, stuttering over it. "Like that. Wanted my own sons, so I could teach them different, but I ain't never got married. But I figure plenty of people have kids they don't even appreciate. Wouldn't hurt for me to pay a little attention to them, when nobody else does."

I don't know what to say. It sounds like bullshit, all bullshit. People don't just *change*, turn from childhood bullies to the neighborhood cupcake dispenser. People don't do something for nothing. That's how Hallmark works, not real life.

The engine of my car clicks and pings as it cools, the healthy sound of a well-tuned machine. And that's the part of the equation that just doesn't fit. Because he *did* do something for nothing.

"I wasn't even nice to you." I can't stop staring.

He hangs his head, like he's embarrassed by that when, by all rights, *I* probably should be. He scuffs at the wet pavement with his toe, kicking a pebble up the street.

"I knew you didn't like me," he mutters. "But you needed me. It felt kinda good, somebody needing me enough that they'd want me around. And your mom . . . never coming out of that trailer, all those bottles stacking up. I thought maybe you could use some company, just like me."

I take a step back, the hose I'm still holding spattering over the hot pavement. "I don't need shit. And let me tell you something else. If you ever touch one of those kids. If you ever hurt them. I'll kill you."

His eyes narrow and he looks hurt. "What's wrong with you, anyway? I knew you were kind of rude, but I thought it was just— But—" He gestures to the car, to the pink water still dripping from my soaked seat. "That looks like blood, is what it looks like. You want to tell me what that's about? Are you in some kind of trouble?"

"I don't answer to you, asshole."

I need him to go away. I can't stand to look at his sallow face, knowing he's been kinder, cleaner than me all along. And I need him to be so afraid of me he doesn't tell anybody what he saw me washing out of my car. I surge forward, the hose wetting his shoes, then his pants, but my eyes holding his with every bit of rage I can still muster up out of my shame. He gapes, not even moving away from the icy spray. He's afraid all right, but he doesn't break and run.

"You think I meant 'kill' as a figure of speech?" I breathe, close enough to his face to rip a chunk off him with my teeth. "Because yeah, that's blood. Still want to test me?"

He points a shaking finger at me, backing away. "You stay away from those kids," he says. "I don't know what the hell you are, or what kind of trouble you're stirring up. Ain't my business. But you come near any of the little 'uns in this neighborhood again, and I'll make it my business. Call the police and tell them about all that blood, fucked if I won't." His shoulders hunch. "What do I have to lose?"

I jerk my chin toward the road and he flinches, but then his jaw sets hard. He turns around and takes off down the street with bounding, lanky strides.

Fuck. Now I've got somebody watching me at work and at home. Too many secrets and nowhere to hide them, and no idea how I could have been so blind about so many things. So many people. I train the hose back on my ruined driver's seat, but it's not washing out any cleaner than when I started, and I don't know what else to do.

CHAPTER

37

Dani

I SQUELCH BACK INTO our trailer, my shoes filled with hose water and leaving pink-tinged smears on the linoleum. There are papers by the door, the stack of options I've been working on to give Jeika something to live for. None of them seem like enough to draw her out of her despair, and I don't know who the hell I think I am, trying to act like I know what purpose looks like for her. For anyone.

I stand in my doorway and suddenly I see the whole place with new eyes. It's the same layout as Eric's trailer, with piles of dirty clothes around the living room instead of just in front of the washer. There's white bread in the kitchen, the same brand that he bought. It's probably going moldy just like his, because it turns lumpy and paste-like in my mouth and I never reach for it until it's those last few endless days before payday.

Why don't we ever clean up? It's not that hard, a fucking broom and a trash bag. It doesn't cost shit.

I stared in through his window, judging every ugly inch of his life and I didn't even notice how much it looked like mine. My toe catches one of Mom's empties when I stride forward and Southern Comfort drips out onto the floor, the smell so sticky I carry it with me on everything I own. I should be figuring out how to get us both out of town before Peter can track me here but abruptly, I'm furious. Maybe if Mom ever sat in the living room with me, I'd have a reason to move the piles of clothes off the couch. Maybe if I didn't have to do her laundry too, I wouldn't let mine get so behind. Maybe if she'd get a goddamn job, I wouldn't be so exhausted from trying to stretch my few measly dollars into a life for us.

"Mom!" I shout it, stalking through the living room and banging into her room without even caring if she might have a man in there.

She doesn't, though. She's passed out with her hair falling over her face and her legs flung in a tangle on top of the sheets. A plastic bowl leans against her knee, tipped almost all the way over where she shifted while she was asleep. Mac and cheese has slid out onto the sheet beneath, forming a deeper orange film across the top where it's been sitting all night. My stomach churns.

She didn't even notice. When did we stop noticing? Our lives, each other. Was it when we lost Uncle Ricky? Because somehow I'd forgotten that even without him, I still have a family.

"Renee," I snap, the emotion tightening my throat squeezing out as anger.

She blinks, the sound of her name waking her when the name of what she is to me failed to rouse.

Her hand sags exhaustedly from her wrist as she pushes back her hair and winces at the light coming through the shaded windows. "What's wrong, sweetie? Are you feeling sick?"

I grab her shoulder and she squeaks, flinching back from me. Her knee tips the bowl the rest of the way and congealed mac and cheese grinds into the sheets.

"I'm not giving you money anymore," I say abruptly. "If you want something, you can work."

She probably won't. In the past, when I cut her off to get her to stop drinking, she did a lot uglier things for money. More dangerous things. But that's her choice. We all have to make them.

Maybe I can be for her what Jeika was to me. The jolt to wake me up and make me realize the person I am isn't who I always have to be. Jeika's death isn't my answer. I'm not even sure an answer exists. But my eyes are coming open now.

My mom's are falling closed again, her lips parting on a heavy exhale that smells like day-old Southern Comfort and unbrushed teeth. I recognize the look from every morning she's dragged herself out of bed, forcing smiles for me and offering to scramble me an egg before she realizes there aren't any in the fridge. It's guilt at first and the dregs of love that have her attempting to make it up to me. Then it'll hit: the realization that she's fucked up more than she thought. Whatever she didn't mean to say last night or what she broke, or just remembering how goddamn long it's been since she's been to a grocery store to buy food for her daughter.

And she crumbles.

She gulps back more booze because she thinks it's who she fucking is. Because she tells herself she's weak and messed up and that's all she'll ever be. The booze is a punishment as much as it's an escape. It's permission never to change. And it happens every goddamn day.

Today, I shake her until her neck snaps back and the bowl bounces to the floor, splattering cheese goo on my bare ankle.

"YOU STILL EXIST," I shout in her face. I'm so goddamn tired of both of us, of the way the guilt over what we've done holds us back from ever changing enough that guilt would be unnecessary.

I throw my arm back toward the mess of our dusty trailer.

"This doesn't have to be your life forever."

Her face twists. She stands up and shoves my hand off her.

"Yeah? Well, it's your shitty life too."

CHAPTER

38

To: MVictimVolunteer@gmail.com
From: FacelessMan00@gmail.com
Date: May 23, 7:34 PM
Re: I want to help

Dear Jeika,

If you still want to help me, meet me at the Starbucks tomorrow. 5:00.

-Dani

CHAPTER

39
Dani

WHEN I GET to the Starbucks, Jeika's there.

I wasn't sure she would be, after everything she saw me do in the desert, all the empty days in between when she offered to help me and when I answered. I chose the Starbucks instead of going back to her house because I wanted it to be her choice. She offered to help me with murdering Eric, and now that I know who he really is, that seems like the most grotesque of all jokes. I can still remember his face: frightened but determined to protect the children of our neighborhood. From me.

Jeika's got on metallic gladiator sandals and shorts, a purse slung over her shoulder and brushing against her hip. The sun's striking gold on her hair and I almost don't stop to pick her up, because I can't shake the feeling she'd be safer far away from me. But no. This is the woman who asked the internet for her very own psychopath. The woman who now wants to help me kill. The woman nobody knows the truth about but me.

Which means no one is left to help her. Except me.

Bile rises in my throat and I clench my teeth against it, kicking the brake too hard when I pull up. The car jolts with its stop, shaking me inside its heavy metal cage.

Jeika ducks to my side window, a lock of hair falling forward to brush her cheekbone. "I didn't get coffees," she says. "I wasn't sure where we were going, and you don't have cupholders, so I thought I'd just wait and—"

I jerk my chin for her to get in. If I unclamp my teeth, I have no idea what I'll say. If I might beg. I dug through the whole internet for answers for her and reread her first explanation email a hundred times, staring at the pieces of why she felt she wasn't enough. What I found feels like a pretty half-assed stand-in for the meaning of life, but it's something she can actually *do*. Someone she can help, who is worse off than her, and doesn't need her to be the best or the smartest or the most accomplished anything. For it to help, though, *she* needs to want it. And if she doesn't, I'll have to peel back all the other layers of bullshit she's been telling herself and force her to see the truth of how the world really works.

She slides inside, nestling her purse down by her feet, and when she tucks her hair back, she frowns.

"What's with all the towels on your seat?"

The blood wouldn't come all the way out. It's like driving a fucking crime scene, the foam all stiff with DNA that could be tying me to any number of murders, if the cops show up at my house to test it. Peter already has my license plate number. He can ask Marilyn for my address whenever he wants. It could happen any day.

But I can't afford another car any more than I could afford to quit my job, not before I have a new one so we can flee. When I told my mom I wasn't going to give her money anymore, I didn't think it would be because I didn't have any to give. But I can't just leave her behind in case Peter takes his vengeance out on her instead. I've been dealing out job applications as fast as I can fill out my name and address, and I just covered the bloody wounds in my seats with beach towels, secured with white medical tape I found in the first aid kit at work. I have no idea how to change my future or protect my mother from what I've done, so I've been researching Jeika's future instead.

There's nothing stopping Peter from coming after me, or from sending handcuffs and sirens my way. I should want him to catch me, to send me to prison. A good person would want to be punished for what I've done, but I don't.

The truth is, I'm just too broke to run.

I could go after Peter before he comes for me, but every time I think about it, I remember Eric's face, frightened but resolute as he warned me away from the neighborhood kids. How utterly wrong I was about which one of us was the villain. If I'm not supposed to kill, what the hell am I supposed to do? I thought all these people showed up in my life as signs of what my purpose could be. But that was just a sickness in me, a lie that I made real so I could live with the sins I'd already committed.

Jeika's forehead creases and she reaches for the towels covering my seat to see what's beneath. I knock her hand back, my blood suddenly pumping. "Don't."

"Um, okay . . ." She sits back, wary.

I drive, stomping the gas harder than I should dare when I'm sitting on a whole seat stained with probable cause, but I need to get the fuck through this. I hurt her, and that's good. It's fine. If she's upset with me, she won't want to be like me and that's the point of all this.

It's only a few blocks to where we're going and I take the corner hard enough to make her grab for the door to balance herself.

"A health food store?" The creases in her forehead deepen, but she keeps her voice light. "You don't strike me as a sprouts and tofu girl."

I spin the wheel and avoid the crowded parking lot, the shiny-haired shoppers with their lululemon leggings and reusable bags. I steer us along the dusty stretch of cinder block wall to the narrow alley in the back, and jerk to a halt in front of the dumpster. With any luck, I won't need the visual aid, but I chose this spot in case Plan A doesn't work.

I turn to her, trying to think past the heaviness that's invaded every part of my body to do what I came here for. It's been a hard few days, with no end in sight. She reaches out and touches my knee, her fingers light.

"What's going on with you, really? Is it Peter? Or that other guy, from the playground?" She squeezes, the denim of my jeans suddenly rough against my awakened skin. "Something about you is different. I'm the one you can say it to, you know." She offers a tentative smile. "I've already heard all the things you're not allowed to tell anyone else, remember?"

The arguments I've practiced for days roil in my stomach, black and hot, like I can feel every bite of food

I've eaten since I was fourteen trying to claw its way back out of my body. All of them stolen because they should have belonged to my uncle, not me. My sweet, sad Uncle Ricky who was just trying to save us from ever hurting as bad as he did. If I'd just talked him through that one hard night, if I hadn't been so fast to reach for a weapon rather than words, who could he have become?

I push her hand away, because I'm not the one who deserves her comfort. Instead, I open the glove box, letting the answer she needs fall into her lap. It's a thin envelope with a single piece of paper in it, and right now, it looks as flimsy as it is.

But so were all the lies I told myself about why I had to kill my uncle, then the next victim, and the next. They were only thoughts, really, and they kept me strong all this time. That piece of paper holds enough hope to keep Jeika alive for the rest of her life, if she believes in it enough.

CHAPTER

40

Jeika

THE ENVELOPE DANI hands me has a logo in the corner: Make-A-Wish Foundation. I run my thumb across it. "Uh, pretty sure they don't grant wishes to people who want to die on purpose."

"Just open it." Dani's pale today, but her eyes are still their same hard slash of darkness. She's even more beautiful with her cheekbones hollow and her eyes shadowed, but it makes me want to bring her piles of fresh fruit and a pillow, and stand guard over her while she lies down to rest. I don't know where she's been for all these days since I last heard from her. From the looks of it, it was somewhere hard, and ugly.

I thumb open the flap of the envelope and unfold the piece of paper. It's an application, with spaces for name and address and a few questions with open lines left for my answers.

"What's a wish granter?" I ask after I've skimmed to the bottom. This feels like an accusation, somehow, like the emails my mom used to send me about all the different colleges she thought I could go to. Someone else's hopes, weighing in my pockets like stones.

"Just what it sounds like," Dani says. "Dying kids send in their wishes to the foundation, and donations cover the costs, but it's volunteers who have to figure out how to make the wishes happen. You don't have to have special skills, or a degree, or be the fastest or best at anything. You just have to make a lot of phone calls and stick with it to get the person what they want most, even when you have to plow through a mile of red tape. Sometimes it's as simple as a celebrity meeting and you just have to figure out how to contact the person, then make travel arrangements. Or, for the younger kids, sort of more of a fantasy idea that you have to figure out how to translate into reality. Like going on a trip with the tooth fairy."

Dani shifts to sit more sideways in the driver's seat, watching me.

"The way you saw Eric . . . I brought you there to show you a person who I thought deserved to die and what you saw was a dad on the playground who was nice enough to bring snacks. You can give that to dying children and their families. Gift them their own little scrap of hope to look to. To see the best in an unfair world, instead of the worst."

My head tips back against the seat, and I let the application fall closed along its folds. I can't look at her. Dani was supposed to be the one who understood. Some job at a charity can't fix me, no matter how many people it helps, because it's not a job I need. I need to *be* the kind of person who could do all those things, and I'm still not.

I can't even grant my own wish—she was supposed to do that.

"It's not about just acting like a better person," I tell Dani. "I've been trying to keep going after everything that happened, trying to be normal, trying to—I don't know, just do the right fucking thing. But nothing's enough to make up for crashing that car or making it look like my mom was driving drunk when she'd never done that a day in her life. I'm not enough to balance those scales." I stare down at my hands tightening on the application, the thin paper crumpling in my fingers and going from smooth to ugly. "This isn't even a career, or some kind of life path. It's just a volunteer gig."

"So what? Some of the most important things you'll do in your life aren't for money. Hell, probably all of them." Her eyes go dark, almost angry. "This is something you could be good at, a way you could make somebody's life better and be worth all the resources your life is using up. It's what you said you wanted. Remember?"

Like it's that simple. Like you can *be* someone else, just because you want to. I look at Dani, and I've never felt so betrayed. Why is she, of all people, trying to give me excuses not to kill myself now?

"You just don't want to do it yourself. That's what this is about. Peter scared you with the whole story about his daughter and now you want out of our deal." I flick the wish granter application and it ricochets off the stick shift and hits her leg. "At least have the courage to say it to my face, instead of hiding behind this crap. If you think *this* is enough to live for, you've never really wanted to die."

Dani's lashes flare, then narrow. "You want to talk about who's hiding behind flimsy shit?"

Her door bangs open and she storms up to the fence surrounding the dumpster, but the latch is secured by a padlock. I get out slowly, not sure where she could be going. She moves back to her car, pops the trunk, and pulls out a full-sized set of bolt cutters.

She props one side of the bolt cutters against her side, sets its teeth against the padlock, and pulls with her left hand. She grunts a little as the handle grinds into her ribs, but then the padlock gives and she bumps the gate open. Once she's inside, she uses the bolt cutters to push the dumpster lid up high enough that it wobbles past vertical and falls open with a crash.

"Look." The order is as staccato and unyielding as the clang of metal. I eye her, wary of the fury washing off her in waves, but I'm too curious not to look. I edge past her and peek into the dumpster. I'm half expecting a corpse, or at the very least some rotten, slimy garbage, but it actually looks like somebody just swept the store shelves into the trash. Whole loaves of bread, boxes of pasta, cookies. Fresh fruit, a bit of wilted lettuce and a wonky-shaped banana.

"Why is this locked?" My nose crinkles. "Most of this food looks fine. Couldn't they give it to a food pantry or something?"

"'You'll eat thirty-five tons of food in your lifetime,'" she quotes my email back to me. "But every sandwich you don't eat doesn't go to another person."

She reaches over the edge and uses the bolt cutters to flick a box of crackers up toward me. I let the box bounce off the edge and fall back in, and I don't take my eyes off her.

"If it doesn't sell by the date some idiot stamps on the side, it ends up here. People go hungry while they lock up giant boxes of food. I read about it in *Grapes of Wrath*, sophomore year. During the Depression, the price of pork was way down, so they let people starve while they cut pigs' throats and buried them in a ditch. Because to those people, it's not about the food. It's about the money. Nearly a hundred years later, and we're doing it again like we haven't learned a thing since the whole world was candles and pig farmers."

Dani swings the bolt cutters in a wide circle and I flinch back.

"If you don't eat the food, it doesn't go to someone more worthy. It goes to a stupid locked dumpster or someone else buys it, maybe somebody who cheats on their taxes or slaps their wife around. If you want it to go to someone who needs it, you have to stick around and send it there. The only one who can make the world into what you want it to be is you."

She's shorter than me. It seems impossible, her looking up at me, but I guess I didn't realize that we've rarely been so close together anywhere outside of her car. And yet when her eyes lock onto mine, I want to shrink from the sheer, furious energy of her. She's like a bomb with the fuse always burning.

"You think I don't feel that?" she hisses. "That wasted food, churning in my gut for so many years when all I did to deserve my place was fry some fucking chicken?

And yeah, it feels like crap. But what are you going to *do* about it, Jeika?"

As hard as I try, I can't hold my ground when she's like this. I take a step back but she stalks along with the movement and the fence looms behind us, a solid barrier. I can't tell if she's angry with me or herself, and I don't know which scares me most. The bolt cutters in her hand suddenly look less like a tool and more like a weapon.

"My mom's parents were killed by drunk drivers when she was eleven." Dani doesn't blink when she says it. "She and my uncle went to distant relatives, then to foster care when the relatives couldn't handle them anymore. A bunch of really bad places, where bad shit happens. My mom's forty-six fucking years old. She could have lived five different lives by now. Led AA meetings. Tried to stop anybody from driving drunk ever again. She could have lived any life she wanted, but she couldn't see past her first one."

The heat ripples up from the pavement beneath us, and I feel woozy but I can't look away from the lock of our eyes.

"Because that's the thing, Jeika. What's unforgivable? You can always start over, but most people don't. They make excuses for why they can't, and *that's* the unforgivable part." She chucks the bolt cutters onto the ground and they slide across the pavement, coming to a rest at my feet like an accusation. "My mom disappeared down a bottle and I've barely seen her since. She only stopped crashing cars when she couldn't afford new ones to crash."

Breaking glass. Screeching metal. The sirens that never come.

I wind my fingers through the chain link behind me and grip just to feel the steel dig into my flesh, so something feels solid.

"In a suicide note, you get to say one thing. One fucking thing. And in a life, you get to say a million different things." Her voice is razor wire and battlefields and I'm losing the war. "What's it gonna be?"

I open my mouth and the next breath catches in my throat. I don't realize I have tears in my eyes until her face goes fuzzy, all the sharp black and white lines of her blurring together.

"I don't *know*, Dani. That's what I've been trying to tell you this whole time. I want to make up for what I ruined, to be a good enough person that it makes sense why I'm the one who lived. But I don't know how." Because all I want is to not be the person I already am.

Something gentle skims my jaw. Her fingers.

I gasp to catch my breath but all the oxygen has fled and in its wake, I tremble.

"Who do you wish you were?" Her voice is quiet now, and I don't know why she sounds afraid. "What's a life you'd be willing to live?"

I hate everything I'm thinking. I hate everything she doesn't know about me. But with her hand cradling my face, somehow I can say part of it out loud.

"It all sounds hollow. All of it." The truth feels as electrified as a fence I don't dare approach, much less cross. "Once, I wanted to be a real estate agent, but now that seems so ridiculous. Plenty of people sell houses, so the world doesn't need me to stick around to do that. I've thought of all the obvious things I could do, to be somebody who makes a difference. Doctor, therapist, an artist or an athlete, as far-fetched as those all are. But I don't think *I* could be any of those things."

It's like Dani knew what I was going to say before I did. She lets her hand fall, but she doesn't step away.

"It feels like bullshit because that's what it is." Her eyes are dark, fathomless. "I think the real problem is you already know that no degree you get and no uniform you put on is ever going to be enough to get rid of that little voice. The one that knows the person you are underneath isn't worth a shit."

I jerk away from her, scraping my arm on the fence in my haste to put space between us. "What's with you today? What the hell did I do to you?"

It's like Dani's reached right inside my mind and found the ugliest part of me and I don't understand why she's throwing it in my face.

"I know because I feel it too."

I spin around. All her steel lines and atom bomb energy have vanished and she's a shaky wisp of smoke. A woman even smaller than I am.

"For a long time, I thought I was feeling nothing," Dani says. "When I killed. But that empty, lightless feeling . . . it's so much worse than nothing."

She raises her gaze back to mine.

"I put innocent people to death, Jeika. I thought I had to, that the universe was saying I was supposed to, but it was only me all along, fucking up. I'm the bad guy. I am." She inhales, and it feels like the whole world trembles when she does. "I don't want to be my mom. I don't want to give up, but I . . . what I've done . . . what I've turned myself into . . . I don't know if there's anybody left that I can be."

I catch her when she wobbles, and I don't know that I would have ever had the courage to touch her if she wasn't falling. Her first sob lands in my neck, and I grip her tight as we sink to the ground. The oily grit of the pavement scrapes my bare knees but we're all tangled together and I won't let her go, no matter where we are.

The things she said keep echoing, like a monster chasing me through the dark that knows everything I've never told a soul.

"Shh," I tell her, and I don't know if I'm comforting her or shushing her because I can't stand to hear another word of what she feels. What I feel.

It's impossible to live with, fucking *impossible*, and yet here we are. All tumbled together on the ground next to a broken lock and a box full of garbage that never really needed to be thrown away.

"You didn't do anything wrong," I tell her. I'd say anything if she'd stop crying. If she'd stand back up with fire sparking in her eyes and swing a crowbar like she could crush the whole world. "You've never killed anyone who didn't want to die."

"Yes," she says, her voice scraping. "I have."

As soon as I remember the three others, the ones whose stories she never told me, I can't breathe. *He pissed me off.* That's what she said, about the one only a few weeks ago.

I fight to swallow against a suddenly dry mouth. Why can't I be angry with her? Even now, even when I know she's done unforgivable things? And more than that, in the deepest, most selfish part of me . . . I know I can't let Dani stop killing now because she's my only way out.

"Please," I whisper. "Please don't make me live with what you can't. I mean, haven't you thought—maybe everything you did was about getting you here, to help me. Maybe I'm your redemption." To rebalance the scales for everything that never should have happened.

"But how can you *know*, Jeika?" She pushes me away, gripping my shoulder so hard it feels like her fingers will punch through the skin. "I thought I was doing the right thing with Peter, with Eric. And it turned out I didn't know anything. What if this whole time, I was supposed to be helping keep you alive instead?"

I shake my head, sooty certainty blackening my insides, staining every breath I take. I can't meet her gaze when all I can see is a body, drained of the person I knew. No justification on earth will ever make that image right. Will make it something that was *supposed* to happen. "You don't understand."

"Understand this." Dani yanks me to my feet and I stumble over the bolt cutters as we pass. "Peter knows who I am, and he has an idea of what I've done. He's not going to let me forget."

She pulls open the door to her car and I catch the handle when she lets it go, afraid she's trying to leave without me. Instead, she rips the towels off the driver's seat.

I fall back, horrified. The pristine seat is dismembered, its skin sliced deeply and the foam beneath stained a rusty red that looks like—but it can't be—

"Peter found out where I work, what my car looks like. He threatened me with my own scalpel." Her arm sags back to her side. "I can't help you, Jeika. If you disappear, he'll go to the cops and I'll die in prison."

"Damn you," I gasp it, because it's not fair that she knows me well enough to use that against me. The tears flood my eyes, but not enough that I can't see the blood soaking her driver's seat, just like my mother's did. "You could deal with Peter, if you wanted to, just like you did before. You *know*, goddamn you. You're my only way out, and you know exactly how I feel, and you're ditching me because of one stupid moment of cold feet."

"I'm trying," she seethes. "Do you understand that? I'm fighting like *hell* to find the right thing here and do it for you." Her face contorts as she glares at me. "And you hate me for it. Of course you do. Well, guess what? I hate me too. But if I do one right thing in my whole fucking life, it will be saving you."

I back away, shaking my head. I know, even if she doesn't, that none of this is real. She'd never try to protect me, never look at me this way, never bring me applications like I could be the answer to anyone's wish.

Not if she knew the truth about me.

"I have to die," I whisper. "And if you won't help me do it clean, I'll do it any way that I can."

CHAPTER

41
Jeika

I BURST BACK INTO my apartment and don't even hit the lights before I'm slamming through cupboards, ripping through duffel bags in the back of my closet to search for a weapon. It's quiet as an abandoned warehouse, both Kia and Cooper gone off somewhere together. This place doesn't even feel like mine—no place does. My body's just this unfamiliar sack of pain I've been dragging from place to place, and I can't do it anymore.

The steak knives I got from the dollar store aren't sharp enough, their serrated teeth chipped and flimsy. I find a box cutter knife under the kitchen sink and pull out the screw that holds it together, the old razor blade inside falling into my lap.

I have to *show* Dani. The things she said today—she talked like she saw every part of me, every shame-ridden thought I didn't think anybody else ever had. But if she really knew all that, she wouldn't be leaving me like this.

She just doesn't understand how much it hurts to live with myself.

I set the razor blade against my arm and push down. Nothing happens and panic flutters that it's too dull, that nothing is sharp enough to save me. Can I find another way to convince her? I don't want to do this, like that first moment of stark unreality when I stuck my head into a noose, an actual noose, and felt the rope against my neck. I just want *out*, and I don't know what else to do.

I drag the blade back toward myself and feel the burn of skin being sliced apart before the blood even starts to well. It hurts, so much more than such a tiny thing should, and I have to force myself to keep going.

How many cuts will it take to panic Dani, to show her even if she tries to ditch out on me, I'll never be okay? I can't accept that a world without my mom in it can ever contain a happy ending.

I wipe off the blade, leaving blood streaked across my shorts, and set the razor against a meatier part of my forearm. This time, I'm expecting the cold inside the burn, the way the skin tugs and resists even as I drag the blade through it.

She has to help me. She has to make all this stop.

The blood is nothing, tiny and undramatic. It drips, doesn't gush, and I flip my arm over and stare at the tiny ridges of veins in my wrist. If I thought it would work, I'd try it right now. But I devoured suicide forums on the internet for days when I failed to hang myself, and that's what finally made me desperate enough to post the classified ad. I've read the stories of all the ways it doesn't work.

I turn my arm over again, but there's not enough blood.

Whatever Peter killed in Dani's car to soak her seat that way, he must have slit more than its arm. He's dangerous, more than we gave him credit for. A memory ricochets through my head: her down on her knees, his gun to her head. The razor blade drops from my shaking fingers, landing among some toast crumbs on the kitchen floor.

Now all I can remember is Dani's misery today, how bad she wanted out of the person she'd become.

I thought I had to, that the universe was saying I was supposed to, but it was only me all along, fucking up. I'm the bad guy. I am.

I don't want her to have to kill, but I need to die.

It takes me two tries to pick up the razor blade because it's so thin. I lay the blade against my skin again, but this time I can't make myself press down hard enough to cut because I can remember her eyes, burning like a torch I want to follow out of the darkness.

She's suffering too, and this will hurt her more. I hurl the razor blade across the kitchen and drag myself to the bathroom, knocking things out of the cabinets with shaking hands until I find a roll of gauze. My hands shake as I wind it around and around my arm.

The beads of blood expand red, blotting out the pure white. I keep wrapping layers on top of them until the cuts are buried like just another secret that I'm never going to tell Dani. I'll wear long sleeves or avoid her until I heal. I'll find another way out, because if she does this for me, I'll make her into exactly what I hate myself for being.

I will never let her feel like I do right now.

CHAPTER 42

Dani

THE PATCH OF shade is small today. Barely enough to hide us both, with my knees tucked up tight next to Jane's as we share the same concrete step and I turn my head away to light a cigarette. Even in the shade, the wind is sweltering hot and I pluck irritably at the sweaty cotton sleeve of the shirt I've got on underneath my uniform polo. Lately we've been taking our breaks at the same time. Before, I would have thought it was because she didn't want to face Marilyn without me there to shield her, but now I suspect she's worried about leaving me alone.

I don't mind as much as I should. The nudge of Jane's elbow is the only thing that can drag me back from the undertow of worrying about Jeika. She took off from the dumpster at the health food store without waiting for a ride or taking the wish granter application with her, and she hasn't answered her phone since. For all I know, she's dead already.

I blow out a long stream of smoke, watching it like proof that my lungs are still working, even though my whole body feels wrong.

"Can I ask you a question?"

I don't respond, then remember that it's Jane, and I actually give half a shit if I hurt her feelings. "Sure."

"How do you know if a guy's your boyfriend?" Jane asks.

I quirk an eyebrow at her. "I'm gay, how would I know?"

She scratches her head beneath the line of the Norma's baseball cap we all have to wear. "Isn't it the same with girlfriends as boyfriends?"

"Sometimes." I resist the urge to check my phone to see if Jeika's answered any of my messages yet. I would have heard the ding of a notification if she had. She must be okay. Has to be. If she were capable of killing herself, she never would have put up the CheepsList ad.

"This guy," Jane's saying. "He's in my church group and sometimes we hang out afterward. We've kissed a couple of times." She darts a look at me. "Last week, he put his hand up my shirt."

I cough on my next lungful of smoke, distracted in spite of myself. "Damn, girl. Get it."

She tugs at the hem of her Norma's apron. "Do you think I should have let him? I mean, I feel like if my mom found out she'd tell the pastor."

"How old are you? Twenty-two, twenty-three?" Her unlined, round face makes it hard to tell, and her mom seems like the impatient yet overprotective type. Jane takes a few extra tries to learn a thing, but she isn't dumb.

Of the two of us, I think it's pretty fucking clear who should be giving the healthy relationship advice.

"Twenty-five?" Her voice rises on the end as if her age is a question for me to answer.

"Did you like it? When the guy did that, I mean."

She blushes, but nods.

"Then I'd say it's your call." I tap the ash off my cigarette and examine it, trying to decide if I actually want another drag. It itches in my throat and feels like nothing on the way in, tastes like licking a sidewalk on the way out.

"I didn't know you smoked," she ventures. Somehow, from her, it doesn't sound like a judgment.

"Never have. My Uncle Ricky used to say it was the only thing that helped him breathe, some days. So I thought I'd try."

"Does it help?"

I shrug. It's not as satisfying as it looks when other people do it. "I'm not sure I like the taste enough to keep it up."

Jane takes the cigarette from me and puts it to her lips, pursing hard as she draws on it. I lean back on the step behind me, waiting for the inevitable coughing fit, but she just makes a face and huffs out all the smoke in one mouthful before it gets to her lungs.

"I don't think I like it." She gives the cigarette back.

I nod. "Then I'd say that's also your call."

I stub out the cigarette and check my phone, telling myself it's to see the time and it's not about if there's anything from Jeika. We've got seven minutes left on our break, and I can't help but think that the clatter of the kitchen beyond the door sounds the same as every day has always sounded. This was my nightmare, ending up working here with nothing else in my life. Nothing to look toward, nothing that I was to the world beyond a hand that was needed to drop the fryer basket into the oil. But today, on the step with Jane, it's almost . . . comfortable. I can't decide if I like that or if I hate it.

"Can I ask you something?"

She looks up. "Of course!"

"What's your story?" I tuck the lighter and the mostly full pack of cigarettes back into my pocket. "You're way too good for this place, but you like it here, don't you?"

She frowns. "Why wouldn't I? I've always wanted a job, but my mom didn't think I could ever have one, because sometimes I'm forgetful. She said I couldn't move out because I couldn't cook for myself. But my life skills coach thought I could learn, so we started working on it. I can make sandwiches, and mac and cheese, and scrambled eggs. I can even use the fryer now, thanks to you." She smiles at me.

"I've been thinking it's time to get out of my mom's place too." I glance out across the parking lot. Mom has been out a lot lately, and I have no idea if that's because of the ultimatum I gave her about money, or if there's something else going on. I tell myself I can't care, that she's got to make her own choices, but these days I'm always aware that any time Peter wants to, he can ask Marilyn where I live, and he could decide to use my mother to hurt me. I check my phone again. "Let me know if you ever want a roommate," I say to Jane. "I might be looking."

"I've been saving up, but I haven't told Mom I want my own apartment. I can't do everything yet, but people on TV never cook at all. They're always eating Chinese takeout, and I can do better than that." She smiles a little. "I'm getting okay at sausage casserole too."

I nod, because she's just like me. Just trying to live her damn life but everybody's got an opinion about what it should look like. There's only one part of what she said that I still can't quite understand. "But like, why *here*? To work, I mean." It's hard for me to see Norma Dean's Fried Chicken as a place that could make anyone happy.

"I make my own money, and we feed people. Everybody needs to eat." A wrinkle appears between her eyes. "Do you think other jobs are better?"

I look at her for a long moment, then look away. "I used to think so."

"What's your story?" Jane asks.

I'm still trying to figure out how to answer that when the door behind us bangs open.

"Three minutes until your break is over, and don't think I won't notice if you two slide in late. I don't have time for that shit today." It bangs shut without Marilyn giving either of us a chance to respond.

Jane's dimples peek out. "Maybe other places *are* better if they don't have a Marilyn."

She giggles and I'm starting to smile too, until I see the car rounding the back of the restaurant.

It's a station wagon.

CHAPTER 43
Dani

PETER'S EYES ARE black pits, festering in his face as he pulls up next to us and rolls down his window.

"Hi!" Jane calls, waving. "Can we help you? The drive-thru window is around the other side." She points to show him the way. I touch her arm to keep her from going over to talk to him, and then I rise to my feet.

I could ask him if he had a nice time getting a new set of keys made for that station wagon. How much he had to spend on a new phone. If he's enjoying the pain in every breath, thanks to the ribs I cracked for him. I could remind him what I'm capable of and maybe scare him away. But I'm so fucking tired, and I can't stop hearing my mother's voice.

Yeah? Well, it's your shitty life too.

"What are you doing here?" I ask Peter, wearily.

"Recognize these?" He holds out a stack of papers, and I see the email address on the top line: **FacelessMan00@gmail.com.**

I reach for the emails and he lets them go, the stack hitting the pavement and scattering. Jane hops up. "I'll get them."

I throw out an arm to block her. "Don't."

She freezes, not used to hearing my tone so sharp.

The A/C unit behind the store kicks over with a roar, and the whoosh of air from its vents catches the papers so they dance and whirl farther. I won't bend and chase them. It's what he wants, and for all I know, he'll hit me with his car as soon as I stray in front of the bumper.

Instead, I stare him down and try to look like the killer I used to be.

"What do you want?"

"You know what I want." He hits the unlock button for his doors. "Get in."

The memory of his gun barrel itches at the back of my mind. Its yawning, open eye black like a future I can't see into. A future that might not exist, if I get in this car.

A wisp of breeze blows one of the emails toward Jane and I stomp it with my foot, trying not to look over, so he won't think to use her against me.

"Um . . ." she says behind me. "Maybe we should get back inside?"

"Go ahead," I tell her. "I'll be in as soon as I clean this up."

I won't turn my back on him to check, but I can track the scuff of her shoe against the concrete. I wait, but the kitchen door doesn't creak open. If Marilyn comes out to check on me and sees me confronting her brother, what will she do? How much would he tell her?

"These aren't evidence," I tell him, because if I don't call his bluff soon, he'll call mine. I lower my voice. "There's no crime. And there's not a single page of that where I agree to do anything."

He grips the steering wheel and I get the distinct impression that if we were alone, he'd be attacking me instead.

"I know what you are," he hisses.

"You don't know as much as you think you do."

My mind races as we stare each other down. I don't know if he's gotten another gun yet, but if he's using the emails as a weapon, it's because he *can* go to the cops, but he doesn't want to. There's some other punishment he'd rather inflict on me.

He leans out the window. "Get in the fucking car," he hisses, spittle flying from his lips with the intensity of the words. "Unless you want me to start shouting right here about everything you've done, you fucking mur—"

"Stop it!" I bark at him. To overpower his words before Jane hears them, more than anything. I throw a glance back and she's pale and trembling, the toe of her shoe turned in like a little kid, but she hasn't broken and run yet. I fucking hate him for barging into her normal, happy life, and the guy is clearly clinging to the last scraps of his sanity. I can't let him hurt her.

"I'm coming," I mutter, snatching up armfuls of paper and wadding them instead of restacking the pages. Words jump out at me from the pages like they're tracing themselves in bold across the surface of my brain.

Scalpel.
Mindfuck.
Serial killer.

I glance back at Jane, as if she could read the print from where she's standing, and I grind down on my teeth because that look gave away my new weakness. Back when I didn't care about anything, or anyone, I would have wadded these emails into his gas tank like a fuse and lit them up with the lighter in my pocket. Fuck whoever happened to be watching.

But Jane's right here within his reach, and the only weapon I have is a 99-cent Bic.

"You better come inside," Jane says, her voice too high and wavering. "Marilyn's going to be mad."

"Ooh, will Marilyn be mad?" Peter jeers and rage flushes over me to hear him mocking her. I shove all the papers through the window and into his face. He curses, batting pages away. I start around the car before he can make it worse, but then he turns to Jane anyway. "If she knew what this bitch really was," he says to her, "Marilyn wouldn't be crying that she was gone." Jane flinches at the curse word, her wide eyes darting to me as I get in the car with him. Everything he just said confirms my first guess. If he hasn't turned my emails over to the police, and he hasn't even gone to his sister to get my address, it's because he doesn't want them to know what he's about to do to me.

He stomps the gas and the car jolts forward with a dizzy rush like it's leaving my stomach in the parking lot behind us. We're alone. Oh God, oh fuck, we're *alone*, the one place I never let a guy like him corner me into.

Excess saliva pools in my mouth and my skin flashes cold, then hot, every exposed inch of it crying out like it's already stripped naked for whatever torture he has in mind. This isn't just some potentially creepy guy like Eric. This is a man who definitely wants to hurt me—wants to actually murder me.

My heart is beating in jolts and jitters and light flickers before my eyes like I might pass out before he even lays a hand on me. I have to scrape it the fuck together, but suddenly I don't remember how I ever did that.

I haven't felt fear like this since I was so young, I didn't even realize I still could. Ever since I was fourteen, I haven't truly been afraid of anyone hurting me, because I knew what I would do to make them stop: whatever I had to. No matter how cruel, how insane. I *knew* what I was capable of.

I'm the one who survives.

It was a comfort. Now it's a curse, because I've had long, excruciating years to measure exactly what surviving cost me and what it twisted me into. How many more people I hurt trying to justify my ends.

I know all the things he might do to me. And I no longer know how far I'm willing to go to stop him.

CHAPTER

44

Dani

"GIVE ME YOUR phone," Peter snaps.

I turn to look at him and then wish I hadn't. He looks weeks worse than he did when I left him writhing in pain in the desert. His eyes are so dark and sunken that they look like they're rotting into his head like an aging jack-o-lantern.

I don't move. My chances of being able to use it to call for help are slim, but it's my *phone*. There are a thousand things in there I don't want him to have. Not the least of which is every email that's ever passed between Jeika and me.

He grabs the back of my neck, his fingers gouging so the pain darts up into my scalp from all the hair he caught along with the grip.

"Don't fuck with me," he seethes.

I grit my teeth until they grind because he can hurt me, but he can't make me whimper. I'm still enough myself that I won't concede that to any living being. The phone, I flick into his lap.

"Unlock it," he says. "Or we're headed right back to give Marilyn all those emails."

I do it, but not for the reasons he thinks. He snatches the phone back and thumbs through it at stoplights. The pictures, first, then a few apps. He's looking for evidence and I'm looking for time. The door handle is right there, and I know I could jump out when he's stopped and buried in my phone, but he will just keep finding me. If I ghost my job, he'll tell Marilyn the truth, and once he does that, she'll hand him anything on me he could ever want to know.

On the other hand, if he calls the police, it's my word against his. I assaulted him; he tried to kill me. I sterilized and buried the scalpel and I've got Peter's gun, with his prints. He's got the emails, somebody's blood soaking my car seat, and the two ads on CheepsList, assuming anyone can dig them out of whatever internet afterlife things go to after they're deleted. If he gets the emails, the cops will find Jeika, and her secrets. She could go to prison for manslaughter and tampering with evidence, but even more than that, I know she doesn't want anyone to find out the real story about the car accident. To know she's been trying, so very hard, to be the next one to die.

Peter's my mess, and I need to clean him up before his chaos spills over into her life.

There's a thrumming in me that calls to Jeika, that can remember her reaching for me. Her tears washing my neck. I want to be the kind of person she turns to for comfort. I don't want to be the person digging unmarked graves, alone with the splintery handle of the shovel chewing into the underside of my arm.

I turn to Peter just as he lurches to a stop in front of his squat ranch house with its dead garden and a mailbox that's half smashed in. The fear awakes again as I stare at his misshapen mailbox, remembering the crack of the crowbar against his ribs. If he gets me inside, he can do anything he wants to me, and the things I'll have to do to stop him will be just as ugly.

My eyes flick to his neighbor's house, the linebacker who chased me down, but he's nowhere in sight. Where's a vigilante to take justice into his own hands when you need one? Then again, since he thinks I was a car thief, I doubt he'd be much interested in helping the likes of me.

"What do you want?"

Peter scoffs. "What? You didn't figure it out when I had a gun to your head?"

I stay quiet, considering. He thinks he wants to kill me, but what he really wants is a cure to his grief. There has to be a way I can trick him into thinking he's gotten it.

"Let me refresh your memory." He reaches into the console between us and withdraws a gun. A semi-auto this time, so even if I get it away from him, I can't hold it and rack the slide to load the first bullet. My ribs clinch tight into my body like they're a living mouth, snapped shut. *I'm going to fucking die today.*

I remember the whirl of my head when I drank the drugged smoothie, and the sadness in my uncle's eyes as he watched me slump deeper into the couch. I remember the bite of the handle of the kitchen knife, gripped so hard it left marks in my palm that lasted longer than Uncle Ricky's final breath.

"You're leaving here one of two ways," Peter says, the pistol gripped in his lap below the level of the windows, so any passing neighbors won't see. "In a body bag or in handcuffs."

I try for a scoff, but my throat's so dry it comes out more like I'm choking. "If you were going to turn me in, you would have driven me right to the police station."

He points the pistol toward the wind-tossed papers in the backseat and I break out in a sweat when the barrel moves past my torso. "I've got the emails, screenshots of the CheepsList ads, my neighbor who saw you break into my car. I've got plenty to ruin your life, but it's not enough for me." He leans close enough I can smell old coffee. "I want a confession."

The wetness of his breath on my face crawls across my skin and I stare him down, pretending I'm not seeing every corpse I've ever made. I can still remember the funeral for the sick boy I killed. Seeing his family so broken by losing him. How would they feel knowing their son didn't pass naturally but that I ended him early?

"I want to put you away for life," Peter growls. "For every fucking filthy thing I know you've done. And if I can't?" He shrugs. "I'll kill you right here."

"Witnesses," I rasp, gesturing at the windows, the quiet suburban neighborhood.

"You don't have kids, so I don't expect you to understand." The bruised skin under his eye twitches. "I've got *nothing* to lose. I can't bring my Hannah back or find the animal who killed her. But I can rid the world of other parasites like you who prey on young women."

"*I'm* a young woman." I slap my hand against my chest, trying to make him see me past his own grief. "If you shoot me, how does that make you any better than that crazy cult guy who took your daughter?"

"She was an innocent. I think we both know what you are." He gestures to the house with the gun. "Now walk, or die. I don't really care that much which."

I want to believe he's bluffing, that he's no more than a grief-stricken father who probably coached soccer and still has construction paper turkeys stashed somewhere, traced from his daughter's small hands. But I see it in his eyes: the same sickness that took my uncle, that lives just behind my tongue, blackening every breath I take. I know my kind, and I know the depths of depravity we can sink to, when we think we must.

I get out of the car.

Peter tucks the semi-auto into the back of his pants and locks the car with my crumpled emails inside. He's favoring his side a little, but the broken ribs don't seem to be slowing him down enough that I'm confident I can take him without a weapon.

I dig my nails into my palm and take a shaky step toward his house, wondering if I will ever feel the sun on my skin again if I walk through that door. If the last grass I ever see will be dead and brown from the latest drought instead of lush and glistening with green. If the last time I ever see Jeika, it will have been when she ran from me, instead of reaching for me.

Some part of me wants to believe that fate planned all of this, that it set this sidewalk under my feet, leading a few scant feet into the house of a man who is about to become a murderer. But these were all my own choices, all me. I wouldn't be here now if I hadn't clicked on the CheepsList ad. If I hadn't picked up that syringe, telling myself I was just speeding the inevitable. If I hadn't seen a woman with a black eye and decided her husband was my problem to solve. If I'd tackled my uncle instead of stabbing him.

I believed I was a killer, so I made myself into one.

Peter shoves me, sending me stumbling closer to the house. He's the one with the gun, but I still have choices, I realize suddenly. I always did, even when I thought I didn't. Especially when I thought I didn't.

I chose to kill instead of save, to end instead of nurture, and now that I can feel the wrongness of my own sins throbbing through my red, wet veins, I get to decide how I'll be punished. Peter's my executioner, but I'm my own jury. I can have a murderer's death, brutal but quick. All I have to do is refuse to confess. Or I can pass into the purgatory of prison, paying for my crimes the way society has decided I should. How long is life expectancy these days? Seventy? Eighty? I could spend *fifty years* in jail, the length of my current life twice over.

He unlocks the door and stale air conditioning chills my skin as I pass out of the sun and into his house. Goosebumps stand out plain all along my arms and the animal part of me wants to run.

The whole place is full of pictures. Framed, on the walls and mantel and some scattered across the water-spotted coffee table. There are whole stacks of them in places, tipping over so I can see the repetition of her face.

Hannah Hannah Hannah Hannah.

Everywhere I look, her light brown eyes follow me. I wonder where her body is rotting now, while her father sits in this tomb and decays in a totally different way.

"Sit," he grunts, and shoves me toward a chair. He's still thumbing through my phone. Looking for evidence or maybe planting some. I try to force my frozen mind forward, to choose while I still can. Long moments slink by, time warped by the pounding of my heart and the silence of this dusty, shadowed house.

All I can think about is Jeika and how lost she was the last time I saw her. The tears jagging from her eyes. How she accused me of abandoning her. Why did I let her ignore my calls? Why did I stay silent when I know how much she needs me? If I really wanted to save her, I should have tracked her down to her house and forced my way inside, stayed with her no matter how much she raged and cried and tried to push me away.

My throat throbs with pain. I just want to see her, to cradle her in my arms the way I was always too afraid to. I didn't think somebody like her would want to be touched by someone like me, but that, too, was a choice. I was choosing to be a person who wouldn't be touched and I've stood alone and cold all these years when maybe there were people who would have reached back with kindness. People like Jane.

Peter looks up and the hatred in his face is a fresh jolt as he tosses my phone on the coffee table and pulls the gun out of his waistband. He thumbs off the right-handed safety, effortlessly, while I watch him make the movement that's impossible for me.

"Who have you killed?" he says.

I look up at him, and I feel long years of guilt and questions sink flat and finally quiet in my gut. It's my choice. It's always been my choice.

It's a wing-flutter of freedom and the falling boulder weight of responsibility all at once to realize there was never anyone else designing my fate for me. No God plotting out the meaning of my life. The universe is asking the questions, in so many different bodies, but I am the answer.

I rise to my feet.

Noise explodes into the moment as the door bangs, shuddering under the pounding of a fist. My head jerks that way. "Hey!" a male voice shouts from the other side. The knob rattles as he tries it, not waiting for an answer. "Open up, we know you've got Dani in there!"

But who would care enough to come after me?

Peter throws a wild glance toward the back of the house, his hand tightening on the gun. I dart for the door, not taking the time to weigh the consequences as I flip the lock and rip it open.

It's my mom on the front porch. Greasy hair thrown back in a hasty ponytail and the exact same upturned nose that sits on my face. The cherry-chemical smell of Southern Comfort oozes from her breath and her clothes and she's clearly already half drunk but she's *here*. Next to her, Eric shifts his weight in that hunched-shoulder, uncomfortable-in-his-own-skin way that he has, a tire iron fumbled into one hand.

"Dani!" Mom grabs my arm and pulls me onto the porch as Eric glares past me into the house, taking a step in between me and Peter.

"Put—" Eric stutters, then his voice comes back stronger. "Put that *fucking* gun down. People know we're here. Lots of people."

He's the worst liar. How did I ever think he could be lying to me about what he was doing with those kids? The last time I saw him we were threatening each other and it makes my head whirl to try to piece together how he could be *here*, with my *mom*. If this is a dream, it's the longest, most specific one I've ever had, but that's really the only thing left that makes sense.

I turn, fear rising through my confusion as I realize the only family I have left in the world is now here, easy revenge pickings for a crazy guy with a gun when all the weapons I have are locked up miles away in my car. But Peter's pistol is dangling at his side as he gapes at the motley little group of us.

I dart back inside while he's still hesitating and swipe my phone off the table.

"Hey!" He starts to raise the weapon and my mother shrieks, "Don't you dare hurt my little girl, you son of a bitch!"

I bolt to the door, crowding my mom back from the dangerous opening while a shaking Eric grips the tire iron in one hand and a phone with 911 displayed on the screen in the other. His thumb hovers over the call button. "We're walking out of here or I'm calling right now," he says. "Don't you try to stop us."

"You don't know what she is," Peter says. "She's a criminal, a killer."

"You're what?" Eric asks. "Forty-five? Fifty? You forced a woman half your age into your car with witnesses. Right now, you got her held against her will, alone in your house with you. That makes you what exactly? A Good Samaritan?" He glares back at Peter, not looking quite so scared anymore. "You oughta be on your knees thanking me that I ain't bashing your teeth in right now, you pervert."

Mom tugs at my arm—my left, even now she only ever reaches for my left—as she backs away from the door. Eric comes with us, phone still held up, not taking his eyes off Peter.

"This isn't over!" Peter shouts past them. "As soon as you leave here, I'm calling the police. Giving them everything I have, and you *know* what I have. There's no getting away from this, not anymore."

Eric flicks to a different app and snaps a picture of Peter holding the gun. "Call all you want, shithead," he says. "Have fun explaining to them why you kidnapped a girl who's young enough to be your daughter." He stuffs the phone in his pocket, keeping his body between us and the house as he urges Mom and me toward his old Chevelle. "C'mon. Let's get out of here."

I back down the steps, not taking my eyes off Peter. I may be escaping right now, but I'm under no illusion that Peter is actually letting me go. Either he'll report me to the authorities or he'll tell Marilyn what I did so he can get my address. Then he can come after me again as soon as Eric goes home and I've got no backup. One way or another, this is going to end today.

CHAPTER

45
Dani

"HOW?" I BLURT as I land in the backseat. My mom's door slams and before Eric's even made it around the car, she's digging in her purse for a water bottle filled with amber-colored liquid. "How did you guys know where to find me?"

"Your phone." My mother swallows, then tucks the bottle guiltily back in her purse as if I won't have seen it. She twists to look at me. "I've had an app in it set to track your location since I bought your first phone." Her hand pats over my hair, touching my face as if she's searching for injuries. It's so strange to be touched by her, and her slim fingers feel more familiar than I ever guessed they could, after all this time. "I may not be mother of the year," she murmurs, "but I still worry."

Eric pulls out, changing gears at such flawless intervals that we hit sixty miles an hour before we're even a block away. I'd forgotten, too, that it was him who taught me how to drive a stick.

"But how—" My speech comes out as disjointed as my thoughts. "How did you know I was in trouble? I wasn't even supposed to be home from work for another two hours."

"Marilyn called me," Mom says. "I'm your emergency contact on your papers at work. Apparently one of your coworkers saw an older man forcing you into his car."

Jane. Warmth flushes through me, and I fight the urge to hide my face like this is too personal of a feeling to have in front of them.

"Marilyn seemed to have her doubts," Mom was saying. "Said she didn't feel comfortable calling the police because she hadn't seen the man herself, and she hadn't heard sounds of a struggle, but your coworker was adamant that he threatened you and you hadn't wanted to go with him."

All those years I've worked at Norma's, and until the last week, none of my coworkers liked me well enough to take their breaks with me. Much less would have cared enough to *do* something if it looked like I was in some sort of toxic relationship with an older guy. If I hadn't fallen apart enough to need her help, Jane and I never would have become friends and I would have been alone today, utterly at Peter's mercy.

"Marilyn asked if I had any idea who it might have been, since the other girl said you talked to him like you recognized him." Mom sends a self-conscious glance toward the driver's seat. "Eric was the only older man I could think of that you knew, when he's helping you with your car and this and that, so I went down to his place. He said he hadn't seen you. That's when I really started to panic and remembered I could track your phone. I haven't had any reason to check it in a while and I wasn't even sure the app still worked—you know how things are always updating and changing and such, and I can never keep up." Her hands fusses at her purse, touching the bottle just inside, but then she closes the zipper firmly. "Eric was worried too, and he offered to give me a ride to help find you."

She gives his arm a little pat. He ducks his head, blushing. My eyes dart between them and then he catches my gaze in the rearview mirror.

"That the guy who did that shit to your car seat?" he growls.

I nod, slowly. "Some asshole. Found me at work and he's been . . . harassing me." I know I need to explain this whole mess somehow. They heard him say "killer" but neither one of them seems to be taking his ranting seriously.

"I was mad, when we talked before," Eric says, the words snapping off abrupt and reluctant. "But when your mom came by, I remembered that you threatened me, said if I ever hurt those kids . . ." He pauses, flicking a glance at my mother. "I figured anybody who would say that couldn't be too bad. Thought you wouldn't have cut up your own seat like that, even if maybe you had—uh, done all the rest, I mean." He stumbles over trying not to say the word "blood" in front of my mom and I wonder, fleetingly, if he has a crush on her or if he's just being as awkward as usual.

I clear my throat, but the words come out easier than they once would have. Before Jane. "Thank you."

He nods, looking even more uncomfortable as he starts to slow back to the speed limit now that we're away from the house. "Can take you down to the courthouse if you want. Get a restraining order. Or maybe you get those from the police, I don't know. Guess we can google it. I have the picture. That oughta help." He stops at a light and I can hear his foot jiggling on the clutch.

I grip the seat, trying to process my sudden freedom. One more chance. How many times in my life have I had one more chance, one more choice, without even realizing it? This time I'm not going to let it slip away.

"I need my car," I say abruptly. "Drop me at my car, at work."

Mom frowns. "Are you sure you're okay to drive after all that?"

"I have someone I need to check on."

The need to see Jeika is a physical ache that's spreading through my whole body with every minute that passes. My ankle bones, and the tips of my fingers, and the quick flutter of breath beneath my collarbone, the awareness in my skin. I should have kissed her. A thousand times I should have kissed her, and a million I should have held her, and I'd give anything, *do* anything in the time I have left, if it meant she would want to live. I could go to the cops first, try to spin things so I'll get off free no matter what Peter tells them, but Jeika could be in danger right now, trying to hurt herself right *now*.

Peter's certainly called 911 by this time, and all the dominos are already tipping. There are so many different ways they could fall and before that happens, I have to try one last time to save her.

CHAPTER

46

Jeika

I SLINK INTO DANI's car. It's the most I've moved in days, and the solid metal of the door almost seems too heavy to pull closed behind me. But once I'm inside, the seat is as broad and soft as I remember, and I don't have to hold myself upright anymore. My tired lids fall shut, just for a second.

"I wasn't sure you'd come." Dani's words are quiet beneath the rumble of the engine, and she doesn't shift out of neutral.

There's a lump that sits at the back of my throat all the time now, and it rises hard at the sound of her voice. The last time Officer Diego called, I nearly answered. I'm utterly out of fight, out of answers. Out of everything.

"I . . ." I attempt, but there's nothing I know how to say. After a minute, she shifts into first, like my swollen-tongued silence is one she understands. Second gear hums smoothly out of first, and my heart beats more easily. She's wearing a polo shirt that says "Norma Dean's Fried Chicken" over the pocket, a matching cap tossed behind the seat, and it looks all wrong. Like seeing a dancer in mismatched pajamas.

I haven't been to work since the last time I saw her, and fat wraps of gauze sit under the sleeve of my shirt that's too heavy for the weather. I'd like to think she didn't notice.

But Dani's eyes are as quick as always. On me, then the rearview mirror. On the cars all around us, at stoplights. I frown.

"Are you . . . is there someone following us?" Her gaze is usually pointed straight forward, pressing undaunted along with her gas pedal.

"Peter tracked me down. I don't know how long I've got."

"Before what?" I sit up straighter. Peter's my fault, and if he's causing trouble for her, I need to find a way to beat him back. He and I are two different sides of the same coin flip: grief turning us until we became something else. He should listen to me, if he's going to listen to anyone. I sort through my sluggish thoughts, trying to make a plan.

Dani gives me a tight smile as she flicks on her blinker and cruises into a big parking lot.

"Don't worry. I know how to buy us some time." She dodges around a line of chain stores, accelerating past their delivery docks, and skids off the edge of crumbling pavement onto dirt beyond. "The desert's a big place."

Her mention of Peter sounded ominous, but she doesn't seem nervous. Just alert.

There's something different about her today. Lighter, like someone lifted the ceiling off her world. My eyes can't stop tracing her. The set of her lips, the upward curve at the edges of her eyes. I've always been drawn to the darkness of her, but now I see the grace.

Dust billows up in a cloud as the edges of the city shrink behind us. I press the heel of my hand to my heart to still the erratic beat that says we're driving too fast, eating up miles and minutes I can't afford.

I don't have a plan yet for how to help her. I didn't mean to see her again until I did, but my brain is all sludge and apathy and all I know is that I can't erase my own pain if it means adding to hers.

For days, I've been trying to come to terms with that, but instead it's like time slowed and stuck right along with me. And now, it's racing too fast, just like this car I'm not driving, speeding out into a desert I don't know. If Peter's hot on her trail, there's only one thing she could be in a hurry to do, alone with me so far out in the dust beyond the edges of civilization.

Just let her.

The smallest, worst part of me whispers in my head how easy it would be to let her finish the job I sought her out for. I won't ever have to know how it affects her. I'll just be gone into the quiet of whatever comes after. It'll be like I never even happened. She's survived murder before; she can do it again. She's stronger than I am.

The lump in my throat is made of wrongness and it won't be swallowed away.

I wet my lips, feeling how rough and chapped they've become, and try to tell her she doesn't have to do this.

But I can't quite make myself say it, and every time I try, it just makes everything hurt more. For me. For her.

So I don't speak at all, and she drives. The new energy in her gathers around us, humming ever sharper, and I have no fucking clue what it's going to do when it breaks.

She jumps from road to road, following a tangle of unmarked two-tracks across the parched dirt until I know I'll never be able to find my way back to Phoenix without her.

The light is slanting low toward sunset when she stops, and the cloud of dust chasing us catches up to the car, drifting gold and blurring the too-sharp lines of the desert as it settles in between us and the burning ball of the sun. I'm squinting against it, so it takes me a minute to see them.

Five crosses.

My chest clashes, the pure animal fear of a body that doesn't want to die quite as much as the rest of me does.

"Graves?" I struggle out through a dry throat, and Dani slants me a look as she opens her door.

"Not quite."

Her phone bleats, an unfamiliar tone that makes me realize I've never heard it ring before, not in all the times we've been together. She pauses with one foot out the door and tugs it from her pocket, checking the screen and tapping back a quick, two-word response.

I'm okay.

I read it over her shoulder but hanging over both of us I can still feel those crosses, slashed in black lines over the falling sun.

"Who's that?"

She glances at me and tosses the phone down on the seat, leaving it behind. "My friend."

Her *friend*? I honestly hadn't realized she had any. She's never mentioned anyone. Where does her friend think she is right now? Probably not out in the desert with five not-quite graves, facing down a murder she no longer wants to commit. *I'm okay*, she said. But is she?

Nothing about this situation says yes.

I pull the door open and tell myself to be brave. One time, when it fucking matters, for *her*. I can be brave.

"Wait."

She turns back, but not all the way. I can see most of her attention is still captured by the crosses. Homemade, and hanging a little crooked from years out in the wind. One much older than the rest. I tug my sleeves down long to hide the plea I carved into my arm. My desperation, hung out there for her to see, before I made myself face everything that would mean for her.

"We don't have to do this." It hurts to force the words out, with the taste of all the onrushing years I don't want and don't know if I can bear. The sentence wavers and quakes like a floor buckling, and damn it, I need her to believe me. "I don't want . . . *you* to have to do this," I say instead.

She smiles, and it's sharp and so full of things I don't understand, space I can't fathom having within me again. Dani squats, swift and graceful, just another dark silhouette in a desert whose shadows are all starting to stretch. Her shape makes sense out here, and I'm the only thing left that doesn't fit.

"I made these," she says. She's looking at the crosses, so I do too.

The shapes seem too simple for all the meaning that symbol bears. One straight line, one set to oppose it. I've never thought about it before, but the whole thing is a crossroads. It makes no sense to me that this is the symbol an entire religion would have chosen to denote suffering, peace, death. The forgiveness of all sins.

Dani sets her one strong hand around the base of the biggest cross and rips it out. I reel a step back. Is she allowed to just . . . *do* that? She pulls out the second, flips it over, and lets it fall too.

"The bodies were long gone when I made these and brought them out here." She stands, looking down. "When I kept coming back to them over and over again." She nudges the ground, the toe of her black sneaker kicking up dirt into the dark puncture marks left behind. "There's nothing actually here. Nothing but what I bring."

She kicks over the other three, then sets a foot on one arm of a cross and grabs the other side. When she pulls, the string tying them together snaps with a puff of dusty old fibers, and the limbs wrench apart. The newest one resists her the longest, but eventually even it gives way. My face twists in a grimace and I cringe as I watch her destroy each marker in turn. I can guess which was for her uncle, but I can't pick out the one for the boy in the hospital. An odd ache throbs in my throat at the thought.

She tosses them down without ceremony and takes a crumpled pack of cigarettes out of her pocket, pushing them beneath the broken pile of sticks. I didn't think she smoked. My head whirls at the evidence of one more thing I didn't know about her.

Dani fishes a lighter from her pocket and flicks it, holding it steady as the flame jumps from lighter to paper, melting through to dry tobacco underneath.

The splinters of sun-bleached wood catch easily, and it's hard to watch the sparks eating them away. I glance back toward the city, and blink when I see headlights bouncing out across the desert. They're pointed away from us, on another one of the endless web of roads to nowhere. Probably someone as lost as I would be if I tried to drive this desert alone.

I clench my teeth and look back to Dani, trying not to remember my mother's face laid against white satin, her hair parted and smoothed in a way she'd never have chosen herself. In my mind, she looks the same, but I know that where she lies beneath the weight of six feet of cemetery dirt, her face is anything but the same as what I remember.

I don't know what I expected to see in Dani in this exact moment, with the firelight flickering mysterious daggers across her skin, but it wasn't sadness. This beautiful woman, with secret friends and cigarettes in her pockets that I knew nothing about. She has a whole life beyond this, beyond me, and something tells me she's starting to realize it too.

"I thought I had to do it," she says, staring down at the shapes that used to be crosses, but are now just a heap of lines, slowly being eaten away into curves and swoops I can't decipher. "And then I thought it had to be for a reason. Until I saw Peter today, a gun in his hand and the light in his eyes as wild as if he might start a cult himself because he *believed* so much that he had to kill me."

I catch my breath, dizziness taking me. He had a gun on her. Today. "How did you—"

She rises, swift and certain, and turns so the flames are at her back and her eyes are on me.

"All these people kept showing up in my life, marked for death. It felt like the universe shoving the question at me in one body after another. *What is the point of you?*"

I flinch at my private thoughts coming out of her mouth. Even now, I feel that question mark. Drawn by the line of contrast between her and me. Her certainty and my muddy despair.

"The universe keeps asking, but it can't answer for me," she says, her eyes aflame with determination. "I am the answer. The way I live is the only answer I'm ever going to get."

I back away. It's too much. Too simple, too intense. If I were anyone's solution, I wouldn't be out in this desert at all. My application is probably still crumpled in her glove box, because I don't know how to fulfill anyone's wishes, much less mine.

But Dani keeps talking. She tells me about a man named Eric, his abusive father and cupcakes and neighborhood kids. About Jane and frying chicken and Holly and the abuse she thought was going to happen. She tells me about being wrong.

"The first body I ever saw wasn't somebody I killed, did you know that?" She glances at me. "It was a man dropped dead between one breath and another in a Walmart. Even sprawled out on cheap tiles, it looked like the most final thing I'd ever seen. I think that's when I started thinking that death could be the end of suffering. For the person, for whoever they'd hurt." She shakes her head. "If I'd been around back then, I could have killed Eric's father, sure. Though death wouldn't have done a thing to actually end his evil. Only Eric could do that, to choose to stop the pain with him instead of passing it on. Death wasn't half as powerful as the stories he told himself."

"Wait, what stories?"

"It was Jane who gave me the idea," Dani says, taking a step away from the fire and closer to me. "When I could barely get out of bed in the morning, she taught me a story to help me remember what I had to do. It was simple, something about blankets or cribs or something, never going to win a Pulitzer, but it was enough to get me through."

Behind her, the sticks are barely more than embers, smoking and quivering as the last few scraps burn away.

"I want to help people find their stories," she says. "Whatever they have to be. Because I was telling myself the wrong fucking thing, all these years. That day with my uncle, I saw that gun in his hand and I thought it was kill or be killed. But Jane never would have thought that, not ever. She just doesn't have it in her. And I think, if I'd been a little more like her, I'd have tackled the gun out of his hand and hugged him and begged him to stay just one more day. To play lightsabers and cook breakfast with me . . . If I'd done that, maybe he could have found a story that made the world a place he wanted to live in again." Her voice begins to shake. "I just . . . since I met you, and Jane, and now Eric, everything looks so much different for me. And I think the light must have been there all along, and I just never knew how to open my eyes."

She closes the final step between us and grips the back of my neck. Even now, my skin jumps awake at her touch.

"I want to help you find your story," she whispers. "Because you're more than this, Jeika."

I shake my head, my skin twisting under her fingers until pain pinches and I wrench myself away.

"What, so I just lie to myself?" I push past her and it's not until I stumble that I realize I walked straight into the fire.

I stomp, suddenly frantic to shake the soot of her old crosses off my shoes. Sparks fly off the disintegrating wood and die in the dry desert air. She's reaching to help me when I look back up at her, glaring because I can't stop my face from twisting with the ugliness of everything I'm thinking.

"You're saying I should tell myself some fucking *story* so I can live with myself and what I've done?" Laughter cracks out of my throat. "Right. Well, then you spin it, Dani. You tell me what goddamn story exists in this world where my sarcastic, funny, beautiful mom bleeds out all over my hands and that's the start to anything good. Any fantasy land where I deserve *anything* but exactly what she got. A fucked-up ending that doesn't mean anything at all." I'm sobbing now, the words ripping out of me on every exhale. "Where do you find a story like that, huh?"

She doesn't move, and I hate her for being strong enough that she can stay on her feet, even against this.

"You make your own damn story." She doesn't blink. "Of a world where one terrible thing doesn't spawn so many more. You stop the ugliness with you, the way Peter didn't."

Peter. The tears suddenly feel cold in my eyes as I remember with a jolt. *I don't know how long we have.*

He's coming after her, and the desert's big, but the world's bigger. She'd be a hell of a lot safer far away from here. But she won't go if she thinks I'm still worth saving. So I need to make her understand that I'm not.

I close my eyes, and the tears breaking down my cheeks are wet like blood.

"I killed my little brother," I whisper.

CHAPTER

47

Jeika

IT'S WORSE, SOMEHOW, that I didn't even remember he was there at first. I had my mother's blood in my mouth. There was so much pain and I was spitting out glass and then I was staggering under the weight of her body and the worst thing I had ever done.

I forgot him, plain and simple. I understand how it happens now, all those parents who forget their baby strapped in the backseat on a hot day and spend the rest of their lives circling that black hole of despair, always wondering. *How could I have forgotten?*

Ray-Ray was so quiet back there with his earbuds and beloved dinosaur game, because I'd brought it along when we picked him up, knowing it was his iPad he really missed enough to come home early from his dad's. When Mom and I were arguing, he was in the backseat playing. When I swerved, reaching for that phone.

I still remember the crisp *click* of the seatbelt right before I saw him. It was the worst moment of all, me leaned in over my limp mother's lap and fighting nausea as I belted her into the driver's seat to complete the lie. That's when I saw there were two bodies, not one. That I hadn't lost my mother—I'd lost my whole family.

There wasn't even any blood. The freckles on his round cheeks were perfect, unmarred. They told me later that the impact alone snapped his neck, his body so much smaller and more fragile than mine. His iPad had been thrown forward and it was stuck between the seats, colorful dinosaurs ambling across the still-illuminated screen. Going on without him like I've never been able to.

"Ray-Ray was in the car too," I whisper to Dani. My judge, my executioner, my very own Faceless Man. The first person to ever know my whole truth.

Dani is still watching me, her eyes never squirming away from the lock of our gaze. I let the truth of my past weight the world between us, and I wait. For her to slap me, to leave me, to bury me. To spin me a tale full of excuses about how I can kill a child with my carelessness and still deserve an eventually happy life of my own. After all, she's murdered too. Arranged her family members' bodies to cover up her crime too. She *knows* it's not okay. She's lived all the miserable years of how not-okay it is. But part of me is still expecting an avalanche of words to explain how anybody could know all of that and still love me. We all lie in so many different ways to be able to live with ourselves.

But she doesn't.

She kisses me instead. Like it's all already true. The best of it, and the worst, and she doesn't deny a fucking thing.

She holds me too. Not just with her left arm, but with her right, the side she always shifts back from the rest of the world. The piece she always keeps a little defiantly hidden, like she's guarding against the rejection of others even before it comes.

Now she reaches for me and my fingers slide over every perfect shape of her and I don't know how it's possible to feel so much *right* all at once.

She almost pulls away and then comes back to kiss me once more, softly, like she can't help herself. My whole body is a heartbeat and I'm as fragile as thin skin.

My eyes come open as we ease apart, and her face is different once again. Dark and light, and severe lines and open, now, in a way it's never been. I can feel clean years unfolding out before this new version of her and I wonder how any one decision can have so much power as whatever it was she decided today.

How many choices are billowing out behind me like smoke, when I didn't even realize I was making them? Like reaching for my phone that night when I should have been watching the road. Reaching for a girl I'd barely met and failing, just for one crucial second among millions, to protect the family who'd been there for me my entire life.

I think of a counselor who once told me, "Everyone deserves to live. Who told you they didn't?" She was right, but not in the way she thought. People don't deserve to live for no reason in that automatic platitude kind of way. They deserve their lives for a million different-shaped reasons that come down at such contrasting angles that you can't see them all at once without spinning around and around and around.

Eric, with his father's fists bringing out years of later kindness to lonely kids. Jane, who just wanted a job, and didn't realize she was blazing a whole new path for Dani's feet to follow. Peter, his love for his daughter gone sour, like a sweet cucumber soaked in vinegar until the tang of it was sharp enough to wake Dani up when nothing else could. Even I can see she's better for it.

Where before there was that black-diamond-hardness at the center of her, now there's a quiet. And it stretches open like the whole desert, whirling around us. It's a future where she deserves her space in a million new ways. And it makes me ache with envy.

I don't know who Dani will be. What name her friends will call her, whether she'll be a doctor or a janitor or a hermit or a god. But I can feel the gathering of possibilities in her and I know even if she never lifts a finger to do anything ever again, the entire human race would be poorer without her.

Light is growing in her face, her cheekbones becoming sharp and her long eyelashes sending lacy shadows across her skin. It's almost like I can see her more intimately than I ever could before she knew the truth about me. And then I realize it's not that at all. It's headlights.

I whip around, my body blocking her the way I should have shielded my little brother. The car that has been bouncing around the distant web of roads is lost no longer. It's here, and behind the blare of the lights, I can see its shape.

It's a station wagon.

CHAPTER

48

Jeika

PETER SCREECHES TO a stop and I throw up a hand to shield my eyes from the headlights. I barely recognize him through the windshield, for all that I've had nightmares about him shoving a gun to Dani's head.

I freeze and at the same time, Dani *moves*. She surges into her car and throws the glove box open. Metal flashes dully as she pulls out a gun, keeping it beneath the level of the dashboard so Peter won't see.

But then she hesitates, the way she holds her body shifting. Changing. I hold my breath, afraid for reasons I don't fully comprehend, waiting to see what she'll do next.

Peter throws his car door open and Dani shoves the revolver into the back of her uniform pants without cocking it. She returns to my side, shorter than me but her shoulders steady like this new version still has no fear in her. Not even of the new, bigger pistol in Peter's hand and the wild snarl twisting his face. Her wrist brushes against mine and my flesh goes electric with the urgency of even that small touch.

"Run," she whispers.

My heart jolts like it wants to obey, even when the rest of me won't.

"Don't fucking move," Peter says, raising the gun with a wince, favoring his ribs. "Either of you." His gaze narrows on me for a second, like he's working through who I might be, but he doesn't get a chance to ask.

"How'd you find me?"

I can't believe Dani can think to ask something like that now. With armed people on both sides of me, my brain is all static made of the starts to plans it doesn't know how to finish. I need to help her disarm him, but I don't have any particular strength or skills. I'm utterly ordinary, nearly helpless without a weapon to even our odds. Where's the crowbar? The bolt cutters? Dani's car has always been a bottomless well of weapons, but now she's not even reaching for the one she has.

"I set your phone to share your location with me." He smiles coldly. "You didn't think I'd put an insurance policy on it when I had it unlocked?"

"Thought you were going to call the cops on me," she says with an edge of sneer to her voice, so unimpressed by him, even with his gun in her face.

"I called them to my house before I came here," he says. "I left my door wide open and all the evidence spread out on my table. Including the map coordinates of where your phone ended up. They're coming for you, no matter what." His cheek twitches. "Except I realized that's not enough. I hate the idea of you getting to live out the rest of your life in prison, eating food paid for by taxpayers as if you deserve a free ride."

He hasn't glanced at me again, and I wonder if he's guessed that I'm the same girl from his emails. If he can see anything past his own grief at all.

"So you're just going to shoot me and wait for them to come catch *you* instead?" she says. "Great plan, asshole."

"Better than letting you get away with murder," he snaps.

That hollow, bleak eye of the gun barrel is staring directly at her chest, and the emptiness of it makes me ill.

I sneak a glance, but her arm hasn't traveled even the smallest bit toward the pistol at the small of her back. She's too smart to give away to him that she has it, but I don't know if she can be fast enough to draw and fire in time when all he has to do is squeeze the trigger. Is he planning to shoot me too? Let me go? Does he think I'm her accomplice? I'm on the edge of panic, gulping down breaths, and I don't get why she's not.

She was calm last time too, but it's a different kind of calm now, and it's churning my stomach. I don't know this Dani.

The kind of Dani who kisses me. The kind who feels like a heavy door falling open. The kind who came back for me instead of skipping town when she knew this man was coming to kill her.

This Dani has priorities I can't fathom. All I can do is hope she wants to save us both badly enough to take him down again. And that she acts fast enough, before he fires or the police get here.

"You can have me," she says and my whole body jerks with the shock of it, my gaze flying to her face. "If you let her go."

He sneers. "You're not exactly in a position to negotiate, bitch."

"She's an innocent, like your daughter."

"And she's hanging out with someone like you why exactly? To be a good influence?" He laughs, actually laughs, the pistol in his hand shaking enough to make me flinch as it moves between both of us.

She takes a step closer. "I know what you really want. So go ahead. I'm not going to stop you this time. You didn't come for her, and we both know it."

I freeze, the cuts on my arms burning and my lips still echoing with her kiss. What is she *doing*?

He sneers. "You think you can trick me into coming close enough so you can bite me again, you rabid little bitch? Think again. I can kill you from here."

"Maybe," she says. "But I know something you don't."

He pulls back the top part of his pistol, something snapping into place and I'm guessing that was him loading a bullet. My pulse leaps and nausea snarls up my throat.

She's stepped a little in front of me, drawing Peter's attention her way. Maybe if he's focused on her, I could . . .

The handle of the gun pokes up from the back of her belt, less than an arm's reach away. I saw a western movie once, so I know how to cock a revolver, but I don't know how to check if it has any bullets. Dani is so much better at all of this than I am, but she should have gone for her weapon by now. It's not like her to hesitate.

Peter stares her down. "I don't care."

"You will," she says. "Because I know, even if you don't, that nothing ends with the murder. There's no peace. It will chew on your insides in places you didn't know there were teeth."

Peter's gun is shaking now and I'm not sure if he can tell that we can see.

"I've killed more than you," Dani says. "I could do it again." She raises her arms, her hand empty, the pistol in her waistband now lifetimes away from being useful. "But this time? I won't."

I ruined my mother's reputation once to slip the noose of consequences before it closed on my neck. I made myself drag her body, her blood seeping into my clothes, with those memories freezing inside my bones. Ruining the future I thought I was saving. That's why I get, immediately, why Dani says it. And everything in me sinks.

I'm not the one who's going to die tonight after all. She is. This beautiful, fierce storm of a woman with that unseen future stretching miles and decades out in front of her.

It's up to me now. *Do it*, I tell myself, visualizing the wild dive for the gun, the fumble, trying to fire it in time . . . But I already know there's no way I could move faster than Peter can shoot, even if I didn't mess up the whole bullet-loading-and-gun-cocking part.

"I'm not going to kill you," Dani says, "because I used to do anything I had to in order to be the one left standing. And now I know, just like you're going to, that there are things you don't want to survive. A version of yourself you don't want to become."

She cocks her head, gaze steady on Peter.

"Look, you decided to go vigilante on the people who can kill, like the one who hurt your daughter. But instead, why don't you find people like your daughter was, who are lost and searching for their answers? Help them find better ones."

"So, what?" he spits at her. "You want me to open a goddamn support group? Are you out of your fucking mind?"

"It's a choice."

"Yeah, well, you don't get a choice." He advances a step closer, waving the gun at us. "Get down on your knees. You and your sick friend too."

I drop, my heart clenching like I can already feel him pulling that trigger.

"Actually, I do," Dani says, and sinks to her knees. Willingly this time. It makes me sick to watch her humble herself before him, but her posture's as strong as it's ever been. "We all do. You can be the person who shoots another young girl, or you can find a different way to change the world that took your daughter." She shakes her hair back, her face clear. "As for me, you have the gun, but I have a choice too. I can be the person who kills you to save myself. Or I can try to save *you*. Even if it kills me."

She shoots me the quickest of glances, and I get it. She's the distraction. *Run* is the last thing she said to me. She's trying to save me, still. But her face is too calm and I realize she may be trying to help me get away, but she's not lying. She's trying to save him too.

My gut twists. I get it—*oh God*, do I understand why she refuses to live with one more death, and I love her desperately for drawing that solid, beautiful line about who she's willing to be. Except I also know without her, we won't win tonight. I can't lose her, and suddenly, I don't want to lose the glimpse of myself I got tonight either. The future I'm just starting to believe in. Because if he has a choice, so do I.

"I won't hurt you, Peter," she says. "Just because I was once that kind of person doesn't mean that's the only person I ever get to be."

He scoffs, the sound bursting out of him in a spray of spittle like something inside him just broke. "You won't hurt me. Fuck that. You *can't* hurt me." He glances back toward town, like he's waiting for something, but the only lights out here are ours. "Listen up, you stupid bitch. Do you really think because I couldn't find the guy who killed my daughter, that I would give up? You think in all the years since Hannah died, I've just been sitting around waiting for a weird classified ad to pop up?" He takes a step closer. "You won't be the first filth I've cleaned out of this world. Won't even be the tenth. You think you have all the answers, but you're so naive you thought this was my *first* time."

My ears start to ring, shock pushing every sound out of the whole desert. Peter is a killer. He's twice as experienced as Dani is, he's bigger than both of us, and she still hasn't reached for her weapon.

"I thought I wanted something more this time," he said. "That since I had hard evidence for once, I could enjoy watching you rot in prison for years on end the way my daughter's murderer never had to." He shakes his head. "But it's not enough."

If he didn't have hard evidence all the other times, how sure could he be that the people he murdered really deserved it? I don't even have a second to dwell on that, because the police are on their way and he just confessed to multiple homicides in front of both of us. Which means he won't hesitate to kill me too.

My stomach jerks like all my organs are cringing inward and for one horrible second, I think I might lose control of my bladder. I can't think, can't react. I can only look to Dani.

She doesn't flinch, not even now. The only sign of her surprise is a slight widening of her eyes. But then she just shakes her head.

"No matter what you've done, the answer's the same. You can let go of your past before it destroys your future." She doesn't blink. "You can."

"I can do one better," he snarls. "I can destroy *you*."

His gun comes up and I snap.

The metal is cold and rough against my hand, the crosshatches of the grip pressing into my palm. I know I'm doing it, I know it as I cock the gun and my finger finds the trigger. I remember everything she said, and everything we've been through, and everything I hate about being the one who lives, and I choose for both of us.

I shoot him dead.

Everything should stop, afterward, but just like last time, it doesn't. There's not even a pause, a respectful moment of silence. Instead, there's a second gunshot as his hand clenches and his pistol goes off, the shot going wide. There's a thump as he hits the ground. There's gurgling and a soggy choking and his feet thrashing in the dust.

Dani doesn't run to him, but I do. I don't even know how to load another bullet, or if the gun does that on its own when you cock it, but by the time I'm falling to my knees next to his bowing body, he's finished. The gun drops numbly from my hand as I watch. The weight of him eases to the ground when his spine goes from convulsing to limp. There's a ragged, bloody hole in the center of his chest, smaller than it feels like it should be.

"She doesn't deserve to die."

The words come out of my mouth one life too late for him to hear me or understand why I chose Dani's future over his. Because no matter what she'd done, she understood there were still choices left to be made, and he was pulling everything down around him into the sucking whirlpool he'd made of his daughter's murder.

I stare down at him, this man who I might not have recognized on the street, who has made himself part of my story. There's something about how the skin of a face droops when there's no one left behind it that makes you realize faces are so much less fixed than you ever wanted to think. It's been the same, every time.

Vertigo takes me, and it's as if all those years of misery are a snake swallowing its own tail, starting all over again. I can't live with this. I already know I can't.

I feel like someone's drawing a knife down the center of me, just like last time. Splitting me into the kind of person who can do these things and the kind who stands back, frozen like if I never blink, none of this will ever have been real.

But this time, Dani's voice cuts through the silence. "It's not who you are," she says. "Not unless you let it be."

I can't respond. They're just words. And he's a fact. Two hundred pounds that used to be a person, lying heavy in front of me

"You think this changes you, and decides whether you deserve to live, whether you can ever do anything that would be enough to make up for taking a life," Dani says. "But you and I are the only ones here. We're the only ones who can tell the story of what happened and why. You get to decide if you're a piece of shit now, or if you're the hero."

"You just said it, though," I say dazedly. "You can be the kind of person who kills him to save yourself. Or you can be better than that. You were. I wasn't."

She snorts. It's such an irreverent, sardonic sound that it snaps me out of the daze, my eyes lifting to Dani's face. "I gambled that he could change. Played a game of chicken that I would have *lost.* If it weren't for you."

A flicker of movement catches my eye, and when I jerk my head that way, red and blue lights roll across the desert, coming in our direction. My heart jolts in my chest. *No.* Peter's cavalry is coming.

Our time is up.

Dani moves closer, her voice low and urgent. "Jeika, listen to me. We can give ourselves up, let them lock away all our future choices. Or we can stay free." She nods to her car. The lean, muscular lines of steel with the engine bigger than anything they build these days. Fast enough to outrun them, especially in this maze of desert roads she knows better than anyone. "And we can find a way to build something good, even on a foundation of shit, the way he didn't."

The tears are making my vision blur. "You know, if you'd have been the one to shoot him, I wouldn't have blamed you. That whole time, I was hoping you would. But now that I'm the one . . ." My heart stumbles, stuttering a beat like a hiccup. "I don't know why it's so easy to forgive you, and impossible when it's myself instead."

"Yes," Dani says. "You do."

She doesn't say more, and the lights are pressing closer, eating up the last few moments we'll ever have together.

"There's only one question left that matters." She pulls me to my feet. "If this isn't the end of your story, what do you want it to be?"

My eyes find hers, and for the first time since I lost my family, I know my answer.

Epilogue
Jeika

WE'RE RUNNING.

I don't even feel the polished hardwood floors under my feet, because my heart is pumping so fast I'm not sure if the *thump-thump-thump* is the beat of my steps or the thrum of blood through my veins.

It feels fresh, bright, *red* and I know I should be afraid in these moments, but I never am. My face is hot beneath the knit, sweat making the ski mask itchy, but I know better than to pull it off too early. Rich people have cameras everywhere.

We slam out the arched double doors in front and I glance back to make sure Dani is keeping up. Somehow, when we started all this, I figured she'd be faster than me, like she is with everything else. In running, at least, I've still got the edge.

A dark flash of movement passes in my peripheral vision and I flinch, fumbling a step. Security? Could tonight's target have had a panic button and silently called the cops? But no, it's my girlfriend passing me, her breath sawing rough but her arms swinging hard, deliberate. Focused.

Hell. I grin as I throw on another burst of speed. There's something in Dani that makes her almost impossible to beat. Never mind if you *should* be faster or bigger or more powerful than her. She cuts through the world like a red-hot knife.

As the man in the mansion behind us just found out.

We vault the low gate at the end of the drive and the car's waiting a block down the street. Those familiar taillights set wide and glowing red, in a boxy shape that Detroit hasn't made in decades. After these past two years on the road, it looks like home.

Jane bursts out of the driver's seat when she sees us, scrambling with relief and hitting the latch to pop the freshly upholstered seat forward so she can get in the back. We've been teaching her to drive, for emergencies, but she has a tendency to freeze up when she's not sure what to do. Not ideal in most driving situations.

I dive into the passenger seat and the tires bark on pavement, Dani shifting smoothly into second gear before I've even got my sweaty mask off. I toss it to the floorboards, breathing hard, but grinning. God, that never gets old.

"Are you okay? Did he hurt you? Did he agree to do it?" Jane's anxious. For the first year, we tried to keep the ski mask nights a secret, but she got suspicious. So we had to come clean.

Dani just snorts. Even breathing hard, she manages to look unruffled. She tugs the mask off her long sweep of hair, letting it rain down over bare, toned shoulders. My gaze catches on the slim straps of her tank top for a moment before I remember to answer Dani's former coworker.

I toss a manilla envelope into the backseat, smug. "What do you think?"

Jane gasps when she sees the thickness of this new stack of bills.

Bad men understand money. They understand self-interest. They don't understand doing the right thing just because it's the right thing.

So we learned to speak their language.

That night in the desert before we ran from the cops, the right words finally found me.

"I want to do good things for good people. Give the bad ones a chance to change. And fuck them up if they won't."

Dani just smiled, darkly. Before she drove like I'd never seen outside of the movies. Tires churning up dry desert crust. Headlights off. Nothing but stars in a cracked-open sky to guide our path out toward this new life.

I didn't know how to even begin to pull off doing what I'd said. But Dani did.

Turns out there's very little that can stand against her special brand of ruthlessness, even once she stopped killing.

She wasn't even afraid to start at the top—the most powerful, corrupt man in the country. As she taught me, it's easy to get them alone when you resemble their preferred prey.

Blackmail is one of our games. Pain is another.

Like the first asshole who we put into permanent paralysis so he had to stick around and watch the ripple effects of all his policies that had bankrupted businesses and destroyed lives and deported innocent people.

I honestly thought it would be harder to evade the police. All it really takes is a new fake ID now and then. We're not exactly Capone, and the Phoenix Metropolitan Police Department doesn't have bottomless resources for cold cases.

"Can you pass me the envelopes?" I straighten, back to business now that my breathing has evened out. Dividing up the money always gives me a surge of satisfaction, like each bill holds a charge of power and we get to deal it out as we please.

We hit the main roads and the car slows, Dani quieting the growl of the engine to match the speed of the innocent people around us.

Jane puts on her gloves before she hands up the money, more latex gloves, and two fresh manilla envelopes to go with it. I stash our half in an envelope with no crime scene DNA or fingerprints on it. The dirty one from the chemical company CEO's mansion gets bagged to be thrown in the trash.

The second envelope, I press against the dashboard to address, using the glow from the red stoplight above.

After-School Snacks LLC
C/O Eric Dennis
1419 Franklin Way
Phoenix, AZ 85001

When I go to tuck the bills inside, I notice one has a drying smear of dark red and I swap it for one in our own envelope. "My bad." Probably best if Dani's old neighbor doesn't have any evidence to tie him to a kneecapping, not that tonight's douchebag will probably be reporting that particular crime. Our crooked CEO fell while jogging, if I had to guess. At least gauging by how much dirt we have on him. Jane has turned out to be very good with a telephoto lens.

Thanks to our generous but erratic contributions—and no thanks to his tendency to ground-stare and stutter whenever he attempts to fundraise—Eric's nonprofit has moved into an old farmhouse with a sagging roof and a big yard and shutters he let the kids paint with rainbows. He sent pics to our last burner phone. Their new place is decorated with a scatter of daisy-shaped throw pillows and soft mats to nap on, the kitchen equipped with sticker-adorned stepstools so the children can help cook if they want to. Cooper was trotting through the background of nearly every picture, fulfilling his role as the beloved mascot and unofficial kid-herder of the organization. He gets plenty of time to run around outside these days, after we talked my old roommate into donating him to the nonprofit.

Eric's after-school program is meant to close the gaps—and fill the bellies—for kids who have shitty parents, but not quite shitty enough for CPS to pull their custody.

An imperfect solution, but one with its heart in the right place. Kind of our specialty these days.

"And where are we headed next, ladies?" Dani asks, the turn signal coming on with a *click-clock* as we approach the freeway interchange.

"How about the giraffes?" I say at the same moment as Jane blurts out, "The Bahamas!"

It's her turn to pick, and she's been talking about the Bahamas ever since she saw the islands on an episode of *Outer Banks*.

She cringes. "We can set up the little girl who wanted to be adopted by giraffes first. Sorry, I forgot!"

"I still want to figure out a better way to do it than a zoo," Dani gripes, as she turns. "Everybody does the damn San Diego Zoo. And she wanted to be *adopted* by a family of giraffes, not just see one."

"I'll have to see if that assignment is still available," I say. "We didn't sign up for it officially."

We weren't sure when we were going to get enough blackmail material on that CEO to move forward, and we try never to take on a wish to grant unless we're free from our other missions. It only took one Make-A-Wish kid passing on before we could wheedle a video game company into animating a custom scene so he could marry his favorite anime character. Now we move as fast as we can, because you never know.

It was Jane's idea to sign up, when she found the old application in Dani's glove box, and we did it under her name only, since her record is clean. But it's fun to make kids' dreams come true, and an outside-the-box kind of challenge to figure out how to grant the weirder requests. I'm aware, always, of their sunken eyes and flagging energy. The moment of joy we bring them doesn't mean they get a happy ending. But it took meeting them in person to know it was worth doing anyway.

"Fake passports are harder to get than fake IDs," Dani comments. "How do you feel about Hawaii?"

"We could put the car in storage for a couple months?" I venture. We swap out the plates from state to state, but it's still recognizable enough it wouldn't hurt to take it out of rotation for a little while. We probably should have done it before, but her classic car is the only constant in our new road-tripping lifestyle. Besides each other, of course.

I reach over and let my hand rest on Dani's forearm, enjoying the flex of muscles under silky skin as she shifts.

"Hawaii!" Jane lights up and I can't help but smile. It's weirdly addictive, making her happy. "We should probably get a new phone first," she decides. "I haven't called my mom this month. She might start to worry."

Dani slides a look sideways to me. If Jane's mom was going to worry, she probably would have started when Jane took off on a road trip with friends, calling from an ever-changing roll of numbers. But turns out Jane's mom's interest in her daughter mostly centered on having someone to order around.

"Yup, no problem" is all my girlfriend says aloud. "I might have a lead on fake passports, actually," Dani says to me in an undertone. "I'll, uh, see how it goes." I can tell what she's thinking. Jane will settle for Hawaii and never complain, but she *wanted* the Bahamas.

I nod, hiding a smile. Knowing Dani, we'll be drinking piña coladas with sand in our shorts before we know it.

The idea of traveling through airport security with a fake passport would have freaked me out once. But a couple of years as a fugitive from the law have taught me that mostly people aren't thinking that much about you. Especially if you're a young, harmless-looking blonde. And it feels like the world is just full of fences and boundaries and reasons you can't do the things you want most . . . until you just *do*. And no one stops you.

It's funny how living by Dani's side has peeled the fear from me. Layer by layer until what's left is all sinew and strength. Purpose. A version of myself I never would have believed in before her.

It's so distant to me these days how I ever thought my best option was to erase myself, when a thousand new threads of possibility unspool for me every time we open a newspaper.

Seeking where we're needed next.

ACKNOWLEDGMENTS

THE DEDICATION ALREADY went to her, but this whole story came from one line she said: "I saw my first dead body in Walmart," so I think Savahna Piercey deserves a second thank you.

Huge thanks to my second agent, Eva Scalzo, for being willing to take a chance on a book that had supposedly used up all its chances. You pulled a fairy godmother miracle out of your hat and found it just the right editing house so it could finally make its way to readers.

This book absolutely wouldn't exist without two people: my first agent and my book coach. Big thank you to Naomi Davis. When I emailed you and asked if this idea was too crazy to write, thank you for lying and saying "no." You not only drank the metaphorical Kool-Aid on this one, you poured the whole pitcher over your head. And if you would have told me "nah" at that first, very vulnerable moment, I would have dropped it and let the whole idea die. Thank you for being willing to shop a book totally outside of your zone of specialty, just because you believed in it—and in me!—so much.

Thank you to Heather Demetrios and Pneuma Creative coaching for breaking me free of the grip of the boggart and making it possible to have the belief in myself to finally complete a draft of this book—not once but *twice*, for very different versions of the book. You did such a good job of busting me out of writer's block that it's been eight years now, and I still haven't had a scrap of writer's block since. Also, the idea you had about writing from the POV of the serial killer character? Mm-hm, that was the right call.

Margarita Montimore, thank you for the idea to make it adult psych suspense, for that Dropbox folder of weirdo guided meditations that expanded my mind enough that I was (almost) smart enough to write a book this brain-bending, and for a four-hour babbling phone call bursting with new ideas for this book.

Thank you to Steph Magister for showing me the things I didn't know I didn't know about psychological suspense, and for brilliant feedback with a light hand.

Margaret Torres talked through this idea with me like a thousand times, and deserves a trophy for having read more versions of this book than anyone on earth. Seriously, I should have been paying you by the hour for the amount of your labor that went into this book. And for the painstaking line comments. I love you for every single "OOF!"

Thank you to Lyssa Mia Smith for being so detail-oriented and encouraging in your feedback and for sharing your immense amount of intelligence and professional therapist knowledge with me. For helping to go over every line to decide when to shade toward realism, and when to shade away from it for the greater good of readers. Very few people have the bravery and integrity to look all these contentious issues in the face and decide how to deal with them, rather than just "writing safe" and saying nothing at all. All the riskiest choices remaining are mine, not hers.

Thank you to Mel Parish for sending screaming gifs and "I stan this book for life" and for being willing to reread when I needed to rewrite "just one more time."

Thank you to Jen K for the positivity pass, and Katie Golding for the best response to a book I've ever gotten in my career and for threatening my life every time I tried to shelve this book. Thank you for all your gorgeous graphics and help with all my marketing, and for the perfect "eyes" to put behind the knife for this cover. Thank you for making this book a cover so we could put it inside a Christmas ornament of my books, well before it ever got a book deal.

Thank you to Kelly Siskind, Gwynne Jackson, Kristin Button Wright, and Keyanna Butler for beta reads.

Thank you to the Book Pipeline Contest for believing in this book and sending it to all their editor contacts. It was a dream working with Ciara, Matt, and Jeanne.

To my husband, who is always so much better at following fiction-writing rules than I am, for helping me figure out how to un-kidnap my main character.

To Mary Helen, whose heartfelt letters about my writing came at a time when I needed it most, to help me believe that my words weren't tossed out into a void and wasted. Thank you for helping me to feel like I mattered. There's not a better gift than that.

Shout-out to Chris and Amy, a beautiful, generous-hearted couple whose dumpster-diving love story was the reason I had to write a Trader Joe's dumpster moral allegory into this novel.

Thank you to AlejAndro Anastasio, for his amazing podcast *One Hand Speaks*, and for being so generous and honest with me about his experience. For explaining the ins and outs of one-handed shoe tying, bike riding, martial arts, and yoga. And for being a perfect role model to prove that Dani's level of badass is realistic.

To my film agents, Jill Gillett and Flora Hackett: your enthusiasm for this project expanded my heart, and it was so fun to see your vision for bringing this one to the screen.

At my publisher, Crooked Lane, thank you to Jess Verdi for acquiring this book and championing it. Thanks to Faith Black Ross for taking over. I've been so impressed with the efficiency and energy of the whole team, especially Julia Abbott, Shannon O'Neill, Thaisheemarie Fantauzzi Perez, Dulce and Beata in marketing and publicity, and Martin Biro in line edits. Thanks to Meghan Deist for a fantastic cover design!

Thanks to Devri Walls for being the very first human to buy this book (sorry, Mom!) and for swooping in to save the day and speed-reading it (twice in a week, you generous soul) when my brain gave out and I could no longer tell good from bad and the deadline was coming either way. I really appreciate your decisiveness and your brilliant plotting brain. But that week, *especially* the decisiveness.

Huge thanks to all my family and friends who helped with the big preorder push! You got this thing off the ground like a rocket!

And finally, thank you to New Orleans, for always raining book ideas down upon my head. Keep 'em coming, baby, there are never too many.